BEDLAM

Also by Harry Adam Knight

THE FUNGUS

BEDLAM

Harry Adam Knight

LONDON
VICTOR GOLLANCZ LTD
1992

First published in Great Britain 1992
by Victor Gollancz Ltd
14 Henrietta Street, London WC2E 8QJ

A catalogue record for this book is available
from the British Library

ISBN 0 575 04995 2

Photoset in Great Britain by
Rowland Phototypesetting Ltd, Bury St Edmunds, Suffolk
Printed in Great Britain by
St Edmundsbury Press Ltd, Bury St Edmunds, Suffolk

Prologue

She awoke abruptly. Something was wrong. She'd always had a sense of knowing when there had been some sort of fuck-up, as Dave put it. Even when it couldn't have been possible to know. Like the time they'd run out of fuel on the M25 with the petrol gauge stuck on half-full. She'd been telling him they'd never get to Letchworth. And they hadn't. Not that it mattered then. In fact, not getting to Letchworth should probably happen to more people. But now she had a sharp sense of something really out of place coming up.

For a start, she didn't know where she was. She was lying on her side on a hard surface, that much was clear. A floor, probably. But whose floor? What had happened? She tried to remember but the effort increased the intensity of the throbbing pain that filled her head. She stared into the dim light, trying to make sense of what she was seeing. It was a wall, she decided. A stained, dirty wall, mere inches from her face.

And then she became aware that she could hear breathing. Hoarse breathing coming from close by. She thought about shifting her position but decided not to. Not just yet. She lay there, dress tight across her hips because it was caught beneath her. Her hair was strewn irritatingly over her face and her left arm, pinned beneath her, dead from her weight upon it.

She made another attempt to remember what had happened. A bit of it came back. She had been walking with Dave. They had their arms around each other's waists and were slowly

*turd-dodging down narrow, and smelly, Relton Passage. They
had been heading for the Indian for a take-away. Then what?
More bits came . . .*

*There had been someone behind them. She remembered now.
Someone walking at a faster pace. She and Dave had automatically started to edge to one side to give the person room to pass
them . . . and then what?*

Nothing. She couldn't remember.

Where was Dave?

*She gave a small, involuntary gasp – furious with herself for
not thinking about him before. Then she went cold as she
realised what she had done. She had made a noise. It was only
in making it that she was horribly conscious of her irrational
determination to be quiet. Her insides contracted in a sort of
ripple from her stomach upwards. She felt conscious of her pants
being on, her groin feeling familiar and not brutalised. For the
moment she knew that things could possibly be worse.*

'Are you awake?'

*A man's voice, speaking in a whisper, and one she didn't
recognise.*

*'If you're awake, turn over slowly . . . but don't make a noise.
You mustn't wake him.'*

Him? Who? Too many whos.

*'Look, I know you're awake because your breathing pattern
has changed and you made a noise. Just turn over quietly.'*

What else could she do but obey him?

She rolled quietly over.

*She quickly glanced around. She was in a fairly large room,
possibly a kitchen-diner that had fallen on very hard times. The
lino was worn and dirty and she couldn't have made out the
pattern had she been interested in doing so. The unlit light bulb
hanging from the ceiling had no shade. What little light there
was came through thin curtains that cut out any view but did
not detract from the sordid surroundings. There was a large
sink, jagged black lines covering porcelain like a fallen cobweb.
Near the sink was a big kitchen table that had dark stains*

running down its legs. There were dark patches on the floor around it . . .

But to her, at first, the main feature of the room was the man. He sat on a chair facing her. She didn't recognise him. But then he had the sort of nondescript face that you could easily forget. He was in his late twenties and was dressed in jeans and a dark blue shirt. Then, beyond him and to his right, she saw a figure lying curled up on a mattress, with his back to her, apparently asleep. The man – it was clearly a man – was wearing a red-striped shirt, light-coloured trousers and had a ski mask over his head. He was lying right in front of a door. The only door. Also lying on the mattress, beside the man, was a bayonet. She sat up, drawing her arms and legs into herself in some unconscious protective reaction.

'Good,' whispered the man. He held out his hands. They were bound together with white nylon cord. Very tightly, she saw as she noticed the red raw look around the cord. More cord was wrapped tightly around his chest, tying him to the chair. His ankles were fastened to the chair legs as well.

'Say nothing,' he whispered hoarsely. His face displayed a desperate urgency. His eyes were wide and were showing lots of white. He looked scared. 'Say nothing and we might live.'

She could feel something filling her chest and throat and pressing hard around her heart.

'That bastard over there' – he flicked his head sideways – 'is going to kill us unless you get him first.'

What? What was he saying? Why was her arm tingling so unpleasantly? What was making her want to explode? To scream and scream . . .

'Come on. Snap out of it, for God's sake. We've got a chance because he thought you'd stay out longer than you have. He's still asleep. Come on.' The man's mouth was a slit from which his words were softly hissing, and his face was an anguished mask.

'Who's he? Who are you? Where's Dave?' Her voice began to rise.

He held out his wrists again in a warning gesture. 'Quiet! I *think Dave's all right if that's who he brought in with you. He took him to another room but I'm pretty sure he didn't do anything. He wasn't gone long enough. But he will do something . . . unless you stop him. You're free. You can get the bastard. You can get us out.'*

She looked at the sleeping figure. 'Who is he?'

The man grimaced. 'From what I've seen in here I'm afraid we're the guests of the Bone Man.'

She suddenly felt giddy. The 'Bone Man' was the name given by the tabloids to the mass murderer who had been terrorising London for the past few months. He had acquired the nick-name when police found his hide-out in a deserted warehouse in the East End. It had been decorated with the bones of several of his victims. The police pathologist said that the number of the bones added up to seven victims, though some of the skulls had never been found. She looked again at the sleeping figure. 'Oh no . . . no.' Terror seized her, filling every cell of her body.

'Listen to me,' said the man urgently. 'You've got to do it!' He indicated with his head. 'There's his bayonet. There, by him. The mad fucker's got careless. Get it and stab him to death.'

'No, I couldn't,' she said, trembling violently. 'Don't ask me to. Please.'

'Look,' he said, his hands clenching, which made the nylon cord bite deeper into his flesh, 'since I've been here he's already killed a woman. After raping her. Do you really want to be the fucking next? I'm bloody sure I don't, you stupid . . . Sorry. Sorry.' He took a deep breath. 'If you don't make a move now it'll be too late. He could wake at any moment.'

She shook her head. 'No. I can't.' Then she thought of something. 'I'll get the bayonet and cut you free, then you can kill him.'

'No way. The chances of you getting over to him, picking up the bayonet, coming over to me and cutting me free without waking him are less than nil. Our only chance is for you to act right now!'

'No . . .' She closed her eyes, trying to will away the whole ghastly situation. But it wouldn't go. And the man's tense

whisper continued, telling her things she didn't want to hear.

'Shall I tell you what he did to the other woman? He tied her spread-eagled on that table there and after he raped her he got a razor . . .'

When the man finished she opened her eyes again. Now she felt very cold. She looked at the bayonet.

The man spoke again. 'You have to do it. To save yourself . . . and to save Dave.'

At the mention of Dave's name she made up her mind. She nodded. 'I'll do it.' But she didn't move.

'Go on,' he urged her. 'Quickly, do it now! For God's sake the bastard is waking up . . .' The figure on the mattress shifted slightly. She held her breath, then began to move slowly across the floor, crawling on her hands and knees on the filthy lino. The figure hadn't stirred again and she prayed that he'd drifted back into deep sleep. She stopped by the mattress and looked round at her fellow-prisoner who was watching her over his shoulder. He nodded frantically, urging her on. She picked up the bayonet, noting how sharp it was. Then, on her knees, she raised the bayonet high, gripping it with both hands. She chose her target: a spot halfway down his left side. She shut her eyes and brought the bayonet hurtling down with all her strength.

The blade plunged deep into the man's side, scraping on a rib as it went. She felt a convulsive shudder conveyed to her through the hilt of the bayonet. She pulled the blade out and, with her eyes still closed, plunged it into him again and again. She was doing it for Dave. And for herself. But she still felt sick.

Finally she stopped and opened her eyes. The figure was completely still, his side a gory mess. Blood had spattered on to the front of her dress. She stood up and turned quickly to the man in the chair, expecting praise, absolution and hope.

But he was standing up too, smiling, loosening the cord he had wound too tightly around his wrists. The cord that had bound his chest and ankles already lay on the floor.

'Poor Dave,' he said. 'Poor dead Dave. I do hope he's not too cut up about it.' Then he laughed.

As he approached he rubbed his bleeding wrists on to his

stomach and smears of blood appeared on his shirt – a blue shirt, she now realised, like the one Dave had been wearing – and his body shook with the pleasure of it all.

Still smiling, he plucked the wet bayonet from her numb hands, then went and roughly hauled the dead man over on to his back. She now saw that he was bound hand and foot. And she knew what she would see even before the ski mask was pulled off his head.

She stared into Dave's dead eyes and then at the man wearing Dave's shirt.

'So much fun already and the night is still young,' he said, reaching for her.

Chapter One

Douglas Scott was having a hell of an erotic dream. The young man with the blond hair and moustache was driving deep into him with every thrust of his hips and Scott groaned with pleasure each time, his fingers digging into the flesh of the man's buttocks. 'Oh, God, Derek . . . Yes, *yes. Ahhhhh!'*

Derek?

Despite the intense pleasure he was experiencing some part of Scott's sleeping brain realised what was happening was not quite right. As he lay there, legs wrapped around the young man's waist, he tried to figure out what was wrong. But the physical distraction of being expertly fucked quickly swept away all other thoughts and he was consumed totally by the exquisite sensations. The orgasm, when it came, was a long and violent one and as Scott's body shuddered uncontrollably he gave a series of high-pitched moans. And even in the middle of all that pleasure it occurred to him that the sounds he was making were unusual. For him, that is.

The young man – Derek – came soon after. Scott felt him spurt inside him and when he was finished he kissed Scott on the lips and collapsed, with an exhausted sigh, beside him on the bed. 'That was great, eh, Doc?'

'Yeah,' whispered Scott. Again he was trying to figure out what was wrong. And as the pleasurable sensations ebbed into the immediate past he was able to focus his mind more clearly. And then he saw what was wrong. He had just been fucked by

a *man*. He, Douglas Scott. Someone who had always regarded
homosexuals – queers, mattress munchers and turd burglars
was how he usually referred to them – as beneath contempt.
He was as hetero as they come. To prove it, he had the repu-
tation of being the office stud – well, he was pretty sure that's
what he was called behind his back by his office colleagues.
Someone who had never ever *ever* had an erotic thought about
another man . . .

The idea that he let himself be fucked by a man – worse, had
enjoyed being fucked by a man – suddenly filled him with
horror and disgust. No, it was impossible!

'No!' he screamed.

He sat up in the bed. The room was now in complete darkness. He was disorientated for a few moments and then let out
a long sigh of relief. He rubbed his sweaty face with his hand.
It had been nothing but a dream. No, a nightmare. He took a
deep breath. And what a nightmare! He'd never dreamt anything like that before.

Aware of his heart pounding, he began to wonder about the
significance of the dream. The fact that he had so enjoyed the
experience while it had been happening deeply disturbed him.
What did it mean? That he was actually a closet queer underneath it all? No, he said to himself, and shuddered with disgust.
The thought of him wanting to feel a man's prick up his arse,
or in any other orifice, was ridiculous. The very thought made
him feel sick and he shuddered again. Then something
occurred to him: while the guy had been sticking it to him up
his backside he had also been thrusting into his . . . his *vagina*.
Yes, the two sensations came back to him very clearly, overlaid
upon each other. When the blond guy had been screwing him
he had had a vagina as well.

He quickly put his hand under the duvet and was relieved
to feel his penis – very small at the moment – and his balls.
Christ, what's the matter with me? he thought worriedly. How
would I know what it feels like to be a woman being fucked by
a bloke? Why would I even dream about being a woman being
fucked by a man? He was wondering if this meant that he

might be a closet transsexual as well as a closet queer when he became aware of something else . . .

He was not alone in his bed.

Someone had sighed and then shifted their weight slightly.

He froze with alarm, then relaxed again. It was Kirsty, of course. Kirsty, the girl he'd met a fortnight ago at the squash club and who he'd been shafting regularly ever since. But how come he'd forgotten she was here, he wondered. He thought back to the previous evening – yeah, he'd met Kirsty in the wine bar after work, as usual, and . . . and . . .

And instead of coming home with him Kirsty had gone off to catch a train to Battersea. She was staying at her mother's tonight.

Then who . . . ?

Some other bird that he'd pulled at the wine bar after Kirsty had left? Yeah, that must be it. But he couldn't remember anything about her. No face or name came up. Christ, he must have drunk a lot. He couldn't even remember giving her one, whoever she was. He really should think about cutting down on his boozing.

He reached out for the switch on the bedside lamp. He turned the light on and looked around.

The young, blond-haired man with the moustache was lying under the duvet beside him. He opened his eyes and smiled at Scott. 'You ready to play around some more, Doc? I know I am.'

Scott gave a yelp of terror and flung himself out of the bed. He landed on all fours, leapt up and ran into the kitchen, snatched the biggest knife from his magnetised knife-rack and ran back into the bedroom. 'I'm going to kill you, you pansy bastard!' he screamed. 'You raped me!'

The bed now appeared to be empty. Scott pulled the duvet off then bent down to peer under the bed, knife at the ready. 'Come out, you bastard! I'm going to cut your stinking prick off!'

There was no sign of him. Scott ran to his large closet, slid open the door and jabbed between his hanging suits and jackets with the knife. The man wasn't there. He checked the bathroom, the kitchen and the sitting room. All empty. Then he examined his front door. It was locked from the inside and the security chain was in place. There was no other way the man could have got out of the flat. Forget the windows – Scott was on the third floor and there were no ledges outside. But even so he made a cursory check of all the windows. All were locked.

Scott began to calm down. He told himself he must have had a 'waking dream', when people think they're awake and see a ghost in their room but in fact they are still half asleep. Okay, this particular dream went on a bit too long but that's all it was – a dream. There had been no young, blond man called Derek in his flat.

He went back into the bedroom, feeling the need to put on some clothes. But first he went and picked up the duvet from the floor. He was about to throw it back on the bed when he paused and stared down at the sheet. So he'd had a wet dream. He already knew that. But what was the significance of those spots of blood? And why, now that he thought about it, did his rectum feel sore? But most importantly: why were there two distinct depressions in the bed?

Douglas Scott was suddenly very frightened again.

That night all the other residents of Hillview House had similar dreams of being made love to by a young man called Derek with blond hair and moustache though only Douglas Scott had the unsettling experience of waking from his dream to find Derek still in bed with him.

The other residents, depending on various factors, such as gender, had different reactions to the dream. For example, sixty-eight-year-old Miss Delia Coope, retired headmistress of a girls' school, woke up in such a distressed state that it brought on one of her angina attacks and during the time it took for her glyceryl trinitrate tablets to work she thought she was going to die. Even when the pain in her chest had lessened, the memory of the dream made her tremble with anxiety. What was wrong with her? she wondered. The very thought of sex had always profoundly disgusted her, thanks to an incident in her childhood that she had long ago buried out of sight from her conscious memory. The dream had brought that incident dangerously close to the surface. Fearful and confused, she began to cry.

Another example: the Stanton family. Emily and Peter Stanton had not been getting on too well for some months. The children, Eric and Suzanne, so sweet as toddlers and in primary school, were now obnoxious teenagers, uncontrollable and openly contemptuous of their parents. Both Emily and Peter had well-paid jobs but these had become precarious. They had both been passed over for promotion and realised, because of their ages, that they would not get a second chance. Their ages; middle-age lay at the source of their problems though their realisation of this was left unspoken between them. Their health was not at its best with the usual niggling wear and tear that middle-age brings. This and their anxiety about their jobs, not to mention the pressures put upon them by the children, was affecting their marriage. Their sex life had certainly been non-existent for some considerable time . . .

. . . until the night of the dream.

The intensity of the dream woke Emily. She was flushed and moist. She reached for the blond man and found Peter instead who was moaning in his sleep. Emily moved her hand under the duvet. She found that Peter was erect and very hard. She squeezed, waking him.

Peter awoke feeling very aroused. And confused. Had he actually been dreaming about being in bed with a man? Then his confusion – and guilt – was forgotten as he became aware that Emily was moving over him, straddling him. He forgot all about the young man. When they were finished they had a short rest and did it again.

At breakfast their children were unusually subdued. Suzanne wore a puzzled expression and kept blushing, while Eric looked as if he'd been pole-axed.

Suddenly, things were looking up for Emily and Peter Stanton.

But while the dream had helped the Stantons' marriage it had the opposite effect on that of two other residents of Hillview House, Philip and Marion Weston. They were in their mid-twenties, both very attractive and successful. They worked for the same advertising company; one of the few to have weathered the recession without too much difficulty. They had only been married for six months and so far everything had been marvellous. Until now . . .

Marion Weston guiltily recalled the dream as she sipped her decaffeinated coffee, then smiled to herself. She wondered who had provided the inspiration for the blond man in her dream. He hadn't looked like anyone she recognised. She couldn't wait to get to the office to tell Sheila, her best friend, all about it. She smiled to herself again as she remembered how incredibly *real* the erotic dream had appeared . . . and felt. It had given her a wow of an orgasm and she was surprised that she hadn't woken Philip up – she was sure she must have made a lot of noise, but if she had he hadn't mentioned anything about it.

She glanced at him. He was very subdued this morning which was not like him. He hadn't touched his muesli or even his coffee; instead he was just staring blankly into space. 'Philip, are you feeling all right?'

He gave a small start and looked at her. 'What?' For a moment or two it seemed to her that he didn't recognise her, then he gave a weak smile and said, 'Oh, sure, I'm fine. Couldn't be better.'

Philip had come to a decision, thanks to the dream. It had shown him the truth about himself, something he had tried to deny for so many years. Now he had to face up to it and stop living a lie. True, it would be bad for poor Marion but better it should all happen now rather than later. She'd get over it.

Yes, the dream had confronted him with his true sexuality and it was now time for him to come out of the closet and declare that he was gay.

When Stephanie Lyell, another resident of Hillview House, woke up and remembered the dream she had laughed aloud. Then she had got out of bed – she slept naked – and gone into the bathroom. After urinating into a glass beaker she had closely examined her eyes, her tongue and her throat, then she took her pulse. Satisfied, she showered and, wearing a white towelling robe, headed for the kitchen for a quick breakfast of toast and coffee.

Twenty minutes later she was emerging from the front of Hillview House, her stride determined and purposeful. She was an attractive woman in her early thirties. She was tall and slim with long, straight black hair that framed her angular, somewhat haughty, face. Today she was wearing a short black skirt, black stockings and black-and-white-striped blouse under a red imitation-leather jacket; the basic fashion uniform of the moment. She was carrying a black attaché case.

She went to the parking area at the rear of the building and got into her maroon-coloured Volvo. At the entrance to the driveway she had to wait, the traffic being very heavy as it always was at this time of the morning on Lower Road. In fact, the traffic was nearly *always* heavy on this road, which was squeezed between the playing fields of Harrow. Across the road, beyond the cricket field, was Harrow School itself, or rather a section of it, and to the left she could see the Hill which gave both Harrow-on-the-Hill and her expensive block of apartments their names. The church spire that emerged from the dense wood on the summit of the Hill looked very picturesque in the clear, cold, early morning air.

Finally a gap appeared in the line of traffic and she swung the big car into it with practised ease. Past the cricket fields Lower Road turned into Bessborough Road. At the railway bridge she swung right into Lowlands Road which, just past the polytechnic, turned into Tyburn Lane. There, on the right, stood Stephanie Lyell's destination, a Victorian monstrosity of a building that was once called the Harrow Asylum for the Mentally Insane – you could still make out those vaguely embossed words in the brickwork of the archway over the entrance – but according to the new sign beside the entrance was now the Harrow Institute for Neurological Research. Older residents of Harrow still referred to it as 'the loony bin', and even older residents called it by its original nick-name that they'd got from their grandparents – 'Bedlam'.

Stephanie drove in and parked in her usual place. As she got out of the car she clipped on her identification tag, then hurried into the building. Her high heels clattered loudly on the worn stone floor of the entrance hall. She nodded to the security man on duty then went straight to her laboratory. It was empty apart from her assistant, Jeff Foster. He was sitting with his feet up on a bench, reading *The Independent* and drinking coffee. He was a slightly overweight man in his early thirties with receding sandy hair. He had a round, pleasant face. 'Morning, Stephanie,' he said, putting the paper down and sitting up. 'You're looking like the cat that has swallowed the proverbial cream.'

'You're spot on, Jeff.' She opened her attaché case and took out a small glass jar. She put it on the bench in front of him. 'For you.'

He picked up the jar and stared dubiously at the fluid it contained. 'Is this what I think it is?'

'Yep.'

'You're so kind to me.'

'I know. I'll give you a blood sample as well. I want the results by lunchtime.'

He sighed. 'So you went ahead and did it.'

'Yes.' She took off her jacket and hung it up, then she slipped on a white lab coat. 'I wanted to be one hundred per cent certain that there are no physical side-effects.'

He shook his head disapprovingly. 'There was no need to take even the slightest risk. That's what the Bone Man is for.'

'You know I don't like that stupid name, Jeff. Call him by his right name. Gilmour. Marc Gilmour. And it's not just the possibility of physical side-effects; I wanted to see, before we use the stuff on Gilmour, if the synthetic BDNFE has any effect on the perception of a normal person.'

'You mean you think you qualify as *normal*?' He shook his head and laughed. 'So what was the result? How are your feelings about me, for example? Any heightened appreciation of my intrinsic worth as a human being?'

'No change at all. I still regard you as a lazy slacker who's unfortunately in the wrong profession. Mine.'

'So the BDNFE has clearly had no psychological effect on you.'

'None whatsoever. Now get off your backside and start running those tests.'

As Jeff rose to his feet the door opened and a lab technician came in. He was a good-looking young man with blond hair and a blond moustache. He grinned at Stephanie. 'Hi, Doc!'

She felt a slight flush on her cheeks as she smiled at him and said, 'Good morning, Derek.'

Chapter Two

Douglas Scott couldn't sleep, unlike the girl lying next to him who was quietly snoring. Laura, her name was. He'd known her vaguely – just to say Hi to in the wine bar – but though she was okay in the looks department she wasn't really his type. Tonight, though, it was different. *Any* woman was his type. And with Kirsty still staying at her mother's place he had made an all-out play for Laura. She'd succumbed, as he knew she would. Two of his friends had already gone the route with her and had given her a clean bill of health. Only thing was that she tended to be a bit clingy, they had warned him. Fine, he'd thought. Kirsty would be available again tomorrow. This one night with Laura would be well worth a few days of hassle, of not answering phone calls and giving her the cold shoulder in the wine bar until she got the message.

God, he'd so needed the reassurance of a woman in his bed after the previous night's events. Although he'd managed to put the memory of the dream out of his mind at least five times in the last few hours it was still very sharp and bitter. Unless he concentrated in blocking the ghastly details out he could relive every shameful thrust of the man's prick into his body . . .

He'd been relieved by his performance with Laura earlier. In fact he couldn't remember when he'd been so bloody good in the sack. Hell, he'd pumped away at her for over twenty minutes and he reckoned she'd come twice before he finally let

loose. Wore her out, he did. With that and all the wine she'd
drunk she was well away. He envied her. He dare not go to
sleep in case he woke up and found Laura had turned into a
man. He couldn't even bring himself to turn out the bedside
lamp.

He turned and looked at her, at her large, flattened breasts
with their very dark nipples. He reached out and stroked his
hand down along her hip and on to her leg, then slid his fingers
into the moist junction of her thighs. If she was a man it was
a hell of a make-up job. He withdrew his hand, sniffed his
fingers then stared at the ceiling. It was at times like this he
wished he smoked. It was one bad habit he'd somehow avoided
taking up.

Smoke.

He could *smell* smoke.

His first reaction was to flinch mentally in expectation of the
appalling smoke alarm going off. The bastard had triggered
for no apparent reason a few times since he'd bought it and the
last time his immediate neighbour, that stuck-up cow *Doctor*
Stephanie Lyell, had made a big stink about it. You'd have
thought he'd set it off deliberately the way she'd carried on.
He waited. There was no shrill beep but the smell of smoke
began to grow stronger. His relief at the silence turned to anger
at the failure of the device. He sat up and cursed it, then finally
it dawned on him that he was in a flat that was possibly on
fire.

He could see the smoke now, curling in around the bedroom
door, blue and rather elegant. He rolled quickly out of bed and
ran to the door. He flung it open and was met with a blast of
heat and smoke. 'Oh shit!' he cried, reeling backwards.

'Wake up!' he yelled as he moved towards the Mickey Mouse
phone on the bedside table. But Laura remained motionless.
'Bloody well *wake up!*'

And he was lying on the bed again, his eyes opening and
immediately stinging. The smoke was billowing into the room
through the open door. What had happened? He must have
blacked out for a few seconds and fallen on to the bed. 'Laura!

Wake up!' he cried, reaching out to shake her. 'Wake up, you . . .' She wasn't there. He sat up, choking, with his eyes streaming. Had the bitch run off and just left him there? Then he remembered that he had come home alone last night. He'd tried to chat up Laura but she'd given him the brush-off. Then what . . . ? His heart gave a lurch, then continued beating again and his bowels churned fiercely. What was going on? Another weird dream?

He wondered if the smoke was part of the dream too. It certainly smelt real but his smoke alarm remained silent. Then, in a distant part of the building, a fire alarm bell did begin to ring. That convinced him. He leapt out of bed, wrapped the duvet around him for protection, and headed for the doorway. From there, one look told him that escape through the living room to the front door was out of the question. Everything was alight, and there were flames running along the ceiling. Then he spotted her. A gap in the swirling smoke revealed a small girl standing in the centre of the room. She was dressed in blue pyjamas and holding a golliwog. She looked terrified. 'Hey, come out of there, you little brat!' he shouted at her, then choked as the burning hot smoke filled his lungs. *How in the hell did she get in?* he wondered as he heaved the duvet over his head and charged into the living room. He reached out for her with his free hand but couldn't find her. Had the silly little bitch moved? He lifted up the duvet and glanced around. He couldn't see anything but smoke. Choking, he pulled the duvet down over his head again and turned away. He'd done his best to save her but now he had to save himself. He headed towards where he thought the doorway was . . . and collided with the wall. *Oh shit!* Panic filled him. His lungs seared with pain with every breath and he felt giddy . . .

He extended his hand and began to feel his way along the wall, hoping to God he was going in the right direction. He was now completely disorientated. And the wall was hot. He yelped as flames licked at his exposed feet and legs, then the duvet began to grow uncomfortably hot and he guessed it was beginning to catch fire as well . . .

His hand found empty space. The doorway. He charged through it. Then he started to scream. The duvet had burst into flames. He flung it from him. The window! Where was the window? Then he glimpsed an area ahead of him that was lighter than its surroundings. By now pain and panic had taken over and his only thought was to escape the flames. He ran towards the window and threw himself at it. Glass exploded outwards and Douglas Scott began his three-storey fall to the ground.

Detective Sergeant Terry Hamilton had ambiguous feelings about doing night-shift duty: he both loathed and liked it. He loathed it because he hated working nights and he liked it because when he caught up with his sleep during the daylight hours he didn't have those bloody awful dreams that plagued the sleep of his nights. This particular night-shift was almost over – another hour to go – and Hamilton was looking forward to a big fry-up when he got home, several large Scotches, and bed. He took a sip of luke-warm coffee, grimaced and tried to concentrate on the report he was slowly typing out. When his phone rang he was tempted to ignore it but after letting it ring several times he irritably snatched it up. It was Sergeant Collins from the Control Room. 'I'm afraid the presence of CID is required, Terry,' he said. 'My PCs on the scene of a fire brigade call-out report a suspicious death. Forensics are being called in on it as well.'

'Christ,' muttered Hamilton. 'My shift's almost over. Isn't there anyone else available?'

'Like who? There's just you and Pat here at the moment.'

Glancing round the empty CID room, Hamilton couldn't argue with that. 'Okay,' he sighed, 'I'll find Pat and get going. Address?'

'It's Hillview House, one of those fancy blocks of flats in Lower Road. Just a couple of minutes' drive away.'

'Right.' He then asked what was suspicious about the death and frowned at the answer he received.

He got up, put on his jacket, picked up his radio and was

heading for the door when Detective Constable Pat Thomson came in, balancing two cups of fresh coffee and a hamburger. 'We're on a call,' Hamilton told him. 'Suspicious death.'

Thomson set the coffees down on his desk, wrapped the hamburger in its serviette and stuck it in his coat pocket. 'So what's suspicious about it?' he asked as he followed Hamilton out of the office.

'Bloke seems to have jumped from his bedroom window to get away from a fire in his flat. Broke his neck in the fall. Severe burns found on his body.'

'Doesn't sound suspicious to me. What do they want us for?'

'They can't find any sign of a fire in his flat,' said Hamilton.

It was getting light when they pulled into the car park behind Hillview House. Apart from a single fire appliance two police cars were also parked there, and an unmarked station wagon that belonged to Forensics. A makeshift screen had been erected around the corpse. The victim had landed on the driveway, missing a flower bed by only a few feet. Tough luck. Hamilton got out of the car and stared up at the shattered third-floor window. Thomson joined him, still munching on his hamburger. 'There *must* have been a fire,' he said through a mouthful of God-knows-what. 'Why else would the poor bastard throw himself through his window?'

An approaching uniform had overheard Thomson's words. 'There was no fire, sir. And that comes from the experts.' He jerked his thumb in the direction of the fire crew who were putting away their equipment and clearly preparing to leave. 'They checked the whole building. Not a thing.' Hamilton looked at the officer, PC Peter Gilden, a youngster who had only finished his probation period a few months ago. It was true what they said about policemen looking younger as you got older. The batch of newer recruits at Harrow Division made Hamilton feel he would be getting his OAP's bus pass any day now.

They walked over to the screens. A grim-faced WPC stood by the entrance. She looked even younger than Gilden. Hamilton and Thomson took a look inside. The man, naked, lay face down, his head twisted to one side. There was a strong smell of charred flesh. Thomson finished the last of his hamburger and said, 'Phew, what a mess.' Hamilton bent down and looked at the man's face which was relatively untouched. His eyes were open but only the whites showed. Most of the body was covered in burns. There were glass lacerations on the shoulders and upper back. A clear liquid seeped from these. The only visible blood was around his mouth and nose. Hamilton straightened. 'If he hasn't been in a fire I'll eat my unsolved cases file.'

Outside, he said to Gilden, 'Forensics had a look at him yet?'

'Yes, sir. They're up in his flat now.'

'Who is he?'

Gilden glanced at his open notebook. 'Douglas Scott. Aged twenty-seven. Works for a firm of City stockbrokers. Single. Lived alone though according to the neighbours there was frequent female company.'

The fire crew had finished and the appliance was slowly backing up to make a turn out of the car park. 'Who called them?'

'A neighbour downstairs. Smelt smoke and set off an alarm in the front lobby. Not alone either. We've questioned all the residents and they all say they smelt smoke in their flats.'

'And that's not all.' It was the WPC. Hamilton tried to remember her name. Carol something. 'Yeah?' he asked.

She glanced at Gilden before answering. 'They all say they were dreaming of a fire before they woke up and smelt smoke.'

Hamilton looked at Gilden. Gilden gave a reluctant nod. 'Yeah, they do.'

'Understandable,' put in Thomson. 'They smell smoke in their sleep and they start dreaming about a fire. Subconscious warning bells.' He wiped a speck of tomato sauce from the corner of his mouth.

'Sounds reasonable,' said Hamilton.

'Yes, if there *had* been a fire,' said the WPC. Hamilton remembered her name now. It was Carol Foster. Recently transferred from Holborn. Good-looking but a bit on the heavy side. 'But there wasn't one.'

'So someone doused the poor bastard with petrol,' said Thomson. 'A pissed-off girlfriend . . . or maybe a pissed-off husband.'

'That's what Forensics suggested,' said Gilden. 'They're looking for evidence, but we didn't see any when we checked the flat after the fire crew gave it the all-clear.'

'You been training in forensics in your spare time?' Thomson asked him, a trifle unpleasantly.

'I've been trained to use my eyes, sir,' Gilden answered stiffly. 'And I didn't see anything that suggested he was set alight in the flat.'

'So what's your explanation?' asked Thomson. 'Spontaneous combustion?'

'Actually, one of the firemen said that, but he was joking . . . I think.'

'There's something else. About the dream, I mean,' said the WPC, hesitantly.

Hamilton noticed that Gilden gave a slight wince. 'What is it?'

'It's nothing . . . just a silly coincidence,' said Gilden.

'I'll be the judge of that,' said Hamilton. He looked sharply at the WPC. 'Well?'

'The residents all said the same thing about their dream. They saw a little girl in the fire. A little girl dressed in pyjamas and holding a . . . a golliwog.'

'A golliwog?' repeated Thomson, and laughed. 'Careful, or you'll have the Race Relations mob on our backs.'

'That's what they all said they saw the girl holding,' said WPC Foster, defiantly. 'That's what the older residents described it as; some of the younger ones didn't know what it was called but they gave the same description.'

'Did anyone recognise the girl?' asked Hamilton, beginning to wish even more that this call had come when his shift had finished.

Foster shook her head. 'No, sir.'

Hamilton gave a weary sigh. 'Well, I haven't a bloody clue

what all that signifies. Come on, Pat, let's take a look at Scott's flat. Maybe Forensics already have the answer.'

Forensics didn't. Burly Mike Emsley, head of the Forensics Department, wiped his glasses on a paper tissue and said frankly, 'I'm buggered if I know what happened in here, Terry.'

'So much for science,' said Hamilton, disappointed. 'Surely you've got *some* ideas. Give me anything. I want to make out my report and go home.'

'Sorry, mate. There's nothing. Look around you.' They were standing in the late Douglas Scott's bedroom. Apart from the broken window and a white duvet lying on the floor, there was nothing obvious amiss. 'When the fire sergeant assured me there had been no fire anywhere in this flat, or anywhere else in the entire block, I figured that the victim had been set alight and he had thrown himself through the window before the flames had caused any damage in here. But if that was so there should be some kind of evidence. We've found no scorch marks and no trace of inflammable liquids anywhere on the floor.'

'So the killer cleaned up before he, or she, left,' suggested Thomson. He was staring down through the shattered window.

'Impossible. If the victim had been doused with any kind of inflammable liquid there would be burnt patches on the carpet, the bed or wherever it happened. And there would be traces of the liquid concerned. We've checked the whole flat thoroughly. Nothing. And nothing to suggest there was anyone else here with the victim at the time of the incident. The fire brigade lads had to break the door down. Three different locks including a security chain. And there's no other way out of here except the windows.'

'How about suicide?' asked Thomson, then shook his head. 'Nah, that's stupid . . . same questions apply, don't they?'

'Yes. Exactly the same. For one thing if he doused himself with something, where's the container?' Emsley went and picked up the duvet, which was lying not far from the broken window. He handed it to Hamilton. 'Take a look at this. Not a mark on it. Yet when our man went through that window he must have looked like a Roman candle.'

Hamilton examined the duvet, then held it to his nose. He said, puzzled, 'I can smell smoke though. Very faint, but I can definitely smell smoke on it.'

'Yeah, so did we,' admitted Emsley. 'And that's not all.' He looked at his young assistant, Paul Kirwan. 'Is it?'

Kirwan closed his sample case and shook his head. 'No. When we first came in here there was a distinct smell of smoke in the room. But it quickly faded away.'

'No smoke without fire,' said Thomson, predictably.

'But this time there was,' said Emsley. 'The only possible source for the smoke was the burned man, which means he was alight in this room, and yet apart from the smell of smoke, there is not the tiniest indication that something had been burning in here.'

'Did the fire brigade boys have any suggestions?' Hamilton asked.

'Only that it was spontaneous combustion,' said Emsley, looking irritated. 'Seems it's a brigade in-joke, spontaneous combustion.'

'What's your professional opinion of spontaneous combustion?' Hamilton asked him.

'Well, I know some perfectly reasonable people who take it seriously, but I'm not one of them. And this case doesn't fit the usual so-called description of spontaneous combustion where someone's body supposedly ignites from within and it burns up completely, leaving just an untouched hand or a foot.' He shook his head in disbelief. 'I mean, it takes four hours for a crematorium to burn a corpse. First they burn it for ninety minutes at 1260 degrees Centigrade. And then they give it another hundred and fifty minutes at 1000 degrees Centigrade. And even then they're still left with bone fragments that have to be crushed by hand. I can't accept that the human body can somehow internally generate temperatures of that intensity. It's absurd.'

'Yeah,' said Hamilton, knowing that he was grasping at

straws but feeling increasingly desperate. 'But our friend down there is only partially burnt. Aren't there cases of spontaneous combustion where people are seen to catch fire on the outside, and don't burn completely up?'

Emsley smiled at him and said, 'Do you ever read anything besides the *Sunday Sport*, Terry?'

'Please, I'm serious.'

'Yeah, sorry. Well, as far as I'm concerned any report of people suddenly catching fire really means that their *clothes* caught fire, and there can be a variety of reasons for that happening. Accidentally splashed with chemicals and such, but as you've no doubt keenly observed, our man wasn't wearing any clothes.'

'So where does that leave us?'

'Speaking for myself, totally mystified.'

'Oh, great,' said Hamilton, with a snort of disgust. He turned to the PC who was standing by the door. 'Did any of the neighbours hear anything from in here?'

'Only one,' said the PC, another schoolboy, and pointed at the wall behind the double bed. 'His next door neighbour on this floor, a Dr. Stephanie Lyell. She said she thought she'd heard him scream, then there was the sound of breaking glass. But at that point, like all the other residents, her main concern was the fire . . . Well, the fire she *thought* was happening . . .'

'I think we'll go and have another word with her,' said Hamilton, starting for the door. 'Thanks for all your help, Mike. I'm sure your autopsy report will be just as bloody helpful.' Then he stopped when he saw the PC shake his head.

'Er, she's not there, sir. She's gone.'

'Gone? Gone where?' Hamilton demanded.

'To work, sir.'

'What? At *this* time of the day? What does she bloody do for a living? Operate a milk float?'

'She's a scientist, sir.'

Hamilton was getting angry. 'I don't give a fuck what she is, she had no right to leave this building. This is a murder investigation! Why didn't you stop her?'

'Er, well, to be strictly accurate, sir, it wasn't a murder investigation when she left. In fact, it wasn't even a "suspicious death" then. In all the confusion, with the fire brigade here and everything, we thought it was a simple case of accidental death. It was only when no one could find any fire that it started to get puzzling . . . sir.'

Hamilton took a deep breath and forced himself to calm down. The schoolboy was right. This was no ordinary situation and in the constable's place he would have probably made the same decision. In a quieter voice, he said, 'I take it you did get the address of her workplace?'

'Yessir. Dr Lyell works for the Institute of Neurological Research. It's in Tyburn Place. That's the road that runs from – '

'I know where it is,' said Hamilton darkly. 'I'll go see her later.'

'Dr Lyell . . . Dr Stephanie Lyell, that name rings a bell,' said Emsley, thoughtfully. 'I've seen it somewhere recently.'

'Let's hope you saw it attached to a scientific paper on spontaneous combustion,' muttered Hamilton. 'We could do with a lucky break on this one.'

Chapter Three

'Golliwogs. Bloody golliwogs,' sighed Hamilton. It was now a few minutes past 11 a.m. and he was going through the statements taken from the residents of Hillview House for about the ninth time. He would have put the shared dream about the little girl in the fire down to some sort of strange coincidence but that telling detail about her golliwog disturbed him. Kids didn't have golliwogs these days. Not for years. He'd checked with a toy manufacturer. Accusations about golliwogs being racist had hit home with the industry – nobody made or sold golliwogs any more. So maybe it was an old golliwog that someone had given her . . .

Christ! He closed his eyes and leaned back in his chair. To hell with the golliwog and the dream; he had to stick to the hard facts or he'd go crazy. And the facts were that a young man was dead. He had jumped to his death to escape from a fire in his flat. His burns proved that. And yet there had been no fire in his flat. That was another fact. Therefore, he *hadn't* jumped to escape a fire in his flat. Then where did he get the burns from?

'Still here, Hamilton?'

He opened his eyes. It was the DCI, Russell Clery. Hamilton didn't like Clery, who was not only much younger than him but a university graduate. Clery was of the New School of British policemen; Hamilton was very much of the Old School. The dislike was mutual. 'Yeah, sir. Still here. I've been trying to put together a report on the Hillview incident but so far nothing adds up.'

'Knock it on the head then, Hamilton. Go home and get some sleep. You're officially off duty so you're not being paid for this.'

The idea of sleep had an overwhelming appeal to Hamilton, but he said, 'I know, but this has got to me, sir. I just can't figure it out. My one hope is that neighbour of the dead man. I'm going to go interview her now, the lady scientist or whatever she is. Maybe she knows something that will make sense of all this.'

Hamilton was surprised to notice a sudden, and very brief, flicker of concern on Clery's face. 'Dr Stephanie Lyell, you mean?' Clery asked him.

'That's her. Works at that old building in Tyburn Lane that used to be the local insane asylum. There's some kind of research unit based there now.' He wondered about the reason for Clery's odd reaction.

Clery said, 'Parrish can go talk to Dr Lyell. You go home. You need some sleep. You look absolutely whacked out. Okay with you, Parrish?'

Detective Constable Philip Parrish looked up from his paperwork. 'Sure, sir,' he said.

Hamilton was feeling very puzzled now. Clery was up to something. He'd never shown any concern for Hamilton's personal well-being in the past. Why would he want to prevent him from seeing this Lyell woman? Well, whatever the reason, Hamilton wasn't going to play ball. He stood up and said, 'Forget it, Parrish. I'll go. It's on my way home.' Then he looked hard at Clery. 'Unless you have some special objection, sir? I promise you I won't fall asleep on the job.'

Clery gave him a look that had sharp, pointed ends. But after a pause he said stonily, 'No objection at all, Hamilton. If you want to spend your free time doing policework for nothing, be my guest.' Then he turned and left the room.

'What the hell was *that* all about?' Hamilton asked his CID colleagues. Nobody had an answer.

*

Stephanie Lyell, furious at the interruption, met the detective in her office. 'Sit down, Detective Sergeant. Would you like a coffee?'

'Yes, thanks.' He was, she observed dispassionately, a beefy-faced man in his mid-forties. From the broken veins in his face she decided he liked his drink. Right now he was looking very tired. She buzzed her secretary and asked for two coffees. 'Now, what can I do for you?' she asked him.

'I'd like to ask you a few questions about what happened last night. I would have asked you earlier this morning but you had gone by the time I arrived. You usually start work so early?'

'No. Today is a rather important day for me and my department here at the Institute. There are last-minute arrangements to be taken care of so I hope this won't take up too much time. Anyway, I had already spoken to one of your officers before I left. I don't think there's anything else I can tell you that I haven't already told him.'

'Maybe. Maybe not. When you woke up this morning you were under the impression there was a fire somewhere in the building?'

'Yes, as I told your officer, I smelt smoke and I could hear a fire alarm bell ringing.'

'And had you been dreaming about a fire before you woke?'

She picked up a pack of Dunhill Menthol from her desk and took out a cigarette, then offered the pack to the detective. He shook his head. 'I've given it up,' he said. 'For the third time this year.'

She lit the cigarette with her gold lighter and drew in a lungful of menthol-favoured carcinogens. 'Yes, I was dreaming about a fire.'

'You saw a little girl in the fire?'

'Yes.'

'No one you recognised?'

She drew again on the cigarette. 'No. I've already told your officer this.'

'I know. But did you know that all your fellow residents in the building had a similar dream?'

This surprised her. 'They did?' Just then her secretary entered with the coffees. She put the two cups down on Stephanie's desk. 'Thanks, June,' said Stephanie. When her secretary had gone she repeated her question to Hamilton. 'The very same dream? All of them?'

'They did. All described the same little girl and the same toy she was holding. A golliwog. You didn't mention any golliwog when you spoke to the constable.'

'No,' she said, distracted. Her mind was racing. 'No, I didn't see any golliwog. You say everyone had exactly the same dream?'

'Yes. Everyone but you. No golliwog in your dream.'

'I don't understand.'

'Neither do I. I was hoping you might be able to shed some light on the mystery.'

She puffed on her cigarette and exhaled a cloud of smoke. 'I wish I could, but I can't.'

'You also told the constable that you heard your neighbour, Douglas Scott, screaming just after you woke up. And then you heard breaking glass?'

'Yes. I did.'

'Anything else? The sound of someone else's voice, perhaps?'

'No. I only heard the scream.'

'And nothing before that?' he pressed.

'No, I was asleep.' She glanced at her watch. 'Will this take much longer?'

'I hope not. Did you know Douglas Scott well?'

'Hardly. I've only ever exchanged a few words with him, and most of them were harsh ones.'

'Harsh?' He raised his eyebrows. 'How do you mean?'

'Because as a neighbour he was a nuisance. Used to play his damn music too loud. We had a few arguments about that – usually at about one in the morning. And, ironically, we argued about his smoke alarm. It went off several times in the early hours of the morning for no good reason. I told him it was obviously faulty and that he should have it replaced but I don't know if he did or not.'

'You didn't hear it last night?'

'Definitely not.'

'I gather then that your opinion of Douglas Scott wasn't too high?'

'I thought he was a yuppie yob. A City lager lout. Basically a cretin who thought he was God's gift to women.'

'So you didn't like him,' said the detective dryly.

'No, I didn't,' she said and smiled. 'But I didn't arrange for his death simply because he played his CD player too loud.'

'You think his death was "arranged"?' he asked quickly.

'Well, there must be something suspicious about it otherwise you wouldn't be here. And I was assured by both one of your officers and a fireman that there had been no fire in Mr Scott's flat.'

'Yes, that's the crux of the whole problem. Why did he jump? And where did his burns come from? Any suggestions?'

She stubbed out her cigarette and thought before she answered. 'No,' she said finally. 'None at all. You've got a real mystery on your hands. Now really, I must ask you to end this interview. I've already given you more time than I can spare. As I said, this is an important day for us here.'

The detective didn't bother to conceal his disappointment from her. 'What's so special about today?' he asked.

'We're expecting a very special visitor.'

'Who? Princess Di?'

'Not exactly. It's Marc Gilmour. I'm sure, as a policeman, you've heard of him. He's more famously known, thanks to the tabloids, as the Bone Man.'

The detective blinked his eyes. 'What kind of joke is this?'

'No joke. Gilmour is arriving here today for an indefinite stay. And when he leaves here he will be, if everything goes to plan, an entirely different man. We think we have made a breakthrough development in the treatment of sociopathic – '

She stopped when she saw the expression on his face. His already florid complexion was getting redder and his eyes were blazing with utter fury. 'You're saying that . . . Marc Gilmour is being brought here . . . to Harrow? To this building?' The words came out slowly, as if he was suddenly finding it difficult to talk.

Concerned, she said, 'Yes, but there's nothing to worry about. We've had experience with dangerous mental patients here before. Our security is excellent. The Home Office has advised your superiors at Harrow police headquarters and they raised no objections. I don't see why – ' Then she gave a start of alarm when the detective let out an explosive yell of *'Jesus Christ!'* and bounded from his chair. For a moment she thought he was going to attack her but he spun round and charged out of her office. She heard the door of the outer office thrown open and then slammed.

Her secretary appeared in the doorway looking shocked. 'What happened?' she asked.

'I'm not exactly sure,' Stephanie answered, feeling rather shocked herself. 'But I seem to have touched a raw nerve.'

'You *bastard!*' yelled Hamilton. 'You knew all about Gilmour going to that damned Institute and you deliberately kept it from me!'

Behind his desk DCI Russell Clery struggled to control his temper. Keeping his voice low and calm he said, 'In the light of past events and your special circumstances I shall forget everything you've said in this office so far, Hamilton . . . but *only* if you stop shouting at me right now and start listening to what I have to say.'

Hamilton slammed his hand down on Clery's desk-top. A photograph of Clery's wife and two children toppled over. 'You idiots! You and the Chief Super . . . agreeing to let Gilmour out of Broadmoor! Agreeing to let him come here! *Here* of all places!'

Clery glanced at the fallen photograph of his family then said coldly, 'Your last chance, Hamilton. One more word from you and your career is down the toilet. Think carefully before you open your mouth again.'

Some kind of automatic survival mechanism kicked in and Hamilton halted his tirade. His shoulders sagged and he sat down heavily in a chair. 'Sorry,' he muttered. He put his face in his hands. 'It's just . . . well, the thought of Gilmour being close by . . .'

'I understand how you must feel, Hamilton,' said Clery, trying, and failing, to sound sympathetic. 'What happened to you was terrible. Terrible. But that was over seven years ago. You've done a sterling job of picking up the pieces. I know that from your record. You don't want to put all you've achieved in jeopardy by cracking up now, do you?'

'But the thought of Gilmour . . . just down the road . . . I can't take it.'

'Neither I or the Chief Superintendent are exactly happy about it either but the Home Office made it clear that raising any formal objections would be a waste of time. They have very high hopes about this new treatment that Dr Lyell and her colleagues have come up with at the Institute.'

Hamilton gave a despairing groan. 'Don't tell me they think they can *cure* that maniac. They don't know what they're dealing with. He's not human – he's a monster.'

'Well, the Home Office thinks differently. So I want you to back off and keep a low profile. And definitely no more visits to Dr Lyell.'

Hamilton removed his hands from his face and looked at Clery. 'But I need to. I still think she holds the key to the Douglas Scott case.'

'That case is no longer your concern. You're on leave, as of now. Go home. Rest.'

'No! I don't need to go on leave – '

Clery held up a hand to silence him. 'You're on leave, Hamilton, and that's official. I don't want any arguments. Since you burst in here you've provided me with enough rope to hang you ten times over. Don't force me to go by the book. Go home.'

Hamilton stood up. 'Yes, sir,' he said dully.

*

Hamilton left the station, crossed the road and went into The Timber Carriage, the pub that stood almost opposite the station. In the saloon bar he ordered the first of what were to be many double Scotches.

Marc Gilmour was watching *Neighbours*. Dr Stephanie Lyell was watching Marc Gilmour. 'So that's the man who murdered, either directly or indirectly, twenty-seven people,' she murmured. The figure she was staring at through the one-way glass was a perfectly ordinary-looking individual. He was in his mid-thirties, of average build and weight, had brown hair and a nondescript face. 'He looks so normal.'

'Fits the general pattern,' said Jeff Blakeley, standing beside her in the observation room. 'If serial killers all looked and behaved like Hannibal Lecter we'd have no trouble in spotting them.'

'True,' she said with a smile. She turned to the male nurse. 'I'm going to speak to him. You know the routine?'

'Yes, Doctor,' said the nurse. He was a large man with very muscular arms. There was a holstered gun hanging from his belt. The gun was an air pistol that fired a dart containing a powerful and fast-acting tranquilliser.

Gilmour looked round as Stephanie and the nurse entered. His expression displayed mild curiosity. Stephanie went over to him and held out her hand, 'Hello, Marc, I'm Dr Lyell, but please call me Stephanie.'

After a moment's hesitation Gilmour took her hand and shook it. Lyell felt it was like shaking hands with a ghost, so insubstantial was his grip. She didn't think she was in any danger. Since being in Broadmoor Gilmour had displayed not the slightest sign of violence. True, there had been one unpleasant incident but Gilmour hadn't been directly involved. Even so, she was happy to know that the nurse was positioned at the door a short distance away, and she wasn't going to take any chances.

She sat down opposite him, providing the nurse with a clear

line of fire at Gilmour, and said brightly, 'I hope you'll be comfortable here. It's a very pleasant room, isn't it?'

He gave her a smile. 'Yes . . . Stephanie, it is. It's very nice. I like it.'

'Good.' She stared into his eyes. They were light brown. She realised she was still searching for some visible indication of what lay within that skull and chided herself for being unscientific. She neither believed in *evil* as such or that the eyes were the windows of the soul. They were just lumps of tissue in which the pupil could change size, or over which the lachrymal glands could vary the amount of fluid, or around which the eyelids could move. Those factors, when seen as part of the whole facial expression, could give the eyes greater emphasis in the face than any other feature. But fundamentally they were just the means, beautifully designed as they were, of getting light into the brain; not of showing things coming out. And Gilmour's brown eyes were perfectly normal. If she could detect anything in them it was a slightly vacuous look. She put this down to the mood-suppressing drugs, mainly haloperidol decanoate, he was on. She intended to drastically lower the dosage of these before she began her own work with him.

'You know why you're here, don't you?'

'Yes, Stephanie. My psychiatrist at Broadmoor explained it to me. You're going to experiment on me with a new drug. A drug that does something to the brain. He said I could refuse if I wanted to but that there was a good chance it would help me. I said I would be happy to participate in the experiment.'

'It's perfectly harmless, Marc, I assure you. We knew it would be but just to make absolutely sure I tested it on myself. And as you can see, I'm feeling just fine.'

Gilmour smiled at her again. 'Yes, Stephanie, you look fine. In fact, you look very lovely.'

Chapter Four

Stephanie was sipping a glass of Chianti and watching *The Late Show* on BBC2 when the buzzer on the intercom in her hallway buzzed. She looked at the clock on her video recorder. It was quarter to twelve and she wasn't expecting company. She got up and went into the hallway. 'Yes, who is it?'

'Detective Sergeant Hamilton, Dr Lyell. I need to speak to you, urgently.'

She sighed, said, 'Oh, all right,' and pressed the button that unlocked the front door of the building. Then she immediately regretted it. She remembered the detective's bizarre behaviour in her office that morning, and she also realised that his voice had sounded slurred over the intercom. It might be that he was drunk. And that might mean he wasn't here on official police business. She waited nervously for him to arrive, and when her front door bell did finally ring she gave a start. She put the heavy security chain into place before unlocking the door . . .

He *was* drunk. He was swaying as he stood there in the corridor, his face was bright red and shiny and his eyes were unfocused. 'What do you want?' she asked warily.

'Need to talk. To you. About Gilmour . . .' He tried to push the door open and the chain went taut. He looked surprised, clearly not understanding why the door wouldn't open. He pushed again. 'Lemme in. We got to talk.'

'Go away. You're drunk,' she told him and attempted to close the door. He pushed back, hard, and she almost lost her balance. His strength frightened her. 'Let me *in*!' he yelled. 'I got to talk to you! You got to understand that what you're doing with Gilmour is wrong. *Wrong*, dammit!' He kept slamming the door against the restraining chain. She backed away, worried that he would either break the chain or that its supports would tear loose from the wood.

'Go away!' she cried. 'Go away or I'll . . . I'll call the police!' It sounded odd to her, even in the circumstances, threatening a police detective with the police. 'Did you hear me?'

Now he was reaching in through the gap in the door, trying to unconnect the chain. It was impossible, of course, and he resumed battering at the door with his shoulder. She turned and ran into the living room. Quickly she looked up 'Police' in the Harrow directory. She expected to find just one number but the directory, despite being local, listed everything from the Transport Police to the Dog Training Establishment. Where the hell was the number for the Harrow station? It was hard to read the tiny print because her hands were shaking. The noise from the hallway became more frightening. She expected to hear the sound of splintering wood at any second. At last she found the number, and dialled it.

Even though she knew the station was only a short distance away in Northolt Road, which ran into Lower Road, she was surprised at how quickly the police arrived on the scene. The thought occurred to her, ungraciously, that it might have something to do with the fact that one of their own was involved. But whatever the reason she was grateful to hear sirens in just a little over a minute after she'd made the call. She returned to the hallway and pressed the button to let them in downstairs. If Hamilton had heard the sirens he gave no indication. He continued his bone-shaking efforts to break the door down. 'You stupid bitch! You don't know what you're doing! Let me *in*!' he bellowed.

She retreated back into the living room. A short time later she heard voices in the corridor. Hamilton stopped battering at the door. She heard him shouting at someone and then sounds of a violent struggle. His shouts slowly faded away as they hustled him down the stairs. Then came a knock on the door. 'Dr Lyell? You okay?'

She went to the door. 'Yes, I think so. Just a moment . . .' She closed the door, unhooked the chain, then opened it again. A man in a wrinkled suit stood there, behind him a policewoman. The man, in his late thirties, showed her his warrant card. 'Detective Constable Thomson, Doctor. I'm very sorry about all this. Can we come in?'

'Of course.' She ushered them into the living room and sat them down. 'Would you care for a drink?' she asked as she poured herself a glass of wine. They both said no. She quickly emptied the glass then sat down on the sofa and lit a cigarette. Her hands were still shaking.

'He didn't harm you in any way?' Thomson asked her.

'No. Just gave me a fright.' She drew on the cigarette. She noticed that *The Late Show* was just finishing on the TV. It had seemed a long time ago that she had been watching the programme. 'What's his problem?'

Thomson didn't answer her question. He said, 'I apologise on behalf of the Harrow Police Force for Detective Sergeant Hamilton's behaviour. And I'm sure the Chief Superintendent will be in touch with you tomorrow to offer his own personal apologies.'

'Yes, yes,' she said irritably, 'but what I want is an explanation for your colleague's behaviour. What is his problem? It obviously concerns Gilmour. I think you owe it to me.'

Thomson glanced at the policewoman and then said to her, 'As Dr Lyell is okay you might as well go back to the station, Diana.' The policewoman raised an eyebrow then nodded. 'All right, sir.' She got to her feet. Stephanie rose too and showed her to the door. When she returned to the living room Thomson was staring at the carpet with a troubled expression. He looked up. 'Actually, Doctor, I will have that drink.'

'Certainly. What would you like?'

'Oh, some of that wine will be fine.'

She poured him a glass, handed it to him, then returned to the sofa. 'Well?'

'It happened over seven years ago, when the Bone Man – Gilmour – was doing his thing. Terry, that's Detective Sergeant Hamilton, was in charge of the special unit at Scotland Yard that had been formed to hunt down Gilmour.'

'Really? *Him?*' she asked in surprise.

'Terry was a different man in those days. Not that I knew him then, but I knew *of* him. He was a high-flyer in the Force – a Detective Superintendent at the age of thirty-six. He'd probably be a Chief Superintendent now if, well . . ." Thomson drank some more of his Chianti. 'Being in charge of the hunt for the Bone Man meant that Terry ended up with a pretty big media profile. It was deliberate policy to try and provoke Gilmour, though we didn't know his identity then, of course, into doing something reckless by bad-mouthing him in the press and on TV. Repeating fake psychiatrists' reports saying that he was obviously a repressed homosexual who had been sexually abused by his mother – that sort of thing. It was Terry who got to say these things and it was Terry who got the messy end of the stick when the plan worked and Gilmour was stung into doing something reckless.'

'What happened?' Stephanie asked. She stubbed out the remains of her cigarette and immediately lit another one.

'One day Terry got a call at the Yard from his wife. She wanted him to come home right away. They had two kids, a boy and a girl, and one of them, the boy, had come off his bike. Nothing too serious, his wife assured Terry, but the kid was pretty shaken up and wanted his Dad. His wife sounded agitated so Terry dropped everything and headed for home. But on the way a little suspicion started growing in his mind – planted there by a policeman's sixth sense, I guess. So he didn't park his car in his own street but in the street behind his house. He was playing it safe, just in case . . .

'What he did was to go through his rear neighbour's house and yard and then climb the fence into his own back garden. He was armed – everyone in that unit was armed, off-duty as well as on. So he drew his revolver, crept up to his house and peeped in one of the kitchen windows at the side. What he saw in the kitchen turned his little suspicion into one hell of a nightmare. The Bone Man was there. So was his wife and one of his kids. It was his five-year-old daughter. She was dead. She'd been stabbed in the neck. There was no sign of his eight-year-old son. His wife was still alive. But the Bone Man had a knife to her throat and was clearly waiting for Terry to arrive home.'

'Horrible . . .' whispered Stephanie.

'Yeah. Well, Terry had no choice but to try and pick the Bone Man off before he had time to use the knife. Terry knew it was going to be a tough shot even though the Bone Man and his wife were only yards away. Terry had had firearms training but he was no marksman. And there was also the problem of shooting through the closed window. The glass might deflect the bullet. But as I said, he had no choice. He took aim and fired.'

Stephanie stifled a yelp of pain as her ignored cigarette singed her fingers. She quickly stubbed it out. 'And?'

'It could have happened to anyone. Like I said, Terry was no marksman. It wasn't his fault.'

'*What* wasn't?' she asked impatiently.

'The bullet hit his wife. Struck her in the head. Killed her instantly.'

"Oh God . . .'

'He fired again. The Bone Man had turned towards the window by then, using Terry's wife's body as a shield. The second bullet clipped him on the shoulder. He let go of the body and tried to make it through the kitchen doorway into the front of the house. Terry's third bullet caught him low in the back and the Bone Man dropped. That's why Gilmour is minus a kidney and his spleen.'

They sat there in silence for a time. Then Lyell said, 'What about his son? Was he dead too?'

'No. He was found bound and gagged in a linen cupboard but physically unhurt.'

'Well, that's *something* to be grateful for,' she said, relieved.

'Not really. I said he was *physically* unharmed but mentally he had been totally wrecked.'

'How?'

Thomson drained his glass. 'It hadn't been the Bone Man who had killed the boy's sister – it had been the boy himself.'

'*What?!*'

'It was a trick the Bone Man had often used – to fool or force someone else into doing the dirty work while he looked on and had a bloody good laugh. Except he'd never done it with kids before. This was a first.'

'God.' Stephanie felt ill. 'But how . . . ? How could Gilmour possibly persuade a young boy to stab his sister to death?'

'He tortured the boy's mother in front of his eyes. He told the boy his mother would stop crying if he would simply stick the knife into his sister's throat. She was gagged and bound to a chair. The kid was forced to choose between his mother and his sister and, naturally, ended up choosing his mother. When he couldn't take any more he closed his eyes and stabbed his sister. Several times. It took a long time to get the whole story out of the boy. On top of the trauma caused by killing his sister he completely freaked out afterwards when he found out that his mother had died anyway. He blamed himself for her death as well as the death of his sister.'

Stephanie pressed her fingers to the sides of her temples. 'I don't remember hearing about this at the time. I wasn't in the country – I was working in the States – but I'm sure I would have read about it in one of the newspapers. Even though it was a British story the Bone Man and his eventual capture was big news there.'

Thomson shook his head. 'No, it was hushed up. For the kid's sake, for Terry's sake . . . even for the Force's sake. It wouldn't have looked good for the long-awaited apprehension of the Bone Man to have been marked by such a total and awful cock-up: cop shoots his own wife while aiming at the Bone Man; cop's son murders own sister . . . No, it was better for all concerned if the truth was dressed up.'

She nodded slowly and said, 'What happened to the son?'

'He spent a couple of years in a mental institution. He lives in Australia now. With his aunt – his mother's sister. I understand he can't remember a thing about what happened that day. He's wiped it all from his mind. But he knows that Terry killed his mother and he hasn't forgiven him. Refuses to have any contact with him. And I hear he's generally in bad psychological shape.'

'And what happened to Hamilton?'

'He went to pieces, understandably. Couldn't work; hit the booze hard. Ended up in hospital suffering from malnutrition and an enlarged liver. When he was released the Force paid for him to enter a clinic and get dried out. Then they took him back on board, though at a reduced rank, and have kept a close eye on him ever since. That was five years ago and he hasn't put a step wrong in all that time. Worked his way up from Detective Constable to Detective Sergeant, though he's not going to go any higher than that and he knows it. And in the four years I've known him I've never seen him drunk. Oh, he drinks all right, but I've never seen him drunk . . . until tonight. That's the effect this Gilmour business has had on him.'

She was silent for a while and then said, with a smile, 'Are you suggesting that tonight's events were all my fault?'

'Oh no, *no*,' he said hastily. 'I just hoped that . . .'

'You just hoped that if I knew the full story I wouldn't press charges against Hamilton.'

'Well, yes,' he said, looking anxious.

'Don't worry, it worked. I'm not going to press charges. Nor will I inform the Home Office what happened.'

She found his look of relief amusing. 'Thank you, Dr Lyell, I really appreciate that,' he said. 'And I'm sure that Chief Superintendent Bradford will say the same thing when he contacts you tomorrow.' He stood up and extended his hand. She rose and shook it. 'I'm sure he will,' she told him.

When Thomson had left, Stephanie poured herself another glass of wine and reflected on what he had told her. It certainly provided a satisfactory explanation for Hamilton's behaviour, but it also changed her attitude towards Gilmour. Suddenly the horrors he had committed upon people had assumed a disturbing reality in her mind rather than being mere academic facts.

During the night Stephanie dreamt of the lab technician, Derek, again. Again he made passionate love to her and again the dream was very intense. Then, to her disgust, Derek turned into Gilmour. She screamed and woke up. She checked the time – it was 4.25 a.m. – then slowly went back to sleep. At 4.30 a.m., on the first floor, Miss Delia Coope hanged herself.

Chapter Five

'You going to be okay?'

Hamilton opened his eyes and focused, with difficulty, on Thomson. 'Yeah,' he grunted.

'You sure? I could hang around for a bit if you like.'

'Nah. You go home.'

Thomson still hesitated at the door. 'You look like shit.'

'I feel like shit.' And that was true. He ached all over, he felt nauseous, his head ached and there was a godawful taste in his mouth. He had spent the night in one of the station's holding cells, sleeping it off. In deference to his status they hadn't shoved anyone else in there with him. Then, after many cups of coffee, Thomson had helped him in the washroom with the futile task of trying to make him look a little more respectable prior to his 'meeting' with the Chief Superintendent. And hadn't *that* been a bundle of laughs? Indefinite suspension on half pay and threatened disciplinary hearing if he so much as passed Dr Stephanie Lyell in the street, much less tried to make deliberate contact with her. Bradford had made it clear that if it came to a hearing he would be off the force. He shut his eyes again. He was only half aware of Thomson's radio suddenly crackling into life and Thomson's acknowledgement of the call. Hamilton was seriously considering handing in his resignation. To hell with everything.

'The place must be jinxed,' said Thomson.

Hamilton opened his eyes again. 'What?'

'That was Sergeant Newman. Thought I'd be interested to know that there's been another incident at Hillview House.'

'Well, it was nothing to do with me,' Hamilton joked weakly, 'I've got an alibi.'

Thomson grinned and said, 'At least this one seems to be a straightforward suicide. An old biddy hanged herself. Her cleaning woman discovered the body about half an hour ago.'

Hamilton sat up a little and frowned. 'No fire alarms this time? Dreams of non-existent fires?'

'I don't know and I don't care. Not my concern, and certainly not yours.'

'Yeah, but you've got to admit it's weird – two deaths in the same building in two days.'

'Coincidence, mate. Now stop thinking about it and get some rest. And for God's sake lay off the booze. I'm going. I'll give you a call later.'

Hamilton sighed. 'Okay. And thanks. For everything.' Thomson had told him about talking to Dr Lyell and persuading her not to press charges.

'No problem. Take care.'

When he heard his front door slam shut Hamilton got up and went into his bathroom. He stripped and got under the shower. He turned the cold tap full on and stood shivering under the icy spray for about two minutes. Then he turned on the hot water and shampooed his head. After drying himself he put on clean clothes and swallowed three aspirin and codeine tablets with a pint of orange juice from the refrigerator. By then he was beginning to feel a little better. He went back into the living room and sat down by his phone. After checking the local directory he dialled the number of the Institute for Neurological Research and asked for Dr Stephanie Lyell.

'It's good of you to see me, Dr Lyell, after . . . yesterday and last night.'

'As I said to you on the phone, Detective Sergeant, there's no need to apologise. Your colleague told me the whole, ghastly story. It's no wonder that unexpectedly learning Gilmour was here on the premises came as a terrible shock to you.'

They were sitting in her office again. He had been relieved when she'd said she was prepared to meet with him again. He'd told her that this visit was completely unofficial and that he'd appreciate it if she kept it to herself. 'Yeah, well "shock" is hardly the word for it. Seven years on and I still relive that day every day. And every day I wish I could go back in time and have another chance at firing that first bullet. If only it was his brains I'd blown out instead of ... of ...' He drew fiercely on the cigarette he'd accepted from her. He hadn't wanted to start smoking again, and he thought menthol-flavoured cigarettes were only for women and poofs, but he badly needed something and it was either the cigarette or a drink.

She watched him with interest. Yesterday she had regarded him as simply a boorish policeman but after what the other detective had told her last night she now saw him very differently. She felt a strong sympathy for him, of course, but she also now saw him as a fascinating case study. 'I don't want to insult you by saying that I understand how you feel,' she told him, 'but I *do* understand guilt. There was a family tragedy when I was twelve – someone died, and it was my fault. So I do know a little about what you've been going through all these years.'

He nodded, and she noted he didn't look convinced. 'I take it you want to talk about Gilmour?' she asked. 'About what we hope to achieve with him here at the Institute?'

'Yeah. I'm curious about this so-called "cure" you're going to try and work on him.'

'It's clear you disapprove.'

'Yeah, because Gilmour is simply an unspeakably evil bastard who should not be alive. Why waste the tax-payers' money trying to cure the uncurable?'

She paused before saying, 'Gilmour is an extreme example of a psychopathic murderer. What such psychopaths have in common is a lack of guilt or remorse about their actions. Otherwise they can be very personable or very dull; they can be extraordinarily intelligent or have the IQ of an amoeba. They can, in short, be like anyone except for that one thing: their inability to empathise. They cannot understand what another human being might be suffering.'

'With all due respect, Doctor,' said Hamilton gruffly, 'I think that's rubbish. They know perfectly well what pain they're causing.'

She nodded. 'Yes, I know. And they enjoy it. But they don't – they *can't* – comprehend what it might feel like to be the sufferer.'

'Of *course* they do. That's the whole point of why they do what they do.'

'You're deliberately misunderstanding me. Empathy goes far deeper than just knowing that another person is suffering. It is sharing the anticipated effects of that feeling as one human being to another. It is the ability to put yourself in someone else's place. Psychopathic killers, like very young children, can't do that.'

'I'm sorry, Doctor,' said Hamilton, 'but this is all double-talk as far as I'm concerned. I don't need to put myself in someone else's place to know that if I punch him on the nose it's going to hurt him. In our society we all grow up knowing that punching someone in the face is wrong and we only do it if we're so annoyed or so pissed, or both, that we forget the rules, or if we're defending ourselves, or defending someone else. All of those are understandable reasons but it's the people who, stone cold sober, deliberately punch you in the face for the sheer fun of it. They like it. And they like it because they're evil.'

She gave a little sigh. '"Evil" isn't a helpful word to a scientist, I'm afraid.'

'You don't accept that there are people who are just plain evil?' he asked her.

'Speaking again as a scientist I find the term far too simplistic. There are people who do evil things, yes, but the idea that they are somehow *evil* in themselves smacks too much of theology rather than science.'

'Well, I'm not a religious man but I believe in people who are actually evil. Christ, I've come across them enough times in my work. There's something about them. You sense it. You have one of them banged up in a cell and the whole station senses it. Like there's something in the air. Just like in here now.'

'Because of Gilmour, you mean?'

'Yeah, because of Gilmour.'

'Let me ask you something – were you aware of this unpleasant atmosphere within the Institute when you visited yesterday? I mean, before you knew about Gilmour?'

He frowned as he thought back to the previous day, then nodded and said, 'Come to think of it, I did feel kind of uncomfortable as soon as I entered the building.'

She smiled. 'Of course you did.'

'You don't believe me?'

'I'm suggesting that your memory is being influenced by hindsight. I'm certainly not aware of any change in the atmosphere here since Gilmour's arrival. And nobody else has commented on any such thing.'

'Yeah, but when you're a cop you become more sensitive to that kind of thing. You develop an instinct.'

'Oh really?' she said dryly. 'Yes, I've heard all about how policemen just *know* when someone is guilty. And it's such an infallible tool. Just ask the Guildford Four or the Birmingham Six.'

He scowled. 'Let's not get side-tracked into *that* area. I'm talking about something different. Surely you must feel something when you're with Gilmour.'

'Nope. I don't like him, I admit it, but that's because I know of his past. But no "bad vibrations", if that's what you mean. Gilmour is simply a man with something missing, and that missing something allows him to do terrible things to people.'

'*Allows* him? That sounds like you think we'd all be like Gilmour if we didn't have this empathy you keep going on about,' muttered Hamilton.

'No. There are a lot of people about who are psychopaths

by definition and who don't go around committing mindless violence. By and large they manage to follow society's rules and conform. Psychopathic killers like Gilmour, I believe, are set off by some sort of trigger, usually when they're young, though not necessarily so. They make the discovery they enjoy hurting things; they like the feeling of power it gives them. Gilmour is a case in point: came from a perfectly normal, if there is such a thing, family. His older brother and two younger sisters are quite conventional, law-abiding people while Gilmour is . . . well, Gilmour. According to the records he had a history of torturing and killing animals from the age of six. At school he was a vicious bully though by then he'd refined his tactics to include mental torture as well as physical abuse.'

Hamilton shrugged. 'So it proves what I said. The shit was born evil.'

'I agree with you that he was born like that, but because of a genetic failing, not a spiritual one.'

'Oh, come on,' he scoffed. 'Are you trying to tell me that Gilmour's a mass murderer because of a genetic defect?'

'That's exactly what I'm trying to tell you,' said Lyell. 'Tests on psychopaths have revealed a common neurological feature – they lack a certain neurotransmitter in their brain. One called BDNFE to be specific. I don't want to sound patronising but you do know what a neurotransmitter is, don't you?'

'Yeah, I think so,' he said doubtfully. 'It's a chemical in your brain . . . something to do with the nervous system.'

'Yes. Neurotransmitters transmit messages between brain cells. There's a whole range of them and each one performs a specific task. We believe that BDNFE provided an essential role in man's development as a highly social creature. A similar chemical has been found in the brains of all the primates with sophisticated social systems involving mutual co-operation in food-gathering, hunting, defence against enemies and so on. We think this is the neurotransmitter that allows the human brain to empathise with fellow human creatures outside of its own personal experience of reality.'

'Well, you've lost me there, Doctor.'

'It's quite simple. BDNFE programs for empathy in the human brain. Gilmour doesn't have any in his, so we inject him with a synthetic substitute and see what happens. We believe we've identified the gene that creates the protein that produces BDNFE within the brain so we've extracted the gene from the DNA of a normal person, inserted it into a yeast cell and let it multiply. The yeast produces BDNFE as a side-product, providing us with a relatively large supply of the chemical. And today we start administering the synthetic BDNFE.'

Hamilton took another menthol cigarette from her packet. He lit it with her lighter and said, 'And this is going to turn Gilmour into a perfect citizen; one safe to be released on to the streets again?' He didn't bother to disguise the contempt in his voice.

'It's not some kind of moral miracle drug, Detective Sergeant. If it works it will give him the empathic capacity of a normal person, and, as you've already pointed out, so-called normal people are quite capable of excessive acts of violence depending on the circumstances. So don't worry – no one has even mentioned releasing Gilmour, no matter what the results of our experiment. Even if they beat our highest expectations there are too many risk factors involved. The required dosage may alter over the years, for example. So don't worry, Gilmour is inside for life.'

Slightly mollified, Hamilton said, 'Just how do you plan to go about testing whether your drug works or not? Give Gilmour a knife and then shove some poor bastard into his cell and see what happens?'

'We have a very sophisticated series of tests that will accurately monitor any profound changes in his personality,' she assured him.

'From the reports I've read the psychiatrists thought he was a low-risk proposition after he'd been in Broadmoor for five years. They did a reassessment on him and pronounced him a . . . well, I forget all the jargon, but it was something about his personality responding positively to the institutional environment.'

'Yes, I've read those reports,' she said briskly.

'And then he persuades that dumb sod to knife a nurse to death.'

'That was never proven, though admittedly the circumstantial evidence points that way.'

'The guy who did the killing was a mentally sub-normal thirty-year-old with a history of bothering little girls but with no history at all of any acts of physical violence. He was rated as completely harmless by the staff at Broadmoor. Then Gilmour got to him somehow. The guy then grabs a woman nurse, locks himself inside an office with her and proceeds to hack her to pieces. Afterwards he calmly gives himself up and tells everyone that he had to do it because of what that nice Mr Gilmour had told him. And he's never said anything much that makes sense ever since that day.'

'I said I'd read the reports.'

'Gilmour is devious and manipulative. Christ, I have enough personal evidence of that. You know what he got my son to do to my daughter! You'll never be able to trust him, no matter what your "very sophisticated series of tests" tell you!' His voice had risen with his anger. Suddenly realising this he stopped and then muttered, 'Sorry, I'm getting out of line again.'

'It's all right. I quite understand. But you must believe me when I tell you that you have nothing to worry about. We know what we're doing here at the Institute and we won't underestimate Gilmour. And if we succeed in this experiment we will have established a major breakthrough in treating psychopathic personality disorders. We might be able to prevent another Marc Gilmour from ever happening again.'

'Yeah, well, I'll believe that when you pull it off,' he muttered, clearly not convinced.

She looked at him for a time then said, 'Would you like to see him?'

'Who? *Gilmour?*'

'Yes. I don't mean meet him in person. Just take a look at him from the observation room. He won't see you. It might help you.'

'*Help me?*' He looked horrified. 'How could seeing that bloody monster possibly help me?'

'Perhaps lay a few ghosts. Help you to see that he is not this terrible demon that you've built up in your mind over the years since those awful events. It will show you that he's just an ordinary man. A very sick one who is still very capable of committing atrocities given the opportunity but basically just a human being.'

He stubbed out his cigarette and stared at the smouldering remains in the ashtray. Then he looked up and said, 'Okay, you're the doctor. I'll take a look at him, but I don't think it's going to make me feel any better.'

Hamilton's stomach muscles tightened as he stepped into the observation room. His emotions were in a turmoil and he badly needed a drink. There was a male nurse sitting there who gave him a curious glance and then raised an eyebrow at Dr Lyell. She said, 'It's okay, Gary. He has official clearance.'

Hamilton went up to the glass panel and peered into the next room. His first impression was how comfortably furnished Gilmour's cell was, then he examined Gilmour himself. Gilmour was relaxed in an armchair and watching television. Some brainless afternoon game show was running. Hamilton stared at Gilmour. He hadn't changed much in seven years. He'd put on a little weight and his face was fleshier but otherwise he still looked the same man who'd destroyed his family. Hamilton clenched his fists.

'What are you feeling?' Dr Lyell asked him quietly.

'How I expected to feel: sick,' he growled. 'I'd like to twist his goddamn head right off his shoulders.'

Just then Gilmour turned and looked towards them.

'It's all right, he can't see or hear us,' said Lyell.

At that moment Gilmour's eyes locked right on to Hamilton's. Then Gilmour smiled straight at him and Hamilton felt a cold shudder run through his body. Gilmour then returned his attention to the television. 'Christ,' muttered Hamilton. His face was covered in icy sweat. 'I've got to get out of here.'

Outside, in the corridor, Lyell touched his arm and said, 'I'm sorry. I made a mistake. I shouldn't have asked you to see him.'

Hamilton was trying to stop trembling. 'How did that bastard *see* me? I thought you said it was one-way glass.'

'It is. There's no way he could have seen you through it. All he can see is a mirror on his side. But, as you say, he's probably well aware that it is an observation window and knows that someone is keeping him under continual watch, as we are. It was just an unfortunate coincidence that you happened to be there when he gave it a glance. He's probably doing that all the time.'

'The bastard fucking *smiled* at me!' cried Hamilton.

'It was just a coincidence. Really,' she tried to assure him.

He leaned against a wall, fighting to control his trembling. He was beginning to feel foolish in front of this attractive woman. 'When do you start injecting him with your stuff?' he asked.

'This afternoon.'

'Any chance it will kill him?'

She shook her head. 'It's completely harmless.'

'Pity.'

In the entrance hall he paused and turned to her. 'I had another reason for wanting to talk to you today. Have you heard about the suicide in your block of flats this morning?'

Her eyes widened with surprise. 'No! I left early as usual. Who was it?'

'I don't know her name. All I know is that she was elderly and lived on the first floor.'

Dr Lyell put her hand to her mouth. 'Oh no! That would be Miss Coope. How awful! Why on earth would she want to commit suicide? She's always seemed a very cheerful sort whenever I've spoken to her.'

Hamilton shrugged. 'Who knows? Maybe the autopsy will show she was suffering from a serious illness. Or maybe it will be put down to the all-purpose reason for suicide – depression. But whatever the reason it strikes me as odd coming so soon after the death of your other neighbour.'

'Yes,' she said, frowning. 'It does seem odd.'

'Can you think of any possible connection between the two deaths?'

She shook her head. 'None whatsoever. Can you?'

'On the face of it, no,' he admitted, disappointed. 'But I have a hunch that there is.'

Chapter Six

After saying goodbye to Dr Lyell, Hamilton walked out into the courtyard and came face to face with one of the last people he wanted to see at that particular moment.

He managed briefly to hold on to the frantic hope that she didn't know . . . but when he saw the expression on her face as she recognised him he knew that she did. Oh shit . . .

'Hi, Josie,' he said, defeatedly.

'Hi, Terry! Well, who's being a naughty boy then? I'd heard you were on suspension, and that it all had to do with this place and a certain lady scientist who works here.'

He gave a deep sigh and took her by the arm. 'Look, can we have a little talk about this? In private?' He began to lead her away from the entrance of the Institute.

She laughed. 'You know me, Terry. Always eager to help the police any time I can. Where shall we go to have this talk?'

He hesitated. He knew he shouldn't drink today but . . . oh, to hell with it. 'Let's go to a pub. The Green Man okay with you?'

'Fine, Terry. Wherever you want.'

Josie Welch settled back in her chair and gave him a smug, self-congratulatory look. 'So what the fuck is going on, Terry? What's with you and the lady scientist? Off the record, of course.'

'Of course,' he said wearily and swallowed a mouthful of

Scotch and soda. Josie Welch was a journalist on one of the
local Harrow papers. She was also a cop groupie. Or rather, a
CID groupie. The word was that uniforms were no turn on at
all for her, but detectives were. Young, old, it didn't matter.
The 'word' about her usually came from either Alan Farris or
John Dayton, both Detective Constables, who openly bragged
about regularly having it off with her. But both Farris and
Dayton were single; Hamilton was pretty certain a number, if
not all, the married men in CID had also experienced Josie
Welch at close range but were keeping quiet about it for diplo-
matic reasons. In the past she had certainly made it obvious
to him on more than one occasion that she was available, but
not recently. She had plainly written him off as a waste of
time. The fact was that Hamilton had been celibate since . . .
since the encounter with Gilmour. It wasn't a willing celibacy
but since the death of his wife every time he had tried to make
love to a woman he'd been completely impotent. No sign of life
at all. He'd long given up trying.

Looking at Josie Welch opposite him, however, made Hamilton think that it might be worth giving it one more try. She
was a pretty girl, with a round, vivacious face, frizzy red hair
and a body that was generous and slim at the same time, which
the best female bodies tended to be, in his opinion. The points
against her were her foul mouth – Hamilton didn't like to
hear young women swearing – and her dress sense. Today was
typical in the latter department: she was wearing a canary-
yellow jacket, a T-shirt with black and white stripes, a red
mini-skirt and black tights covered with white polka dots. The
effect was set off by a pair of huge, dangly, green earrings and
her large, pink-tinted spectacles with round red frames. She
looked like a presenter from a children's TV show.

The one other negative thing against Josie Welch was that
she couldn't be trusted. She was underhand, devious and quite
ruthless. She would make an ideal journalist on a major tabloid
paper: which was her burning ambition. Still, in his position
right now he had no choice but to talk to her and throw himself
on her probably non-existent mercy.

'How much do you know?' he asked her.

'Only that you threw a major wobbly in the DCI's office yesterday morning, got spectacularly drunk, tried to break into Dr Lyell's flat in the evening, spent the night in a cell and got suspended this morning with strict orders to stay away from the same lady scientist, or else.'

He regarded her sourly. 'Well, I can't add much to that. Am I going to read all about it in the *Harrow Examiner?*'

'Oh no, I wouldn't do a thing like that to you. Besides, I've been asked to spike the story.'

'By who?'

'By your DCI, Clery. He said he would greatly appreciate it if I kept quiet about it. I took the hint.'

'I see.' Well, Clery wouldn't want any bad publicity about one of his own detectives. Might reflect badly on him, and Clery's relentless crawl up the promotional ladder was all that mattered to him. Idly, he wondered if Clery had ever sampled Josie's wares, and then decided no, he wouldn't have.

'It's all to do with the Bone Man, isn't it?' she asked.

He winced at the mention of Gilmour's tabloid nick-name, then nodded.

'Look, I know about what happened to your family, Terry. I know it must be hard for you to talk about this stuff. Don't do it if you don't want to.' She sounded sincere and compassionate. She was good at that. People believed her, opened up and spilled everything then got a shock when they read what that really nice girl had written about them in her paper.

'It's okay,' he lied back. 'What do you want to know?'

'What's going on with the Bone Man at that Institute? I know he's there but that's all. I'm getting stone-walled. I rang and asked your lady scientist for an interview but she said no. That's why I dropped round in person, to try and see her.'

He drank more of his Scotch then said, 'They're doing an experiment on *Gilmour*' – he stressed the name, hoping she'd pick up on it, stop calling him by his filthy nick-name – 'trying to turn him into a model citizen.'

Josie hurriedly reached into her large shoulder bag (a shiny green vinyl job covered with large pink flowers) that was sitting on the floor beside her seat and got out a notebook and pen. 'Fucking hell . . .' she said, and wrote rapidly in the notebook. 'What methods are they going to use? Aversion therapy? I saw a bootleg video of that movie that's banned here – *A Clockwork Orange* – and in that they strapped this psycho into a chair with his eyes forced open and – '

Hamilton shook his head. 'No, nothing like that. They're going to use a drug.'

'And if it works, what then? Are they going to let him free?' She was looking excited. Hamilton guessed she was seeing big headlines with her by-line beneath them.

'Dr Lyell says no, whatever the results of the experiment.'

She looked disappointed and then sucked thoughtfully on the end of her pen for a few moments. She had full lips and was wearing lipstick of a very bright shade of red. Hamilton couldn't help but find the gesture erotic. Then her expression brightened. 'Well, even so, it's still a major story for my paper: Britain's Worst Mass Murderer Secretly Moved to Local Medical Institute. People will be outraged.'

'Yeah, probably.'

'Well, *you* certainly were when you found out. When Pat Thomson and a bunch of uniforms got to the lady scientist's flat they found you trying to batter down her front door. You put up a hell of a struggle when they grabbed you, ranting and raving and carrying on like a – '

He held up a hand to halt her flow. 'It's all right, you don't have to tell me. I was there, remember? And yes, I did go completely off the rails. It was the sudden shock of finding out that Gilmour was in the same building that afternoon while I was interviewing Dr Lyell about another matter. But I've calmed down now. And the Doctor kindly agreed to forget the matter. After today's talk with her I'm pretty confident that there's nothing to worry about. I'm still not happy about Gilmour being in the vicinity but that's my personal problem. I don't think the general public has any cause for concern. Security at the Institute is tight and Gilmour is kept under constant watch.' He wished he really felt as confident as he was trying to sound but he had to dampen down Josie's enthusiasm for the story.

His efforts seemed to be working. She was looking disappointed again. 'Even so,' she said, 'the public should have been told about it.'

'The Home Office thinks otherwise,' he told her. 'And I suspect that if you print the story your editor may suddenly find himself in very hot water with the government.'

She thought about that for a while. Then she screwed up her face and said, 'I guess you're right. Fuck. It's such a good story.'

Hamilton felt relieved. 'Well, I think it would be best for all concerned, including you, if you just let it lie.'

'And for you too,' she said pointedly.

'Yeah,' he admitted. 'For me too.'

She pushed her empty glass towards him across the table-top. 'I think you owe me another drink.'

'Sure. Same again?'

She nodded and he got up and took the glasses to the bar. He ordered another Mud Slide for her and double Scotch for himself. When he returned to their table with the drinks she said, 'You mentioned that you were interviewing your lady scientist about another matter yesterday. What was it?'

He was happy to tell her, pleased that she had apparently agreed to drop the idea of a story on Gilmour. 'It was about that suspicious death at Hillview House yesterday. The young guy who threw himself out of his third-floor flat, apparently trying to escape from a fire that didn't exist. You know all about it, I presume?'

'Sure. I covered the story.'

'Well, Dr Lyell was his next-door neighbour.'

'Really?' Her eyes lit up and Hamilton could picture her devious little tabloid mind revving into overdrive as she ran through all the possible angles that this new information might signify.

He smiled at her and said, 'No, I doubt that Dr Lyell was having an affair with Douglas Scott, threw petrol over him in a jealous rage and set him alight. But I admit it would make a nice story for you if it was true.'

She pouted. 'So why were you interested in Dr Lyell?'

'I just wanted to talk to her about it, ask if she'd heard anything suspicious that night. She said no. And today I wanted to ask her about the other death at Hillview House. The suicide this morning. To find out if she could suggest any connection between the two.'

'I'm already ahead of you there,' she said, triumphantly. 'I've been trying to find an angle on that all morning. I went to Hillview House as soon as I heard about the old lady and interviewed all the residents – all the ones that were home, that is.'

He was immediately interested. 'You have? What did you find out?'

'Well, not much,' she admitted, 'but there's something definitely fucking weird about that place. All the people I spoke to were in a bad way.'

'How do you mean?'

'Shaky. Distracted. And I don't think it was just because of the two deaths in the building. Something else seemed to be worrying them. In one case the reason was obvious – a young woman tearfully told me that her husband had walked out on her the day before. Announced he was gay right out of the blue and left.' Josie laughed. 'Fucking way-out, hey?'

'Yeah,' he grunted. 'So what else did you find out?'

'Only that three of them all mentioned that they'd had a rough night because of bad dreams.'

'*Dreams?*' he asked eagerly. 'What kind of dreams? Did they say they dreamt of fires?'

'Nope. They wouldn't say anything about them. Only that they were bad.' Josie frowned. 'It was funny but I got the impression that everyone I spoke to was *embarrassed* about something.'

'Yeah?'

'Yeah. Hey, do you think they're all in it together? Maybe they all belong to a witches coven, or a devil-worshipping sect.' Her eyes sparkled at the thought. 'The guy and the old lady wanted to drop out and the others killed them. What do say?'

He couldn't help smiling. 'Make a great headline, wouldn't it? "Satanic Cult Found in Harrow Block of Flats!" But no, I'm sorry, I don't think so.'

'Shit. So what's your brilliant theory then?'

'I don't have one yet. I just know there's a link between the two deaths but so far I can't spot it.'

She sucked the end of her pen again. 'There's one obvious thing they have in common.'

'What's that?'

'Well, the guy jumped out his window and the old lady hung herself. Don't you see? Both of them were desperately trying to *escape* something.'

He stared at her. 'That's true,' he said slowly. 'We know what Douglas Scott was trying to escape from – a fire . . .'

'Except there wasn't one.'

'Yeah. But what was the old lady trying to get away from? No one you talked to today mentioned another false alarm about a fire, did they?'

'Nope. Hey, maybe the place is haunted! They both saw something so horrible they had to kill themselves.'

'Christ, Josie, do you ever stop thinking like a tabloid reporter and visit the real world?'

She bristled. 'Anyway, what's all this got to do with *you* now? You're on suspension. You're off the case.'

'I know,' he said, regretting that he had undone all his good work by getting her back up. 'But it's got under my skin. It just doesn't make sense and I don't like it when I can't make sense of something. I like everything neat and tidy in my job.'

'Yeah, well you did a hell of a job yourself yesterday in messing up your own job,' she said sarcastically.

'I know. Look, Josie, I'd appreciate it a hell of a lot if you didn't tell a single soul at the station about seeing me at the Institute this afternoon.'

She gave him a speculative look. 'Just how appreciative are you prepared to be?'

He thought it would come to this. 'As much as you want me

to be,' he said, hoping that when the crunch came he could manage something better than a limp dick. He suspected that Josie would not find such a non-development amusing. Not to mention satisfactory.

She put her hand over his. 'How about coming back to my flat and proving it?' she asked.

'I'd love to,' he said, and to his surprise he was feeling more than a little turned on by her.

'Great.' She quickly finished the remains of her drink. 'By the way, in case you're worried, I'm not HIV positive. I've been tested recently, and these days I'm into safe sex only.'

'Oh, good,' he said weakly as she grabbed her lurid shoulder bag and stood up. Then he asked her, 'Er, aren't you going to ask about me?'

She laughed at him. 'Oh, Terry. I know all about *you*. So I don't think I have anything to worry about. Come on, let's go!'

She had started getting out of her clothes as soon as she'd shut the door of her flat. Harrison quickly discovered that everything that Alan Farris and John Dayton had said about Josie was not the usual male fantasising and exaggeration but absolutely true. She was a one-hundred-per-cent-proof sex maniac. They had first made love right there on her living-room floor, right after she had produced a handful of condoms from her lurid shoulder bag, then, after a couple of drinks, on the kitchen floor and then in the bathroom. He had no idea what she had against beds.

He was in her unmade bed now. Alone. She was somewhere else in her small flat, presumably dozing as all was quiet. Strange girl, he mused. But certainly an arousing one. To his relief he had, for the first time in seven years, succeeded in maintaining an erection. He doubted if he figured very highly on Josie's sexual ratings system but personally he was pleased with his performance. Or rather, performances. Okay, the first one had been a bit rushed but that was to be expected. Performances two and three had been spot on. The thought of the third occasion, with Josie bending face down over the edge of the bath, caused his penis to stir again. It couldn't have been very comfortable for her but she seemed to have enjoyed herself.

He wondered why, after seven years, he had suddenly regained his potency. Was it simply because of Josie? Was it because her rampant sexuality, her complete lack of inhibition, acted upon him as an aphrodisiac? Or was it because of something else? Like seeing Gilmour again? Had Dr Lyell been right when she'd said the experience would be good for him and would help him to lay some old ghosts that had been festering inside him for the past seven years? Possibly . . .

Then he remembered, only too clearly, the smile Gilmour had given him through the one-way glass and his veins seemed to fill instantly with ice water. He shivered and his half-erect penis promptly shrivelled.

No, he had not laid any ghosts today. Only Josie.

Chapter Seven

Stephanie Lyell didn't return home from the Institute until after 9 p.m. She showered, changed into a casual shirt and jeans and then opened a bottle of white wine, a reasonably priced Chablis. She cooked herself a light supper, a piece of sole which she simmered in white wine – not the Chablis – along with slices of mushrooms and a lot of garlic, and then ate it in the living room while she watched the ten o'clock news on ITN. She then watched a movie on Channel 4, *The Last Detail* starring Jack Nicholson, while she finished the Chablis. She began to nod off towards the end of the film so decided to give it up and go to bed. First she went into the bathroom and gave herself an injection of BDNFE in the arm.

In her bedroom she locked the door, draped her discarded clothes across a chair and then fell gratefully into bed. As usual she slept naked. She switched off her bedside lamp and quickly slipped into a deep sleep.

Two hours later she woke abruptly.

She lay there in the dark, listening to her racing heart and wondering what it was that had awoken her. A noise from the street below perhaps? Or some disturbance in the building? She lay perfectly still, listening, and trying to determine why she felt so frightened.

Then it occurred to her – perhaps she had heard a rat in her bedroom. She had a serious phobia about rats. It went back to her childhood, though she could never remember if it had a

specific cause. But whatever the reason rats absolutely terrified her.

She listened anxiously, waiting to hear the dreadful pitter-
patter of rodent feet. True, she had never seen a rat inside
Hillview House, but she did know that they had been sighted
in the rear garden and that the council had sent a man round
to lay down rat poison on more than one occasion. It wasn't
impossible that a rat had somehow entered her flat.

But she could hear nothing, apart from the ticking of the
bedside clock. She began to relax. A simple case of the night
fears. Calm down, she told her still-racing heart, there's nothing to be afraid of. She sat up, clutching the duvet protectively
to her breasts. She reached out towards her lamp and switched
it on.

'Hello, lovely Stephanie,' said Marc Gilmour.

She stared at him blankly, refusing to believe the evidence
of her own eyes. He was sitting in the chair on which she had
thrown her clothes. He gave her a shy smile. 'I really appreciate what you're doing for me, Stephanie, so I decided to come
round in person and demonstrate my gratitude.'

Stephanie still couldn't react. Her whole body seemed to have
shut down from the shock, with the exception of her heart
which was racing away faster than ever. Her eyes moved from
his smiling face to the knife that he was absently toying with
on his lap. She recognised it as one of her own from the kitchen.
A serrated steak knife. Its blade gleamed in the light from her
bedside lamp as he rotated it.

'Oh God, this isn't happening,' she heard herself whisper.

He smiled at her again. 'It's happening all right, Stephanie,'
he told her. 'And all thanks to you, in fact.' Then he let his
eyes rove over her. 'You're a very beautiful woman, Stephanie.
But I guess you know that.'

She pulled the duvet up higher. 'How did you escape?' she
asked, in the same whisper. 'It's impossible. You couldn't have
got out.'

'Oh, but I did, lovely Stephanie, I did. As you can plainly
see.'

'How?'

'Magic,' he smiled.

'How did you get in here?'

'Magic,' he said again.

'*Why* are you here?' she asked, though she really didn't want to know the answer to that one.

'I told you – to show my gratitude for what you've done for me.' Then he glanced down at the knife he was playing with. He stopped rotating it between his fingers and held it up. He stared into the blade. 'You're interested in me. You want to know what goes on in my head. You want to know how I can do the things I do. As an act of gratitude I'm going to give you a demonstration.' He stood up.

'No!' she cried. 'Stay away from me!'

'But I'll be doing you a favour, Stephanie. And as a scientist you'll find it very enlightening.' He started towards her.

'No!' she screamed. 'Get away from me!' She shut her eyes. '*GO AWAY!*'

Something landed on the carpet with a soft clunk.

She opened her eyes.

Gilmour was gone.

She sat there, still holding the duvet up as an insubstantial shield. Her every nerve-ending was shrieking and her heart was pounding so hard she thought she would die of a heart attack before Gilmour could lay a finger on her. She was sure he was playing a game with her. Hiding somewhere. He had to be crouching down at the end of the bed. It was the only possible place. She tried to move but she was literally frozen with fear. Out of the corner of her eye she could see the phone sitting on the bedside table. So close yet so far away. She knew that if she tried to reach for it Gilmour would come leaping up at her . . .

'Where are you, damn you?' she said in a shaking voice.

The room was silent apart from the continued ticking of her alarm clock. She wondered if anyone had heard her scream. Perhaps a neighbour was calling the police at this very moment. But no, the flats were well sound-proofed. The only sounds she'd ever heard had come from the flat next door. Douglas Scott's flat, and he was certainly in no position to call the police on her behalf.

'Come out, damn you! Show yourself! Stop torturing me!' she cried, and then had to suppress a hysterical giggle. Torturing people was what Gilmour was all about. 'Oh shit,' she said in a kind of a half sob.

Time passed. She had no idea how much. The clock ticked on.

The clock. She turned her head slightly. Her alarm clock was a big brass one with two bells.

To hell with this, she decided. *I'm not going down without a fight. Fuck Gilmour. Fuck him for doing this to me.* She reached out and picked up the clock, then raised it over her head. It was reassuringly heavy. She was ready to either throw it or bring it down on Gilmour's head. 'Come on, Gilmour. Show yourself.'

More time passed. Her arm began to get tired. Her heart continued to pound. Where the hell could he be?

Finally she could stand it no longer. Gathering her resolve, she took a deep breath then flung back the duvet and leapt out of the bed. She charged round to the end of the bed, prepared to brain Gilmour with the clock.

He wasn't there. But the knife was. It lay there on the carpet. She bent down and quickly picked it up, expecting Gilmour's arm to snake out from under the bed. It didn't. She retreated to the centre of the room and then, holding both knife and clock ready, leaned down and peered under the bed. No Gilmour.

She was beginning to feel puzzled. She looked round the room. There was nowhere else he could be hiding. The curtains were too short. The wardrobe. Unlikely. It was packed solid with her clothes. Even so she warily checked it out. As expected, no Gilmour. Discarding the clock, she pulled a house-coat out from the log-jam of clothes and put it on. Her heart continued to race and she was full of adrenalin. What the hell was going on? She hadn't imagined Gilmour, or dreamed him. She had been wide awake. He had been right here in her bedroom.

Then she went to the bedroom door. The key was still in the lock, and the door was still locked. She looked at the knife in her hand. She went back to the bed and sat down. She stared at the knife for a time and then picked up the phone and punched out the number of the Institute. 'Stewart? It's Dr Lyell. Gilmour just turned up in my flat. How the hell did he get out of the Institute and why didn't someone call me the moment his absence was discovered?' She frowned as she listened to the reply. 'Look, I know what I saw! Gilmour was here! Right here! He threatened me with a knife!' She listened again. 'Well, then he just kind of vanished . . . Look, just go and look in his room! He was here, dammit! And now he's somewhere out there, on the loose!'

She waited impatiently while the male nurse went off to check on Gilmour. She hadn't imagined it, Gilmour *had* been here. It hadn't been some kind of hallucination. But how, she then asked herself, had he got out of her bedroom? At the moment she had no answer . . .

Stewart finally returned to the phone. She listened with mounting disbelief as she was told that Gilmour was asleep in his bed and that according to Malcolm, the nurse who was on duty in the observation room, he hadn't stirred for hours. She slammed the phone down, feeling angry, embarrassed and very confused. What was going on? Was she losing her mind? That would be ironic, one of the country's leading biochemical neurologists losing her own marbles.

Still clutching the knife, she went and unlocked the bedroom door. She turned on the living-room lights. The room was empty, as she knew it would be, as was the kitchen and the bathroom. And all the locks were in place on the front door. She found her cigarettes, poured herself a very large brandy, sat down in an armchair and started to smoke. And think.

Terry Hamilton woke up feeling strange. His head felt fuzzy. It wasn't the usual alcohol-induced fuzziness, it was something different. Unsettling. He propped himself up on his elbows and looked around. He was in an unfamiliar bedroom and lying naked on unwashed sheets. Beside him a naked woman lay sprawled face-down asleep. Her slim, freckled back rose and fell with her breathing. He wondered who she was. Her red hair obscured her face. He brushed it aside. Nope, he still didn't know who she was, though she did seem vaguely familiar. He tried to piece together the events of the previous day. And failed. It was all a blank. He sat up and gently turned the girl over on to her back. She moaned but didn't wake. She had a very nice body, he noted, but right then sex was the furthest thing from his mind. He gazed down at her face, and very slowly fragments of memory began to stick together, forming a name. *Of course*, it was Josie Welch, local girl reporter and tremendous pain in the neck. But how come he was in bed with her? Apart from the obvious reasons, that is.

He got out of the bed, and stretched. Joints crackled. He looked about for his clothes but they were nowhere to be seen. He finally found most of them in the living room. His watch he found in the kitchen. It was just past 7 a.m. He drank several glasses of tap water and still felt thirsty. More bits of memory stuck together and formed pictures. He remembered making love to Josie. Several times. And he remembered being in a pub with her. The Green Man. Had they met there, or somewhere else? Why had they met? Who had propositioned who?

Another thing struck him. He was on night-shift so he should have been at work last night. Clearly he hadn't been. Shit. Clery would have his guts. He looked around for his radio but he couldn't find it anywhere. What had got into him yesterday? He must have got pissed, run into Josie, got even more pissed with her in The Green Man and then come back here. Great. After all the years of keeping his drinking under control and not putting a step wrong at the station he'd gone completely off the rails for the second day in a row.

He finished dressing and returned to the bedroom. Josie was still asleep. He patted her on the bottom, draped a sheet over her and left. He found his car parked down the street. As he got in he wondered what to do. Go straight to the station or go home first to have a shower and a change of clothing? He decided on the latter and started the engine. As he drove he was aware that the strange feeling he'd noticed when he woke was still with him. He felt nervous and uneasy. It was as if he knew that something was very wrong but couldn't remember exactly what. He was then distracted by the sight of a young man sitting on the kerb ahead of him. The man was dressed in a full evening suit complete with bow tie. And as Hamilton drove by he saw that the young man was crying.

He considered stopping and asking what the problem was but decided against it. The bloke had probably been to a party, got drunk and then had a fight with his girlfriend. Tough luck for him, but not a police matter. Besides, Hamilton had problems of his own.

A short way on he saw another odd sight. It was a plump, middle-aged woman wearing a short, see-through nightie and fluffy pink slippers. The woman was clearly naked beneath the nightie but she was calmly walking along the footpath as if she was fully dressed. Hamilton shook his head in bemusement as he passed her. Bloody daft, he told himself.

When he pulled up in front of his flat he could hear a burglar alarm clanging away further up the street. A milk float was sitting in the middle of the road but there was no sign of the milkman. He entered his flat. Inside he could hear his next-door neighbours having a screaming match. That wasn't unusual, but their early-morning rows were always accompanied by the high-pitched wailing of their two-year-old daughter. He couldn't hear the kid this morning. He stripped off his clothes and had a shower, shaved, then put on clean underwear, shirt, socks and a different suit. While waiting for the kettle to boil for coffee he switched on the TV set to watch the news on BBC1. All he got on the screen was interference accompanied by the sound of static. He switched over to ITV. Same thing. And on BBC2 and Channel 4. Damn, he said to himself. Either the TV was on the blink or the problem lay with the aerial. He went back into the kitchen and turned on his transistor radio. And just got static on every station he tried. It was then he began to get seriously worried. What had happened? The Third World War? Had someone forgotten the Cold War was over and pressed a button somewhere?

He went to his phone and was relieved when he picked it up to hear a dialling tone. He rang the station. More relief when someone, finally, answered. 'Yeah, what do you want?' a listless voice said on the other end.

'This is DS Hamilton,' he said. 'Who's that?'

There was a pause and Hamilton could hear other phones ringing in the background, then, 'PC White, if you really want to know.'

Hamilton's unease deepened. 'Put me through to CID,' he ordered.

'Why? There's no one there.'

'What are you talking about?'

'There's no one there. There's no one anywhere here. Just me. And I think I might as well go home now . . .'

'Hey, wait! What's happened? What's wrong?'

The phone went dead. He hung up and looked at his watch. Half-past seven. He decided to forgo the coffee. Switching off the kettle he hurried out of the flat and got into his car. The milk float was still standing unattended in the middle of the road. And the burglar alarm was still clanging away down the street.

He drove towards the station, uneasily aware that there didn't seem to be any other traffic on the roads. Something terrible *had* happened, but what? Suddenly he spotted something moving very fast out of the corner of his eye. He slammed on his brakes just in time as a red post office van came hurtling out of a side street and shot across the road just in front of his car. He was immediately filled with a murderous rage. He put his foot down on the accelerator and as the car jumped forward he spun the wheel, determined to give chase to the van. And when he caught up with it he would force it off the road, drag the driver out and . . .

In his rage and mindless haste he misjudged the sharp turn
he was trying to make. The car mounted the grass verge on
the corner and the next thing he knew he had driven into a
small tree. '*Shit!*' he cried, thumping his fist on to the wheel.
Then, as abruptly as it had flared up, his rage evaporated. He
sat there, shaking and frightened. He no longer felt in control
of his own emotions.

When the shaking stopped he continued on his way to the
station. A short distance on he saw a lone pedestrian, a man
in a black track suit, jogging along the footpath. He slowed the
car until he was pacing the jogging man, rolled down the
window and called out to him. 'Hey, I want to talk to you! Hey!'
But the man didn't acknowledge his existence; he just kept
jogging. 'Hey!' called Hamilton again. 'I said I wanted to talk
to you!' Then he added, 'I'm a police officer!' But still no reaction. The man seemed to be in a world of his own. Muttering
with disgust, Hamilton gave up and drove on.

Northolt Road, when he turned into it, was devoid of traffic
and normally, by this time of the morning, it would have been
very busy. He turned into the station driveway and drove
through the tunnel that led to the car park at the rear of the
building. There were plenty of police vehicles there – cars and
vans – but no private cars that he recognised. He got out of the
car and looked around. Nothing stirred. He sniffed the air. He
hadn't noticed it before but there was an unpleasant smell
hanging about. He tried to identify it and failed.

He could hear the phones ringing as soon as he entered the
station through the rear entrance. Every available line seemed
to be tied up. There was no one in the custody suite and he
continued through into the clerical section. Empty as well. 'Is
anybody here?' he yelled. His voice echoed loudly but, apart
from the ringing phones, that was the only sound in the place.
Constable White had been telling the truth. The station was
apparently deserted.

He went back to the euphemistically named custody suite
and into the row of holding cells. But all the cell doors were
open and every cell was empty. He then checked the interview

rooms but they were all empty too. He looked briefly into the canteen – empty – then went to the Control Room – empty – then headed upstairs. The CID section was equally devoid of life. He was staring distractedly around the CID room and trying to come up with an explanation – *any* explanation – for what was going on when he heard the reception buzzer ringing.

He hurried back downstairs and through the clerical section to the front of the station. Yes, he could see someone through the glass. A woman. He went to the reception counter and the woman, who was in her early thirties, tall and with long black hair, appeared extremely relieved to see him. 'Thank God!' she cried. 'I was hoping I'd find you here!'

He regarded her warily. She was acting as if they knew each other but he was certain he'd never seen her before in his life. And the woman realised this because her face fell. 'You don't recognise me, do you?' she asked.

'No,' he told her. 'Who are you?'

She sighed. 'I was afraid of this. Look, please let me in. I have to talk to you. About what's happening.'

'What do you know about what's going on?' he asked her suspiciously.

'Not too much. Just a theory. But it's vital that you listen to me. You're probably the only person around here now who can help! So please let me in!'

He deliberated for a few moments then decided to comply. She didn't look dangerous and maybe she could throw some light on today's weirdness. He pressed the door-release button and the woman pulled the door open. As she came in he saw that she was carrying a black attaché case. She gave him a strained smile. 'Thank you,' she said. She took the attaché case to a nearby desk and placed it there. 'Please take a look at this,' she said as she opened the case. 'You'll find it very enlightening.'

Puzzled, he peered inside. It seemed to be full of medical equipment: plastic-shrouded hypodermics, phials containing liquids, bottles of pills . . . 'What am I supposed to . . . ?' he began and then gave a yelp of alarm as he felt a stab of pain in his right bicep. He glanced round and saw that she had plunged a hypodermic deep into his arm and was in the act of injecting its contents into him. Instantly he was seized by that murderous rage that had filled him in the car after the near miss with the PO van. 'Bitch!' he cried and shoved her away, then he plucked the hypo from his arm and hurled it across the room. The woman had fallen backwards on to a desk. He went for her, his rage exploding through him. 'Bitch! You tried to kill me!' His hands went round her throat.

'Detective Sergeant Hamilton, it's me, Stephanie Lyell! Hamil – ' She couldn't say any more because now his thumbs were pressing into her windpipe. He bared his teeth at her in a snarl and squeezed her neck as hard as he could.

Chapter Eight

The tremendous pressure around her throat was suddenly gone. Fighting against the waves of darkness that were sweeping over her she rolled from the desk and fell to the floor on her hands and knees, desperately trying to suck air into her lungs. Just when she thought she was about to die her constricted windpipe began to function again and she was able, just barely, to breathe again. Strong hands lifted her from the floor and she was eased into a chair. She wiped tears from her eyes and looked at Hamilton who was leaning over her, an alarmed expression on his face. 'Are you all right?' he asked her.

She managed to croak a 'yes' in reply. She gently massaged her throat.

'Christ, I don't know what's wrong with me,' he said in an anguished voice. 'First I had this tremendous urge to kill you . . . I was seized by this overpowering rage, like before . . . then I heard a man's voice booming in my head . . . "Not her!" he said, and suddenly I'm myself again.' He wiped the back of a hand across his sweaty forehead. 'I must be going crazy . . .'

'You still don't recognise me?' she gasped.

He shook his head.

She frowned. 'I was sure it was the injection that stopped you . . . What can you remember about yesterday?'

'Yesterday . . . ?' he said blankly.

'Do you remember seeing Marc Gilmour at the Institute?'

'Of course I remember . . .' Then he stopped. 'I don't understand,' he said, staring at her in astonishment. 'I remember Gilmour *now*, and suddenly I recognise *you* but earlier today I'd forgotten both of you! Christ, now I remember how I met Josie Welch! It was outside the Institute, after I'd talked to you . . . Jesus Christ, I'd even forgotten about the Institute! *And* my suspension . . .' He looked at her with stricken eyes. 'Doctor, what the hell is happening to me? Am I really going mad?'

'Don't worry, it's not just you, it's all the unlucky people who got swept up by Gilmour when . . .' She stopped and glanced nervously at the front door. 'Look, let's go back to my place. At least it's still secure. I'll tell you there what I think is going on. And then we're going to have to figure out what we can do to stop it.'

'Yeah. Whatever you say.'

'Before we go, can you lay your hands on any guns?'

'Guns?' he asked with surprise.

'Yes. I don't know what your experiences have been so far today but it's getting wild out there. My car was stoned on the way here. We're going to need weapons.'

'Well, if you say so,' he said, sounding dubious. 'Wait here.'

Hamilton, his mind reeling every time he tried to get a handle on the day's events, went upstairs to the Chief Super's office. He knew that the keys to the gun cabinet were kept in the Chief Super's desk. The drawer was locked, of course, and Hamilton had to break it open. He got the keys and then went to the Duty Sergeant's office where the gun cabinet was located. The cabinet contained six Smith and Wesson Model 10 .38s, each one with an identity tag, and boxes of ammunition. He took two of the .38s and two boxes of ammunition, relocked the cabinet and went back downstairs. Dr Lyell was peering nervously out of the front door. He could hear distant shouting. And screaming. 'What's going on?' he asked.

'Sounds like a riot,' she said and turned towards him. 'Did you get the guns?'

'Yeah.' He patted his bulky pockets. 'I guess with this little stunt my police career is well and truly over.'

'I don't think your superiors are in any position to give a damn. Let's see them? Are they loaded?'

'Not yet,' he said as he put the two revolvers and the boxes of ammunition on a desk. It felt odd to handle a gun again. He hadn't touched one since that day seven years ago. She picked up one of the guns and looked at it. 'Heavy,' she commented. 'Show me how the thing works and then how to load it.'

He demonstrated to her how to release the safety catch and pull back on the trigger until the hammer hit home on an empty chamber. She tried herself and grunted from the effort. 'God, the trigger is stiff,' she complained. Holding the .38 with both hands she repeated the action several times then gave the gun back to him. He showed her how to load it then he loaded the other gun. She put hers into her attaché case. He said, 'Are you sure we're going to need them?'

'From the way things have gone rapidly downhill out there I'd say we definitely are. And we need them for another reason apart from self-protection. We're going to have to kill Gilmour.'

'Kill Gilmour?' He stared at her. 'You keep mentioning him. What on earth has he got to do with what's happening today?'

'If my theory is right – everything. And we may no longer even *be* on earth. And it's all my fault.'

'I don't know what you're talking about,' he said, looking at her as if she were crazy.

She decided not to unload too much on him all at once. She desperately needed his co-operation. She couldn't afford to alienate him. She said, 'I'll try and explain everything when we get back to my flat. Now let's get going. We'll take my car.'

Though reluctant to leave his own car behind he followed her out of the front entrance and over to her Volvo which was parked nearby. He noted that the unpleasant odour in the air had grown stronger. Also that there was now a kind of murky haze as well which gave the early-morning sunshine a curiously sickly tinge. He could still hear shouting but there was no one in evidence in the immediate area. And in the distance,

82 *Harry Adam Knight*

behind the Hill, he saw a pillar of black smoke rising up. He estimated the fire must be located in Harrow-on-the-Hill's main shopping precinct.

'Is it just Harrow that's gone crazy today or the whole of London?' he asked her. 'I was beginning to think World War Three had started.'

She'd opened her door but paused before getting in and looked around. 'From my attempts to drive out of Harrow I suspect the Effect is localised but I don't know for certain.'

'The *Effect*?'

'That's what I call it. Typical scientist's trick. You stick a label on something and it creates the illusion you understand what it is.' She gave him a bitter smile and got in the car. He climbed in as well.

'There's one other thing, Doctor,' he said as she started the engine.

'Yes?'

'Call me Terry.'

'Oh, right. Terry it is.' She gave him another smile, a more friendly one this time. 'And please call me Stephanie.'

They made the short drive to Hillview House without seeing anyone in the streets. When she'd parked behind the building Stephanie looked carefully about before opening her door. 'Seems safe, but keep your eyes sharp,' she told Hamilton.

She relaxed somewhat once the heavy front door of the building had closed behind them. 'What about your neighbours?' he asked.

'Can't raise a peep from any of them. I thought I heard yelling coming from the floor below early this morning but I've rung every doorbell and if there is still anyone in any of the flats they're keeping very quiet now.'

They took the elevator to the top floor. 'Sit down,' she told him when they were in her flat and all the locks on the door had been secured. 'Want a drink?'

'Yeah. Please.' He asked for a Scotch and ice with plenty of soda. He was very thirsty. She fixed the drink for him, poured a large vodka and ice for herself and lit a cigarette. She kicked off her shoes and sat down on the sofa, curling her feet up under her. There was now severe bruising around her neck, he noted guiltily. *Christ*, he'd come a hair's breadth away from killing her. The rage he'd felt consume him so totally still scared him.

She stared into space and said, with a sigh, 'Where do I begin?'

He gave a helpless shrug. 'Start wherever you want. I'm completely in the dark.'

She thought for a while and then said, 'I started to realise what might be happening after Gilmour appeared here last night. In my bedroom.' She indicated the closed door behind her.

'Gilmour got out?' he asked incredulously.

'That's what I thought at first. He certainly seemed real. He was solid, because he carried a knife in from my kitchen. Through a locked door, however. When I screamed at him to go away – I was utterly terrified, needless to say – he simply vanished, though I didn't immediately know that. I thought he was hiding somewhere. But he had gone. Then I phoned the Institute and was told Gilmour was still in his room.'

'So what did you see?'

'I wasn't sure at first. I was certain for a brief time that Gilmour had escaped, despite what Stewart, the nurse at the Institute, told me. Then when I'd calmed down I thought maybe I'd suffered from a sort of hallucination as a result of overwork. Gilmour had been at the centre of all my thinking of late so it seemed logical that I might hallucinate about him. The knife I might have unconsciously brought into the bedroom myself. It seemed the only logical explanation. I went back to bed and tried to sleep. It was impossible. Then I began to think about what had happened here at Hillview House during the last few days – Douglas Scott jumping to his death, Miss Coope hanging herself and all that talk from the other residents about their dreaming of a fire.' She paused and stared at the glowing end of her cigarette. 'Then I remembered something you'd told me the first time you came to my office. About all the residents mentioning they saw a little girl in the fire. With a golliwog.'

'Yeah. But you said you couldn't even remember dreaming of a fire.'

'And I still don't. But remember yesterday when I said I understood some of your feelings about what had happened when you . . . you accidentally shot your wife. I mentioned that there had been a family tragedy when I was twelve and that I was responsible.' She stubbed out her cigarette and fell silent.

'What happened?' he prompted.

'There was a fire,' she said, without looking at him. 'My younger sister, Gloria, died in it. She was just seven years old. My parents had gone out and I was responsible for looking after her. I . . . I accidentally started a fire. With a cigarette. I had started smoking on the sly. A lot of the girls in my class were doing it. It was cool and all that crap. According to the fire investigators I must have left a burning cigarette on the edge of an ashtray and gone out of the room for some reason. It rolled off and set alight some newspapers on a coffee table. The fire spread. I was rescued by a neighbour who came in through a window. Gloria wasn't so lucky. She got trapped in the living room and died.' Lyell lit another cigarette.

'I'm sorry,' Hamilton told her. 'But what has this got to do with anything?'

'Until today, I haven't been able to remember the details. For years I buried what happened that day deep inside myself. Oh, I knew there had been a fire that had killed my little sister and that I was responsible but I couldn't . . . I wouldn't *let* myself remember exactly what had happened until, as I said, today.'

'So?'

'Don't you see? The dream everyone in this building experienced? It was mine.'

'Yours? How can you know that?' he asked, disbelievingly.

'Because this morning I recalled your mention of the golliwog. And I remember now that Gloria's favourite toy was a golliwog. It was her constant companion. She had it with her on the day she died in the fire.'

They stared at each other, then she added, 'This was back

in the days before golliwogs became ideologically unsound, of
course. You never see them about any more, do you?'

'No,' he said slowly. 'You don't.'

'So it was *my* dream everyone shared here in the building. I
was broadcasting it as I slept.'

'I don't understand. What do you mean by "broadcasting"?'

'The other residents were picking up my intense unconscious
thoughts.'

'You're saying you're telepathic?'

'It's not telepathy. It's something else. You remember I told
you about that substance we're using to experiment on Gilmour
with. The synthetic neurotransmitter called BDNFE?'

He nodded. 'What about it?'

'I've been taking it myself. By injection. To see if the size of
the dosages produced any side-effects, and to see if having extra
BDNFE in my brain produced any changes in my perception.
I intended to compare its effect on me with its effect on Gilmour
who, as I explained, was born without the genetic capability to
produce any natural BDNFE of his own.'

'You've lost me,' admitted Hamilton.

'Terry, I first injected myself with the drug the night before
last.'

'I see,' he said, as the implications struck home. 'I mean, I
understand the connection even if I don't understand the *how*.
You're saying that this BDN whatever it is has altered your
brain in some way?'

'Yes, I am. Somehow it amplifies my will, *broadcasts* it so
that it affects other people.'

He rubbed his chin and frowned. 'But you said this stuff
occurs naturally in our brains, with the exception of nutters
like Gilmour. How can giving yourself an extra dose of it
suddenly turn you into a human TV channel?'

'That I don't know,' she admitted. 'Maybe it's to do with
the increased dosage, or perhaps there is a subtle molecular
difference between our synthetic BDNFE and the real thing. I
need access to my lab, and that I don't have. All I know is

that by continuing to inject myself with the drug I have some immunity from the Effect, as you do now.'

'Me?' he asked.

'Oh, for goodness sake!' she cried in a flash of irritation. 'Stop being so dense! Why do you think you remember everything now? I injected you with BDNFE at the police station, you bonehead!'

'Oh,' he said, and touched the place on his arm where she'd jabbed him with the hypodermic. With everything else that had happened he had entirely forgotten about it. 'That's right . . . you did.'

'And I'll have to inject you again in four hours or you'll fall back under his influence,' she muttered.

'His?' he asked, aware that he was still sounding like a dense bonehead.

'*Gilmour*, you idiot! I told you we're going to have to kill him. All this is his doing!' She waved her arms around. 'He's causing all this. And he's got access to an unlimited supply of the synthetic BDNFE while all we've got is enough to last for another twenty-four hours. Then we've had it.'

He was desperately trying to make sense of what she was saying. 'You mean that Gilmour is doing what you were doing in your sleep, except on a much greater scale?'

'Ah, the penny has dropped at last! Yes, you stupid policeman, that's exactly what is happening!'

'But we're not dreaming,' he pointed out, deciding to ignore the insult.

'No, and neither is Gilmour any more. He's taken conscious control of the Effect. That's why we have to kill him! Are you with me?'

'Well,' he said hesitantly. 'If all you've said is true, then yes. Or, at the very least, put him out of action.' He stood up. 'So let's go to your institute right now.'

Her shoulders sagged. 'No use. I've already tried that.'

'What do you mean?'

'The Institute isn't there any more. It's gone.'

Chapter Nine

Mrs Mary Spencer, sixty-seven years old and a widow, was sitting in an armchair in her small living room. She didn't want to be there but she had no choice. She was paralysed. She wanted to close her eyes but she couldn't. She wanted to block her ears with her hands but she couldn't. She wanted to turn her head away but she couldn't. It was as if invisible hands held her head, forcing her to look at what she didn't want to see. She wanted to scream and this she could do but she had been screaming so long her voice was hoarse and barely audible.

She was having to look at her cat, Mooksie. The neutered nine-year-old cat was the most important thing in her life. She would have died for it. And now she was having to watch Mooksie eat himself alive. Mooksie clearly didn't *want* to eat himself – between bites he would howl in the most awful, terrible way – but he would continue ripping at his own flesh and fur. Right now he was pulling his intestines out of the gaping, ragged hole he had ripped in his belly. She knew he would keep on gnawing at himself until he was dead. And then, without a moment's respite, it would begin all over again. Mooksie would suddenly be alive and complete and then he would start eating himself again. Mrs Mary Spencer had been watching this grisly process all morning. And she knew that if she was forced to endure it one more time she would go totally insane.

And she did.

*

'Gone?'

'Yes. Completely. There's just empty land where the Institute used to stand.'

'I don't believe it.'

'Gilmour has changed the rules on what is now possible and impossible,' Stephanie told him. 'He's in control.'

'But *how*? I don't understand any of this!' Hamilton got up from his chair and strode over to the main window that looked out over the Hill. 'Are you saying that Gilmour is influencing our thoughts in the same way that your dream influenced the other residents?' He gestured at the yellow haze that hung over Harrow-on-the-Hill. 'Are you saying that all this is Gilmour's dream and we're sharing it against our wishes?' He turned back to her. 'Well?'

She was looking very tired now. Her previous anger towards him had evaporated. She said wearily, 'I think it's more than that. Much more. Remember Douglas Scott?'

'Of course.'

'You saw his body. He was badly burned, wasn't he?'

'Yeah. So?'

'Don't you see? He didn't merely share my dream about the fire, he *experienced* it. For real.'

Hamilton rubbed his forehead as he tried to comprehend what she was saying. 'The fire was for real? But there was no sign of any fire damage in the flat.'

'I know, I know. The fire was real but not in this reality, only in the reality I had inadvertently created and pulled him into. Scott had the misfortune of being in my immediate vicinity. The other residents merely had the same dream. What's happening with Gilmour is the same thing only intensified a hundredfold ... maybe even a *thousandfold*. Why, I don't know yet.'

'Look, you're the scientist and I'm just the stupid policeman, as you put it, but even I can see you're talking pure rubbish. Gilmour is controlling our reality? That's *crazy*!'

She nodded. 'I agree. But as I said, the normal rules no longer apply ... and we're at the total mercy of a crazy man.' She gave a deep sigh. 'I understand how you feel. I had a lot of trouble coming to terms with the situation myself. This helped.' She leaned forward and picked up a hardback book that had been lying on the coffee table in front of her. As she opened it at a book-marked place Hamilton read the title: *The Invented Reality* by Professor Simon Ian Childer. 'Professor Childer was one of my lecturers at university,' she told him. 'He's the top man in our field and was a great influence on me.' She began to read aloud: '"Everything but the brain itself – the rest of the body and the outside world – is part of the mental model created by the brain. As the physicist Arthur Eddington observed: 'Mind is the first and most direct thing in our experience, and all else is remote inference – inference either intuitive or deliberate.' What actually comes to our senses is energy in the form of vibrations of different frequencies . . . modern physics would describe them simply as heaps of statistical probabilities. These radiations trigger neural codes, which are made by the brain into a model of the external world. This model is then given subjective value and, by a trick of brain functioning, projected outwards to form the subjective world."' She closed the book. 'Did you follow that?'

'Yeah, I think so,' he lied.

'Professor Childer's theory is that what we perceive of as the external world is a collective construct. You've heard of the term "consensus reality"?'

He nodded.

'Well, it means we all have an equal share in creating and maintaining it. Until now. The synthetic BDNFE within Gilmour has altered his brain. It's providing him with an edge over the rest of us. His projected subjective world is overpowering the consensus reality. It's no longer a "consensus" any more, it's Gilmour's reality. At least, it is in this locale. God knows how far his influence can extend but I'm pretty certain that the Effect is localised. For the time being anyway.'

Hamilton turned and stared out the window as he digested her words. He noticed, distractedly, that the sickly yellow haze was so thick around the summit of the Hill that it blocked out the church tower. Then he turned back to Stephanie. 'Okay, if what you say is true, how come we don't have the same power as Gilmour to alter reality? We've got the same stuff in us as well.'

'Yes, I've been wondering about that. The BDNFE gives us protection against Gilmour, but that's it. I've tried various experiments but I can't alter a damn thing. Yet I know now that it was because the synthetic BDNFE was in my system that I was able to make Gilmour go away last night. And it's clear that not all my dreams were affecting Scott and the others in the building, only the one about the fire. And that was because it involved me powerfully on a subconscious level. To exploit BDNFE you have to tap into your deepest emotions, and we can't do that at will.'

'But Gilmour apparently can. Why?'

'I just don't know,' she admitted. 'Yet.'

'Great. So what are we going to do? Try and get outside help? I mean, I can't understand why emergency services from outside the area aren't pouring in. Surely it must be obvious to people outside Harrow that something is seriously wrong.'

She took a deep breath. 'You're still not fully comprehending the situation, Terry.'

He gave a forced laugh. 'I'm not comprehending *any* of this, Doctor . . . I mean, Stephanie. I'm trying to, believe me, but I can't help thinking that I'm going to wake up somewhere and find that I'm modelling the latest style in designer strait-jackets.'

'I know how you feel, but believe me when I tell you this is really happening.'

'Then explain to me why we can't just hop in your car and keep driving until we're out of range of this damned Effect and then get help.'

Stephanie lit a cigarette. 'I tried driving out of here. It didn't work. That's why I'm pretty sure the Effect is localised. And why I believe we're stuck inside Gilmour's own specialised reality.'

'What's he done? Set up road blocks?' asked Hamilton.

'Nothing so simple. What happened was that I first drove up Roxeth Hill Road and turned right into London Road, heading towards town. But the next thing I knew I was driving in the opposite direction. *Back* towards Harrow-on-the-Hill. And I certainly hadn't turned the car around myself.'

'That's impossible!'

She smiled sweetly at him. 'Yes, Terry. You're getting the picture now. Anyway, I tried again and the same thing happened. I tried different routes out and each time I'd suddenly find myself heading in the reverse direction. Sometimes on entirely different roads. I estimate that Gilmour's private world is about one and a half to two miles in diameter. And it is completely cut off from the rest of the world.'

He asked if he could pour himself another drink. She told him to go ahead. As he headed towards the drinks cabinet, he said, 'What about the phone? Have you tried that?'

'Same thing. You can get local numbers – nobody answers but the phone does ring – but nothing outside. Try it for yourself. Call a number in Central London.'

After pouring himself another large Scotch and soda, Hamilton went to her phone and dialled Scotland Yard. He waited. Finally he put the phone down.

'Nothing?' she asked.

'I got canned music. *The Girl from Ipanema.*' He sat down. 'So we kill Gilmour, right? But first we've got to find him. And your goddamned Institute. How in the hell can he hide an entire building?'

She shrugged. 'Like I said, he's making up the rules now.'

He thought for a bit. 'Well, no use hanging about here. Let's get started. First I want to check out where the Institute used to be.'

'You don't believe me?'

'Yeah, but I want to see for myself. But before we start shouldn't you change into something more suitable? Things are likely to get dirty out there.'

She glanced down at herself, taking in her short black skirt, black stockings and discarded high-heel shoes on the floor.

'Yes, I see what you mean. I'll change.' She got up and headed for the bedroom. 'I won't be long,' she told him as the bedroom door closed behind her.

She wasn't. She returned wearing jeans, a baggy denim jacket and boots. She picked up her attaché case, took the .38 out and slipped it into her jacket pocket. 'Let's go.'

They went back downstairs. They saw and heard nobody on their way out of the building. Outside, Hamilton sniffed the air and grimaced. The stink was getting worse. He stared up at the thick yellow murk that covered the top of the Hill. 'I still find it hard to believe that all this is happening just because of Gilmour,' he told her seriously.

'I know what you mean. The last time I felt this degree of unreality was back in 1979 when I woke up to find Margaret Thatcher was Prime Minister.'

He rounded on her. 'What are you talking about? Thatcher was the best thing that ever happened to this country! And the way she was betrayed by her own people was disgusting!' he said hotly.

She held up a hand. 'Sorry. Just trying to lighten the mood. Wrong joke. I should have expected . . .' She didn't finish.

'Expected what?'

'Forget it. Come on, let's get the car.'

A couple of minutes later they were pulling out on to the deserted Lower Road. 'All those mornings that I've cursed the traffic along here,' she said. 'And right now I'd give everything to have it all back as normal, jams, tailbacks and everything.'

He grunted something in response. He was still annoyed about her Thatcher jibe.

The streets continued to be deserted as they entered Bessborough Road. 'Where do you think everyone is?' he grudgingly asked her.

'The lucky ones are still in the real world. As for the unlucky ones, I shudder to think.'

'What do you mean?'

'You know Gilmour's personality profile. He enjoys, most of all, manipulating people into hurting each other. Now he's got a whole town to play with. Think of the fun he's having.'

Hamilton thought about it and whispered softly, 'Christ.' Then he jumped as something exploded against the passenger window near his head. He turned quickly. Someone had thrown an empty bottle at the car. He could see the glass fragments falling on the road but there was no sign of the person who had thrown it. His hand automatically went to the jacket pocket which was being pulled down by the reassuring weight of the .38. His fingers closed around the butt but he didn't draw the revolver. They reached the junction at the railway bridge and turned left into Lowlands Road. Hamilton looking around for any sign of life. Then, as they were passing the park that lay on the lower slope of the Hill, he spotted something and told Stephanie to stop. She did so. 'What is it?' she asked.

He pointed across her to the park. She looked and said, 'Oh God.'

Three naked bodies were hanging by ropes around their necks from the branches of a tree beside the road. All were men and all were black. From the two who were facing the road they could see that they had been castrated.

Hamilton and Stephanie sat silently in the car for nearly a minute, just looking. She was the first to speak. 'Looks like Gilmour's influence is unleashing some old, familiar hatreds. Maybe fuelling them somehow . . . amplifying them.' He had no idea what she was talking about. He was transfixed by the sight of the three mutilated bodies hanging from the tree in the heart of cosy, respectable Harrow-on-the Hill.

The car moved forward. He kept staring at the bodies until they were out of sight. Tyburn Lane was just a short stretch of road that linked Lowlands Road with Kenton Road and was dominated by the red-brick building that was the Institute which stood on the corner. Or rather, it *had* been. Hamilton saw that Stephanie had been telling the truth. The Institute had vanished.

Stephanie turned into the driveway which came to an abrupt end where it reached the point of running under the missing archway that led into the non-existent courtyard. Now there was just bare earth in front of a large hole where the Institute's extensive labyrinth of foundations and cellars had been. They got out of the car and went to the edge of the hole. They could see the ends of pipes and electricity conduits extending from the edges of the hole. They had been sheared off when the building had vanished. 'Well, wherever he's taken it he's without light, heat and water,' said Hamilton, desperately trying to find something positive to say.

'I'm sure that will seriously inconvenience him,' she said with heavy sarcasm.

He didn't hear her. He stared worriedly down into the hole and then up at the yellow miasma that was the sky over Harrow. Then he said, speaking more to himself than her, 'No, I'm not buying any of this. It isn't Gilmour, it's *me*. I went on a bender and now I'm back in the drying-out unit suffering from one hell of a withdrawal symptom. Or maybe I got so drunk I walked in front of a car or choked on my own vomit and I'm dead. And this is Hell.' It had all reminded him of a book he'd read a long time ago. *The Third Policeman*. Actually, he'd started reading it because he'd been under the mistaken impression that it was a crime thriller but by the time he'd realised it was nothing of the kind he'd been hooked by its compelling weirdness. And he still remembered the unnerving moment when he realised that the central character was dead and in Hell . . .

Stephanie's hand delivered him a stinging slap across the side of his face. He turned and cried angrily at her, 'Why the hell did you do that?'

'You were starting to ramble. I need your help, Terry, so pull yourself together.' She rubbed the palm of her hand on the front of her jacket. 'Besides, I've wanted to do that for a while now. I'm glad to see it worked.'

He put his fingers to his stinging cheek. 'Well, it certainly pissed me off. But how can you convince me all this isn't happening in my own mind, like I said? It would be a lot easier to take that this is all some kind of bad trip I'm having rather than the idea that Gilmour has taken over Harrow-on-the-Hill.'

'Then what's the reason for me being in your bad trip, Terry?'

'I don't know. I just happen to be dreaming about you, that's all.'

'Not for any erotic purpose, I trust,' she said and gave him a razor-thin smile.

Both his stinging and his non-stinging cheek grew hot. 'No, of course not,' he protested.

She laughed and said, 'Well, that is a relief. Now look around you, Terry. And listen too. Have you heard a single train go by since we've been here?'

'No,' he admitted.

'Or a plane?'

He shook his head. And Harrow-on-the-Hill lay directly on the flight-path for aircraft heading for Northolt Airport.

'It all goes to prove my theory, Terry. We're cut off in this place. Gilmour has created his own little universe.'

Hamilton thought about this, then glanced at the hole in the ground where the Institute had stood. 'You mean, back in the real world, there's a big hole like this where all of Harrow-on-the-Hill used to be?'

'No, I don't,' she said, a trifle impatiently. 'This place is a kind of copy – a reproduction of Harrow-on-the-Hill that Gilmour has created. An alternate reality. But they'll know something is wrong in the real world, because suddenly a hell of a lot of people simply vanished within the radius of Gilmour's influence. Who knows how many. Hundreds, probably. Maybe even more.'

He scratched his head. 'Why didn't he simply bring everyone in the area with him?'

'I suppose there's a limit to how many he can handle at any one time. He may have become a god in this place but he's not God.'

Even more alarmed, he said, 'You mean Gilmour's like God in this place? He's everywhere at once?'

'In a manner of speaking, I guess so. But don't forget that

his god-like powers don't extend to us ... not yet, anyway, which is why it's up to us to find him and kill him. As quickly as possible.'

'But shit, how the hell do we find him? Drive around until we happen to see the Institute? And how do we know if it's even visible? If Gilmour has the powers you say he does he could have taken it anywhere!'

She shook her head. 'No, both it and he are in the vicinity. I know it. This is close to where the Effect is the strongest. I can feel it in my skin ... the hairs on my arms ... it's like being close to high-voltage wires. Can't you feel it too?'

'Yeah,' he said, after a couple of moments. 'Yeah, I do.'

Gilmour was definitely close by.

Chapter Ten

Mrs Cathy Hudson, aged thirty-two, sat in front of a cooling cup of tea and pondered on the reasons behind her very un-typical actions earlier that morning. She simply couldn't understand why she had done what she had done. All right, so Bob did have many irritating habits. *Extremely* irritating habits, like his persistence in farting as noisily as possible when in bed . . . and his refusal to clean the bath after using it . . . and his constant sneering about her favourite TV shows . . . his insistence on showing her every new porn magazine he bought even though he knew full well they disgusted her . . . Well, yes, the list of his faults was pretty long. But even so she had no idea she felt quite *so* strongly about them. But she must have . . .

She picked up her cup and took a sip of the cool tea, adding more blood stains to the handle.

What other reason would there be for her to have got up while he was still asleep this morning, fetch the electric carv-ing knife from the kitchen, plug it in beside the bed, switch it on and then use it to cut open Bob's throat?

She felt no guilt or remorse about what she had done. Only a mild surprise.

It was all very strange.

And even if she had murdered her husband because of his bad habits that didn't explain why she had then taken the carving knife into first her five-year-old son's room and then her seven-year-old daughter's room. She stared at the blood on her hands.

That was a *complete* mystery.

Detective Chief Inspector Russell Clery awoke gradually from a disturbed sleep to the pleasurable realisation that his wife, Laura, was lying nude on top of him and gently grinding her pelvis into his own. As he began to respond with a rapidly growing erection it did occur to him that it was very unusual for Laura to take the initiative in their love-making. And on a weekday too.

He ran his hands down the sides of her body . . . and immediately knew something was very wrong. Her body was too slim . . . and too small. He forced open sleep-glued eyes. And found himself staring into the face of his twelve-year-old daughter, Melissa.

'Melissa!' he cried in horror, even as he felt his erection sinking into her.

She grinned at him, revealing blood-stained teeth. 'Hello, Daddy!' she said brightly. Then she sank those blood-stained teeth into his throat.

They decided to drive into the nearby town centre of Harrow-on-the-Hill. Hamilton wanted to check out the source of the smoke that was still billowing into the sky. They turned left from Tyburn Lane into Station Road and Hamilton saw that the column of smoke was ahead of them on the right. The building on fire turned out to be the big video rental store that had previously been a toy shop. Stephanie pulled up on the other side of the street, on the corner of College Road. There didn't appear to be anybody about. Hamilton drew the gun from his pocket then got out of the car. He immediately felt the heat from the fire on his face. Stephanie joined him. She too had taken out her revolver. 'Be careful with that,' he warned her.

'It's all right . . . the safety's on.' She looked around. 'Not a soul in sight.'

'Good. Let's hope it stays that way.'

The roof of the burning building collapsed with a loud crash and smoke and flames billowed out across the road. They both shielded their faces with their arms. Then sparks began to rain down on them. Coughing they hurriedly got back in the car. Stephanie started the engine and drove slowly up College Road towards the station.

They both heard it. A woman's piercing scream. It seemed to be coming from within the shopping mall opposite the station. Hamilton jumped out of the car as soon as Stephanie had braked and ran across the street. Stephanie followed him. The automatic – when they worked – sliding doors at the entrance of the mall had been smashed down and there was broken glass on the floor of the foyer. Hamilton paused at the top of the stairs that led down to the main section of the mall. The woman was still screaming but he couldn't see anyone. Because of the way the screams were echoing around the empty mall it was hard to work out where they were coming from. He ran down the stairs. And saw them to his right, in the entrance to a menswear store. Two men and a woman. One of the men was holding the struggling woman down by her shoulders while his companion raped her. That was bad enough but what disturbed Hamilton even more was that the two men were uniformed police officers.

'Stop it! Leave her alone!' he shouted as he ran towards them. The rapist stopped moving and peered round over his shoulder. Then he smiled at Hamilton. 'Hi, Terry! You want some of this too? I'm just about finished.'

Hamilton recognised him. PC Shore. He recognised the other uniform too. PC Gilden. He was smiling at Hamilton as well. Hamilton slowed to a walk. Shore turned back and resumed his thrusting into the woman. Hamilton walked up to them and swung the .38, butt first, at the side of Shore's head. The butt made a solid *thonk* sound as it slammed into his skull just behind his left ear. Shore said, 'Uh,' and collapsed on to the woman who continued to scream. PC Gilden looked at Hamilton with surprise. 'Why did you do that?' he asked.

Hamilton pointed the gun at him. 'Let her go, stand up and back away, slowly,' he said in a voice shaking with anger.

PC Gilden did so. By now Hamilton was aware of Stephanie standing beside him. 'Cover him. Shoot the bastard if he tries to run for it.' He put the gun in his pocket and squatted down, then he roughly rolled Shore off the woman. Another shock. All the woman was wearing was a ripped shirt and a jacket. A policewoman's jacket. He recognised her too. WPC Foster. Carol Foster.

'Christ,' he muttered as he stared at her. Her cheeks were bruised and swollen and there was blood around her mouth. She stared back at him with animal eyes. At least she had stopped screaming. 'It's okay, Carol. It's all over now. You're safe.' He reached out to her, intending to assist her to sit up. He was taken by surprise when she grabbed his hand with both of hers. Then he screamed with pain as she sunk her teeth into the edge of his hand. The pain exploded through him. He tried to pull his hand free but he couldn't. The pain was intolerable. Tears filled his eyes, blinding him. He punched out with his free hand. Made a connection with her face. Punched her again, harder. She let go of him. There was a gun shot. Loud. His ears rang. *'Shit!'* he yelled. He blinked furiously, trying to see. Then, through a blur, he saw two retreating figures running through the mall towards the St Ann's Road exit.

'Are you all right?' asked Stephanie as he stood up.

'No,' he said, staring at his hand. WPC Foster's teethmarks formed a perfect arc on the edge of his hand. He turned it over and saw a matching mark on the palm side. Blood was beginning to flow. The bite was deep. 'Nasty,' he heard Stephanie say. He looked again at the fleeing pair. They had almost reached the exit. The half-naked Carol Foster was ahead of Gilden. Maybe he was chasing her. Right now Hamilton couldn't give a shit. 'You shot at him?'

'Over his head,' she said. 'When he started to run. I couldn't just shoot him.' She looked pale and anxious.

'No.' He wrapped some paper tissues around his hand. They

were instantly soaked with blood. She said, referring to his hand, 'I'm going to have to take care of that.'

'Can you?' he asked, doubtfully.

'I am a trained doctor. But what I don't have are the necessary instruments. Or drugs. You could do with a shot of penicillin. And a tetanus shot too, just to be on the safe side.' She frowned. 'Now where is the nearest doctor's surgery to here?'

He thought, then said, 'There's one just around the corner in Headstone Road.'

'Let's pay it a visit. Come on.' She strode away. Hamilton glared down at the unconscious figure of Constable Shore, who now looked rather ludicrous with his trousers and underpants around his knees and his prick a flaccid pink slug against his thigh, then he followed her out of the mall.

The doctor's name, according to the metal plate beside the door, was B. Rajendram. No one responded to the doorbell so Hamilton kicked the door in. His hand hurt like hell and was still bleeding copiously. And he was in a very bad mood. The reception area and the waiting room were empty. The surgery door was locked. Hamilton kicked that open too.

Stephanie found what she needed and quickly got to work on his hand. She cleaned the wound, sutured the deepest of the bites and put a dressing and bandage around his hand. Then she gave him two injections. It was all over in a matter of minutes. Hamilton was impressed. As he put his shirt and jacket back on she rummaged through the shelves of the absent doctor's drugs cabinet, selecting certain items and putting them in her attaché case. 'Might come in handy,' she told him.

Outside, in the corridor, she sniffed the air. 'You smell that?' she asked.

'Yeah. Something cooking.'

A staircase at the rear of the building led to a flat over the surgery. Presumably the doctor and his family lived there. At the top of the stairs Hamilton called out, 'Hello! Anybody home?'

There was no answer. The smell of cooking was very strong now. Cautiously, holding the .38 in his left hand, he began checking the rooms. Stephanie followed him, also holding her gun. The flat appeared to be empty. The final room they entered was the kitchen. It too was empty. On the kitchen stove stood a large pot. Boiling water was bubbling out of it and running down the sides. Hamilton went to the stove and looked into the pot. Black hair swirled in the boiling water. He turned off the gas. 'Bloody hell,' he muttered. Stephanie came to his side and peered into the water. She said nothing.

The pot contained a woman's head. It was impossible to tell her age or what she had looked like. The cooked flesh of her face was coming off her skull in tatters.

'Mrs Rajendram, I presume,' said Hamilton grimly.

'This has Gilmour's fingerprints all over it,' said Stephanie. 'He used to boil up the bodies of his victims to get their bones as trophies. That's why the tabloids called him the Bone Man.'

'I never liked that name. It had working-class connotations.'

They both whirled round. Gilmour was perched on the side of the kitchen table, swinging his legs. He grinned at them.

Hamilton fired. He did it without thinking. A china plate on a sideboard behind Gilmour exploded into fragments. Gilmour kept grinning. Hamilton fired again and scored a cup this time.

'You're wasting bullets,' Stephanie told him. 'He isn't really here. Not in a physical sense.'

'Pay attention to the lovely Stephanie,' Gilmour told him mockingly. 'She's talking sense, Terry.'

Gilmour's use of his first name disturbed Hamilton almost as much as his sudden manifestation. 'You know me?'

'But of course, Terry. How could I forget the man who nailed me? It was nice of you to come to see me at the Institute yesterday.'

Hamilton's skin crawled. Gilmour *had* seen him. Right through the one-way glass. And that was *before* Stephanie had injected him with her damned drug.

'This can't go on,' Stephanie told Gilmour. 'You won't be able to sustain all this indefinitely.'

'I don't see why not, lovely Stephanie. Members of your staff are busily manufacturing more of your delightful magic juice even as we speak. But you and Terry, on the other hand, have only a limited supply. And when it runs out I'll visit you for real. I'm really looking forward to that. You both mean a lot to me.'

'Yeah, and I'm looking forward to getting my hands on you for real,' snarled Hamilton. 'I'm going to break your fucking neck.'

'Brave words to hide your quaking fear, Terry,' said Gilmour, with a smile. 'Inside you're all quivering jelly. I can feel it.'

Hamilton couldn't help firing the .38 at him again. Another plate hit the dust. Gilmour glanced at the wreckage over his shoulder then turned, grinning, back to Hamilton. 'Good shooting.'

'Marc, where is the Institute?' Stephanie asked quietly.

'Around, Stephanie, around,' he said, and winked at her.

'Stop all this, Marc, please. You need help. And I promise I'll do everything I can to help you.'

'You've already helped me, lovely Stephanie. And as a reward I have a special treat in store for you. When the time is right. And now, for the moment, au revoir . . .' He began to fade away. As he did so he sang, in a high childish voice: 'I'm the King of the Castle, and you're the dirty rascals . . .' He then did a respectable Cheshire Cat act, leaving just his eyes and his grinning mouth in the air for some seconds before vanishing entirely.

'Good special effects,' said Stephanie sourly.

'Bastard.'

'If he was telling the truth it's as I feared, he's got my people with him in the Institute, forcing them to keep him dosed up with BDNFE.'

'We've got to find him.'

She looked at Hamilton. 'Yes, Sherlock. Good thinking.'

The car was surrounded by children. Young children, ranging in ages from between five and seven. There must have been

over thirty of them. All turned to look at Hamilton and Stephanie as they emerged from the doctor's surgery. All were completely silent. All had the same expression in their eyes –
hunger. Hamilton froze and took the revolver out of his pocket,
intending to fire a shot in the air to frighten them if they made
any menacing moves. But from the look in their eyes he knew
these kids would not scare easily. They were beyond that.

'Hello, children!' said Stephanie in an unnaturally cheery
voice. 'What are you doing here?'

None of them said a word. *Christ*, thought Hamilton, *next
she'll be asking them why they weren't in school. If they had
been to school today it was probably to eat their teachers.*

Then, unexpectedly, the children fell away on either side,
leaving a wide passageway that led to the side of the car. The
invitation was clear. Hamilton wasn't sure he wanted to accept
it, but Stephanie obviously did. She took him firmly by the arm
and said softly, 'Come on. We can't just stand here.'

They walked slowly through the crowd of silent, staring children. Hamilton could have sworn that one of them licked his
lips as they passed. They reached the car. Stephanie opened the
door and got in. She slid over to the driver's seat and Hamilton
hastily followed her. He slammed the door shut with relief and
immediately locked it. Then, as Stephanie started the engine,
the children started to whoop and yell . . . and at the same
time every one of them produced a knife and proceeded to wave
it about. Hamilton feared the worst but, in spite of the cacoph-
ony of menacing sounds, the children in front of the car melted
away on each side and Stephanie was able to drive through
the crowd of shrieking, knife-wielding little monsters.

'Another gesture from Gilmour,' said Stephanie, when they
had left the kids far behind them. Her voice was shaky.

'Did you see? Some of them had blood on them. On their
chins.'

'Yes. I saw.'

After a while he said, 'When all this is over – when we've
put a bullet in Gilmour and he's dead – will everything just
snap back to what it was like before?'

'You mean everyone, including us, will just wake up and think they've had a bad dream?'

'Yeah.'

'I seriously doubt it. Think of Douglas Scott. When I caught him up in my dream and he died, he stayed dead.'

'Yeah,' said Hamilton, and he lapsed into silence again.

They drove aimlessly around Harrow-on-the-Hill, hoping they would see something that would point the way to Gilmour. They saw no such thing. They saw a few people lying on the roadsides, presumably dead, and had the odd stone thrown at the car, but that was all. Finally Stephanie said that they might as well return to her flat and thrash out a plan of action over a meal. En route they stopped at a petrol station so that Stephanie could top up her tank. Hamilton, gun in hand, warily stood guard while Stephanie operated the fuel dispenser but no one appeared.

Hillview House was just as ominously silent as when they had left it. They rode the lift up to her floor without speaking. Hamilton felt depressed and anxious. No matter what Stephanie said he persisted with the hope that it was all a bad dream from which he would soon wake. But when, damn it, *when*?

He followed her into her flat . . . and immediately drew his gun. The flat was filled with the smell of cooking. Then he heard a sound from the kitchen. A clatter of dishes. Stephanie looked at him, eyes showing alarm. He raised a finger to his lips and then walked quietly towards the kitchen door.

He looked in. A woman was standing at the sink with her back to him. She was washing dishes.

He stepped into the kitchen. She glanced over her shoulder at him, then gave him a tired smile. 'Hello, Terry,' she said. She turned and began to peel the rubber gloves from her hands. He stared at her in shock.

'Who is *that*?' asked Stephanie, as she came into the kitchen.

After several moments Hamilton was able to say, despite his suddenly very dry mouth, 'Stephanie, I'd like you to meet Judith. My wife.'

Chapter Eleven

'Your *wife*?'

Hamilton stared helplessly at the woman by the sink. Yes, it was Judith all right. His wife. Whom he had accidentally shot dead over seven years ago.

She put the rubber gloves on the side of the sink and came towards them, hand outstretched. 'And you are?' she asked Stephanie.

'She's Dr Lyell. Dr Stephanie Lyell,' Hamilton told her.

'Pleased to meet you, Mrs Hamilton,' Stephanie said stiffly. They shook hands. Hamilton wanted to throw himself out of the kitchen window. 'You're very attractive,' his wife told Stephanie. Then she frowned at Stephanie's neck. 'What nasty-looking bruises! What happened to you?'

'An . . . accident,' said Stephanie.

'Someone tried to strangle her,' Hamilton told her.

'Goodness,' said his wife and turned to him. She looked him slowly up and down. 'Tsk, tsk,' she said, and then, 'You've put on a lot of weight. You obviously haven't been looking after yourself, have you?'

'Uh, no, Judith, I haven't,' he admitted. 'Things have never been the same with me since . . . well . . .' He didn't continue.

'Well, you two go and sit down. I know it was presumptuous of me, being in a stranger's home and everything, but I thought you would be hungry when you returned so I've made you both some brunch. I warn you I had to make do with what I could find in the refrigerator. With all due respect, Miss Lyell, you seem to shop like a man who lives alone.'

'Uh, sorry, Mrs Hamilton. I never seem to find the time.'

'Can't be helped now. I'm sure that trying to find an open shop around here today would be a nightmare. Now you two go and sit at the table. I won't be a jiff.'

Dutifully, Hamilton and Stephanie returned to the living room. She gave him an enquiring, incredulous glance. He shrugged his shoulders. They sat down at her dining table. There were already table mats and cutlery in place. Hamilton didn't know if they had been there when they'd first come into the room. He hadn't noticed them. Stephanie stared at him. 'She's really your wife?' she whispered.

'She certainly *seems* to be,' he whispered back. He ran a weary hand over his face. 'God, I need a drink.'

Stephanie got up. 'A large Scotch?'

He nodded, and she went to her drinks cabinet.

When Judith bustled into the room carrying two plates Stephanie was sitting down again and Hamilton was sipping gratefully at his drink. His wife made tut-tutting sounds when she saw the Scotch. 'Really, Terry. At *this* time of the day? And you know how you get when you drink whisky.'

The seven years plus seemed to melt away. He recalled that hectoring tone of hers as if he had last heard it yesterday. He muttered, 'Like I said, things have been rough.'

'Your liver must be like the sole of an old football boot,' she said as she put the plates down on the table.

Considering her complaints about the contents of Stephanie's refrigerator Hamilton saw that his plate was filled to overflowing. Strips of bacon, sausages, a fried egg, a fried tomato and a slice of fried bread. Wherever Judith had been for the last seven years the latest findings on the dangers of high cholesterol levels hadn't reached her. He had been feeling vaguely hungry before but the sight of all that fried food made his stomach queasy. He drank more Scotch. 'Tuck in,' commanded his late wife, and returned to the kitchen.

From the expression on Stephanie's face as she regarded

her plate and its contents she shared his feeling about eating Judith's meal. They exchanged a glance and she grimaced. He gave another shrug. Judith returned, carrying a tray. It had a tea pot and cups on it, as well as her own plate of fried food. She poured them each a cup of tea then took a sip from her own cup. 'Ah, there's nothing like a good cup of tea,' she said, closing her eyes as she savoured the taste. Then she began digging enthusiastically into her meal. Observing her, Hamilton told himself that it was logical she would be hungry; after all, it had been a long time since her last meal. He bit back a laugh that could have easily turned into a fit of hysterics. He sliced off a small piece of bacon and put it into his mouth. It was tasteless but very greasy. He wondered if this was real food or something that had been created by the Effect. Stephanie had similarly started playing with her food. They exchanged another glance.

Judith, between mouthfuls, said to Stephanie, 'You have a lovely flat, Dr Lyell. How do you manage to keep it looking so neat and tidy, considering your lack of time for housekeeping?'

'Er, I have a woman who comes in three times a week, Mrs Hamilton.'

'Oh, please call me Judith. She doesn't shop for you?'

'No, just cleans and does the laundry . . . Judith.'

'Have you ever been married, Dr Lyell?'

'Er, please call me Stephanie. And yes. I have been. Some time ago. He was an American. A fellow doctor, though he was a neuro-surgeon. It didn't work out. I'm divorced now.'

'Any children?'

'No. Neither of us wanted children. That was one of the few things we both agreed on, it turned out.' She gave a forced smile.

Judith looked disapproving. 'Forgive me, but I can't understand why any woman wouldn't want to have children. To me it seems that giving birth is the most important thing that can happen to a woman in her entire life.'

'I respect your opinion, Judith, but I don't agree with you as far as *I'm* concerned. I've never had any desire to have children.

And even if I did I don't think, unlike many professional women, that I would be competent enough to combine my career with raising a child.'

Listening to this conversation, Hamilton's sensation of unreality intensified. There was no denying that this person *was* his wife. Exactly as she had been seven years ago. The same face with its faded prettiness, the same brown hair done in the same short style. She was even wearing the same blue summer dress that she had been wearing on that day he'd shot her. And she was wearing that same, familiar expression that he knew so well. Her 'martyr look', as he used to call it to himself. That look that suggested she was bravely coping despite everything. And once again he experienced that old guilty feeling that what she was coping with was all his fault . . .

Looking at her sitting at Stephanie's dining table, he remembered something that he'd consciously suppressed all these years – the fact that he'd fallen out of love with Judith. There was no other woman involved, he'd simply lost all desire for her. He remembered what he'd felt for her – how *much* he'd felt for her – in the beginning of their relationship and in the early years of their marriage. But somewhere along the way one of them had changed. He was firmly convinced it was her. He couldn't pinpoint the beginning of the change but slowly, after the children had come, she had turned into a younger version of her own mother. The children were the most important thing in her life, and after them came the house, and way down the list came him. And yet she could still make him feel that the situation was all his fault. That he'd failed her in some way. But whoever's fault, their existence together had become a series of tedious automatic duties, the only thing of mutual interest in their marriage being the kids. At the time of her death he couldn't really remember the last occasion he'd enjoyed making love to her . . . And now he realised that, by the end, he'd even come to be repelled by her.

No wonder he had felt guilty whenever he'd looked at her. And now that guilt was stronger than ever.

'Judith,' he said suddenly, cutting into her continuing advertisement for the joys of motherhood, 'how much do you know? About, I mean, what happened to you.'

She turned to him. 'Well, I know you shot me, dear,' she said, and gave him a quick smile. 'I know you didn't mean to, of course. You were trying to shoot that dreadful man but instead you shot me. In the head.'

Stephanie put her knife and fork down on her plate with an abrupt clatter. She took her cigarettes and lighter out. 'Excuse me, do you mind if I smoke?' she asked his wife.

'Well, we have a rule not to smoke at the table. Not that I ever smoke at all but Terry smokes like a chimney. Unless, as he always promised to, he's finally given it up. But, of course, this is *your* place, Stephanie, so feel free.'

'Thank you,' said Stephanie. She hurriedly lit a cigarette. Hamilton could see she was agitated. He finished his Scotch and yearned for another one. Instead he indicated to Stephanie that he would like one of her cigarettes. She slid the packet and the lighter across the table to him. He lit a cigarette under his wife's disapproving gaze.

'So you haven't given up smoking,' she said. 'But that comes as no surprise. You never did have any willpower.'

'I did give up,' he protested, 'For a while . . .' Christ, he wasn't going to argue with her about his damned smoking. 'Look, what else do you know? About what's happening here . . . and about . . . yourself?'

'I only know that I was dead and that now I'm not,' she said brightly.

'Doesn't that strike you as a little . . . unusual?' he asked.

'You know me, Terry,' she ate a piece of fried bread, 'I always take life as it comes.'

Christ, another of her damned mother's platitudes, he thought angrily. 'Judith, this whole situation is downright unnatural. You admit that, don't you?'

She gave him her best martyr's look with her best brave smile thrown in, complete with a suggestion of trembling in the lower lip. 'Aren't you pleased to see me again, Terry?'

That caught him off guard. 'Uh, yes, *of course* I am, Judith.'

'How's Matt?'

Another jab to the vitals. Matt was their son. 'Uh, okay, I guess. Your sister hasn't written in some time. You know he's living with Jan, don't you? In Sydney?'

'I knew. Don't ask me how.' She sipped her tea. 'When did you last see him?'

'Not since your sister came and collected him. That was over six years ago.'

'You haven't gone to visit him at all?'

'For one thing I couldn't afford to ... for another I don't think he'd be happy to see me. He kind of blamed me for ... everything.'

She put down her cup and covered her eyes. Her shoulders began to heave. She was crying. 'That *dreadful* man,' she sobbed. 'What he made Matt do to Pam ... horrible ... *horrible ...*'

Hamilton wondered what he should do. Get up and comfort her? He had to admit that the thought of touching his dead wife – even though she appeared to be well and truly alive – filled him with deep unease. Then, to his relief, he saw Stephanie rise to her feet. *That's right,* he thought, *just what's needed – a bit of womanly mutual support. Thank you, Stephanie. I owe you.*

But Stephanie said, 'I think you and your wife need to be alone, Terry. I'm going for a walk.' And she strode quickly out of the room.

'What!' He jumped up from the table and caught up with her in the hallway. He grabbed her arm. 'Are you mad? You can't go outside! It's too dangerous!'

'I have the gun. I'll be fine. I'm not going far. Just for a walk around the back garden. I really can't take any more of her. She gives me the shudders.'

'What the hell do you think she does to *me*? Christ! And you're leaving me to deal with her on my own.'

She pulled her arm free. 'She's your wife, Terry.'

'Jesus, Stephanie, she's *dead!*'

'Not any more, it seems,' she said and opened the door. Then she was gone. He returned, resignedly, to the living room. Judith was wiping her eyes with a paper tissue. He wondered vaguely where it had come from.

'Your friend has gone?' she asked.

He sat down and stared at the greasy mess on his plate. 'Yeah.'

'I didn't mean to upset her.'

'You didn't. She doesn't feel well. Needed some fresh air.' That was a laugh. The air outside was thick with that yellow crap.

'Oh. That explains why she hardly touched her food.' Judith paused, then said, 'She's very attractive.'

'Yeah. You've said that before.' He desperately wanted another whisky.

'Are you . . . sleeping with her, Terry?'

He looked at her and saw that it was a serious question. He got up and went to the drinks cabinet. 'Don't be ridiculous. She wouldn't be interested in me in that way if I was the last man on earth.' Then it occurred to him that, the way things were going, he might just end up being that. He poured whisky all the way to the top of the tumbler. 'Anyway, sex hasn't figured very high on my list of interests these past seven years.' *Apart from last night*, he thought. And he wondered what had happened to Josie Welch after he had left her flat. Was she still alive? He took a large swallow of the Scotch.

As Stephanie waited for the lift to arrive she lit another cigarette. The click of the lighter coincided with another click. She turned. The door to Douglas Scott's flat was open. Just a few inches. She frowned. She was sure it had been shut when they'd passed it on the way in. She walked back down the corridor towards it. 'Is someone there?' she called. She stopped in front of the door. All she could see through the gap was blackness. She smelt something though. Something bad. She took a step closer, taking the gun out of her pocket.

'Hello, Dr Lyell,' came a throaty whisper from behind the door.

'Who's that?' she said, nervously. She took hold of the gun with both hands, ready to pull the trigger. The cigarette was clamped between her lips and the smoke was getting in her eyes.

'It's me, Dr Lyell,' came the whisper. Then the door slowly swung open. Standing there was her former next-door neighbour, the late Douglas Scott, and he looked the worse for wear. He was naked and horribly burned. The blackened and broken blisters on his body leaked colourless fluid and he was holding his head at an impossibly odd angle. The smell of charred flesh overwhelmed the smell of her cigarette. 'Shit,' she muttered and pulled the trigger.

Nothing happened. Then she remembered the safety catch. But before she could release it Douglas Scott grabbed her. Then she was hauled off her feet and dragged into the darkness of his flat. She heard the door slam shut behind her with a terrible air of finality.

Chapter Twelve

Josie Welch arrived at the offices of the *Harrow Examiner* in a highly confused and worried state of mind. 'Where the fuck *is* everybody?' she asked herself aloud, not for the first time that morning, as she gazed around the empty, open-plan news and features department.

She had woken up feeling very strange. She was pretty positive she had brought a man back to her flat the night before but for the life of her she couldn't remember who. That was a bad sign, not to mention a scary one. Maybe she should ease up a little. No more funny pills for a while.

Then, when she had turned on her radio there was nothing but static on every station. Same with the TV channels. This was when she had started to feel afraid.

She began frantically dialling phone numbers, but not one of the people she tried to call answered their phone. She then tried ringing the Harrow police station. No reply there either. She'd dressed hurriedly and gone out to her car. It was all very quiet in the usually noisy street. No yelling kids. No crying babies. Not even any crying mothers. What had happened? Nuclear war. She decided to drive to the office. Surely there would be someone at the paper who knew what was going on . . .

At first she thought the roads were entirely deserted but then she was greatly relieved to see a touch of normality in the form of a red double-decker bus coming towards her as she

drove along Pinner Road. Then, as it drew nearer, she saw that
its driver was a very small boy – his head barely visible above
the steering wheel. As the bus sped by the tiny driver gave her
the finger.

Something was definitely very wrong.

As she'd driven on the strange feeling in her head had grown
more pronounced. It felt as if someone had broken into her
skull as they might do into her flat and were now violently
rummaging about in there, throwing open cupboard doors,
emptying drawers and generally rooting through her mind
with scant regard for her mental belongings. It occurred to her
she might be going mad.

And now she found the office deserted too. 'Hey, is anybody
fucking here?' she shouted at the top of her voice. But wasn't
surprised when no one answered. She walked over to her desk
and sat down resignedly. What could she do next, she wondered? Check out the police station? Then she noticed the copy
of the *Harrow Examiner* lying on her desk. The headline on the
front page made her go very cold. It read: 'LOCAL JOURNALIST
BRUTALLY MURDERED.' She read the text beneath it. 'The body
of *Harrow Examiner* journalist Josie Welch, aged 23, was discovered by colleagues today on and around her desk at the
newspaper's premises. A police spokesman from the Harrow
Division said, "The victim was hacked to pieces by someone
wielding an axe. It was a particularly nasty and brutal murder
and whoever was responsible is clearly a very sick, evil and
highly dangerous individual. Miss Josie Welch was a fine journalist with a bright future in the profession. She will be greatly
missed, especially by all the lads in CID."'

Josie had stopped breathing. She looked at the paper's date.
It was today's.

Then she heard the swish of the axe blade behind her.

Judith returned to the living room after having taken the
plates out to the kitchen. 'You're just like your friend. You
hardly touched a thing. Such a waste of good food.' She sat

down and looked at him. 'Have you seen any recent photographs of Matt?' she asked.

'Yeah. Jan sends me photographs of him fairly regularly. The last ones I got just before Christmas.'

'How does he look?'

'Fine,' he answered, uneasily. He remembered Matt's sullen expression as he glared into the lens of the camera. He obviously knew who the photograph was for. Hamilton could feel the hate. Also, the boy didn't look well. His face was drawn and thin. He knew from Jan that the youth was still being prescribed anti-depressants.

'He must be quite big now. He'll be sixteen next birthday, won't he? Or have I got my sums wrong?'

'No, you're right. He'll be sixteen.' Hamilton was feeling increasingly uncomfortable, sitting there chatting to the woman he'd shot dead years ago. He wished Stephanie hadn't taken her cigarettes with her. And he hoped she'd return soon.

Stephanie opened her eyes. She was confused for a few moments, then it all came back to her. Being dragged into Douglas Scott's flat . . . by Scott himself. The door slamming shut. The darkness. The gun being plucked from her hands . . . and then nothing. Her head ached. She presumed he had hit her, probably with the gun, knocking her unconscious.

'Ah, that's good, *Dr* Lyell. You're back with us. I didn't want to start without you.'

The bedside lamp had been turned on. Scott was standing at the end of the bed, leering down at her. He looked worse than ever. It wasn't just his burns and his broken neck . . . he was beginning to decompose. She tried to move but couldn't. She was tied, spread-eagled, to his bed. And she was naked. Nor could she call out. Something had been stuffed in her mouth. A dirty sock, by the taste of it.

'Not so high and mighty now, are you, *Doctor*?' Scott sneered. 'Beginning to wish you'd been a bit more neighbourly to me, eh? Beginning to wish you hadn't called me a "yuppie yob", a

"City lager lout", a "cretin who thought he was God's gift to women"?'

She noticed then that he had an erection. And like the rest of him, apart from his face, his penis was charred and blistered. She struggled against whatever was tied around her wrists and ankles but it was useless. She was totally helpless. He came round to the side of the bed and leaned over her. She could smell his stench and her stomach rebelled at it. She knew she didn't dare vomit – with the gag in her mouth she'd choke to death. *Go away!* she willed desperately. *Go away! Get out of here! Vanish! I command you!* But he persisted in existing. She wondered what had gone wrong. She still had the BDNFE in her system. It should still be providing her with protection against Gilmour . . .

'And I bet you're regretting all those complaints about me playing my music, eh?' He reached down and put his hand on her left breast. She shuddered violently at his touch. His hand felt cold and slimy. 'And I bet you're *really* regretting that letter of complaint about me that you sent to the landlords, eh?' He squeezed her breast, hard. She groaned.

'Like it, do you? Yeah, I thought you would, you stuck-up bitch. I always thought what you needed was a bloke to treat you rough and fuck your brains out at the same time. Teach you how to be a real woman. Well, here I am.' He let go of her breast and slapped her face, hard. Her eyes filled with tears from the pain. Then she felt his hand on her again. It moved down across her stomach, leaving a slimy trail as it went. She pictured pieces of dead flesh flaking off it. She writhed and struggled. His hand kept on moving. *No! No! No!* she silently screamed. The thought of his fingers inside her was just too disgusting to bear. But, slowly, the unbearable happened.

'Pam would be thirteen now . . . if she'd lived.'

'Yeah, she would be, but she didn't so she isn't.' He couldn't take much more of this. She was driving him crazy, raking through his deepest wounds, pulling off the scar tissue. He'd poured himself another large whisky, intending to get drunk.

He was also worried about Stephanie. She shouldn't have gone off on her own.

The phone rang, taking Hamilton by surprise. 'Bloody marvellous,' he said as he got up. 'The whole place has gone to hell in a bucket but British Telecom is still operating as normal. Still, stands to reason, I guess.' He picked up the phone. 'Hello?'

'Hi, Terry! How you doing?' A cheery voice. And one he recognised . . . and loathed. *Gilmour.*

'Now what, you bastard?' he snarled. 'Obscene phone calls?'

'You've got me wrong, Terry. I'm calling to do you a favour. I have some information for you. It concerns our mutual friend, the lovely Dr Stephanie Lyell.'

The late Douglas Scott was straddling her, his rotting groin above her face. The stench was appalling. He had pulled the gag from her mouth, after warning her that he would kill her if she tried to scream. Now her mouth was clenched shut. He prodded her lips with the tip of his decaying, burnt penis. 'Go on, Doctor, open up. You owe it to me, *Doctor*. After all, you fucking killed me. You and that fucking dream of yours. So open up wide, Doctor, and take your medicine.'

She kept her teeth clenched. Her eyes were squeezed shut as well. She kept willing this ghastly creature to disappear but he stubbornly remained on top of her . . .

He hit her hard on the side of her face. Involuntarily, she opened her mouth to cry out from the shock and the pain. Immediately, the foul and shitty thing was pushed into her mouth. Sick with revulsion, she started to gag. Scott thrust his swollen, encrusted penis down into her throat, choking her. Her body convulsed against her unyielding bonds as Scott's laughter filled her buzzing ears. 'Now *that's* more like it, *Dr Lyell!*'

Dimly, she heard a banging sound. Then another one. Jesus Christ help me! she silently screamed. She'd give anything for just one more breath of air . . .

Scott's penis was pulled roughly from her mouth. She

gasped for breath, his stink still making her gag. She couldn't let herself vomit . . .

Voices. Then gunshots. In the room. What was happening? Coughing and hacking, she strained to raise her head from the bed.

Hamilton had made the mistake of trying to kick the door down. But the doors of Hillview House, unlike those of the doctor's surgery in Headstone Road, were built to provide security. He only succeeded in severely jarring his foot and his leg. He then put the barrel of the .38 close to the lock and, hoping that the bullet wouldn't ricochet into him, fired. The lock shattered and he was still alive. He kicked again. The door flew open and bits of lock flew across the hallway. He charged inside, heading for the bedroom. Its door wasn't locked. He flung it open and charged inside, gun ready.

Stephanie, he saw, was tied up naked on the bed. He noted that she had very white skin even as he reacted in shock to the creature on top of her face and what it was doing to her. The thing turned and looked at him over his shoulder. Or rather, its head *lolled* back over its shoulder. And Hamilton recognised the late Douglas Scott who he had last seen lying dead on the ground three storeys below. Now he was looking even more dead.

'What the fuck do you want?' asked Scott as he rose from Stephanie's face and then slowly got off the bed. Hamilton could smell him from the bedroom doorway. He didn't want to think about how bad the smell was in Stephanie's position. He advanced on the creature. The creature advanced on him. Hamilton said the first words that came into his head. 'Douglas Scott, I am Detective Sergeant Hamilton and I am placing you under arrest. I must warn you that anything you say will be taken down and used in evidence against you.'

Surprise flickered in Scott's eyes. 'You fucking moron,' he said, contemptuously. 'You can't arrest me – I'm *dead.*'

'I sure hope so,' said Hamilton, and fired. He aimed high, intending to avoid hitting Stephanie if the bullets passed straight through Scott as they had with Gilmour. But they didn't. The first bullet hit Scott in the throat, blowing a large hole in it. The second hit him in the forehead. The top of his head powderised from the impact. There was no blood. Scott looked surprised, then raised his hand to the top of his head and felt around in the empty cavity. 'Bastard,' he said to Hamilton and vanished. Not slowly, the way that Gilmour had, but instantly.

Hamilton spun round, suspecting some sort of trick with Scott reappearing elsewhere in the bedroom. But no. There was nothing. Then, behind him, he became aware of Stephanie coughing and spluttering on the bed. He pocketed the gun and went to her. Her face was dark red and she was shaking her head from side to side as she spat and coughed. 'You okay?' he asked. She didn't answer. He realised that, considering the circumstances, it hadn't been the most intelligent question he could have asked her. He wondered what to do first. Untying her was a pretty good idea for a start, he decided.

He got to work on one of the cords around her wrists. It was tied to the leg of the bed. The knot was tight and as he struggled with it his wounded hand began to jab with pain.

'Hurry up, will you, damn it!' Stephanie cried.

He took out his pen-knife and began sawing at the cord. He cut her wrists free first and then got to work on her ankles. He carefully kept his eyes averted from her naked body as he sawed away. She was still making spluttering and hacking sounds. Finally he was finished. She sat on the edge of the bed and leaned forward, clasping her head between her hands. Then she vomited noisily on to the carpet. He went into the kitchen to get her a glass of water. He was still wary about the dead Douglas Scott popping up again but the flat remained empty. He returned to the bedroom with the water. She was still leaning forward on the side of the bed, head between her hands. He held the glass out in front of her. 'Here, drink this,' he said and at the same time tried to give her a reassuring pat on the shoulder, but she jerked away from his touch. She did,

however, accept the glass of water. She drank some of it then
threw up again.

Feeling embarrassed and downright useless he went to
Scott's closet, found a dressing gown and draped it around her
shoulders. Then he began picking up her clothes from the floor
and laid them out on the bed. She was now sobbing quietly to
herself. He said, 'Look, Stephanie, when you're feeling up to it
I think it might be a good idea if we got out of here.'

She stayed silent and he was beginning to think that she
hadn't heard him when, abruptly, she stood up and pulled the
dressing gown tight around her. 'Yes, you're right. Let's go.' She
strode out of the room without looking at him. He hurriedly
gathered up her clothes and followed her. She was waiting
for him in the hallway. She still wouldn't look him in the
eyes. 'What happened to your gun?' he asked her.

'I don't know and I don't care. A fat lot of good it did me.'

'Wait,' he said and went back into the living room. He
glanced around and spotted it lying just under an armchair.
He picked it up and returned to Stephanie. She opened the door
and they walked in silence to her flat.

When they entered Stephanie's living room his wife looked
first at Stephanie and then at him. She raised her eyebrows.
'And what have you two been up to then?' she asked.

He wanted to smack her. 'Stephanie has had a very bad
experience,' he said coldly. 'She was attacked by a . . . man.'

Judith made a tsk-tsking sound of sympathy. 'Oh dear. I'd
better go and make her a nice cup of tea.' She disappeared into
the kitchen.

'That's not Judith, it's her fucking mother,' he muttered. He
turned to Stephanie. Her face was now white. Her eyes were
glazed. He guided her over to the sofa and made her sit down.
'Forget the tea, you need a large Scotch.'

'No,' she murmured. 'A brandy. A very large brandy.'

He put her clothes down on the sofa beside her and went and
poured her a brandy and then got a large Scotch for himself.
He was about to sit down in an armchair when she said, simply,
'Cigarette.'

'You've got them,' he told her. 'They're in your jacket pocket, beside you.'

Still not looking at him, she shook her head. 'No, I can't touch those clothes. *He* did.'

Understanding what she meant, he got up and removed her packet and lighter from the jacket. He gave her a cigarette, lit it for her then lit one for himself. He left the pack and lighter on the arm of the sofa. Then, on reflection, he picked up the bundle of clothes and dropped them on the floor.

He went back to his chair. After a while he said, uncomfortably, 'How do you feel?'

'How do you think?' she snapped.

After a long pause he asked, 'Did he rape you? As well as the other, I mean?'

'No. I guess I got off lucky, eh?' she said bitterly. Then, after an even longer pause, she raised her head and looked at him directly. 'Thank you.'

'Uh, you're welcome.' He drank his Scotch.

'How did you know?'

'I got a phone call.'

'From whom?' she asked, surprised.

'Gilmour?'

'What?'

'It's true. He rang me and said you were being attacked in the flat next door. I presumed he was just playing some kind of sick game with me but I thought I'd better check to make sure. I'm glad I did.'

She frowned. 'Why would Gilmour bring Scott back to life to attack me and then alert you to my danger?'

'I have no idea,' he admitted. 'He just told me what was happening to you, wished me luck and hung up.'

'And deliberately spoilt his own rotten fun as a result . . . weird.' She shook her head. 'And I can't understand why the BDNFE didn't protect me against Gilmour's creature.' Then she glanced at her watch. 'Which reminds me, we'd both better have another injection in a half an hour.'

'Maybe Gilmour is getting stronger.'

'Maybe,' she said, doubtfully. She grunted and stubbed out her cigarette. 'We've got to find the bastard.' She rose to her feet. 'But first I'm going to take a bath. Perhaps two.'

She left the room and a short time later Hamilton heard bathwater running. At the same time he realised that the kitchen was oddly quiet. Judith in a kitchen automatically produced a high-decibel clatter. He got up and went to the kitchen door. He opened it and looked inside. The kitchen was empty. Judith had gone.

He felt very relieved.

Chapter Thirteen

'I've got a theory,' said Hamilton. He was feeling more than a
little drunk. And he was still clinging to the wild hope that at
any moment he would wake up in a detoxification unit and
discover that all this was nothing but an alcoholic delirium.
Then again, he remembered having a similar hope about one
day eventually waking up from the horrors of the real world.

'So let's hear it,' said Stephanie. She had changed her clothes.
Now she was wearing black jeans, black shirt and black leather
jacket. Her hair was pulled back from her face in a tight
pony-tail and she looked very severe. But her face was still
extremely pale.

'We assumed that Judith's appearance – manifestation – was
the work of Gilmour. Right?'

She nodded and drew deeply on her cigarette.

'But what if she wasn't? What if she was *my* creation? You
said that we had no conscious control over the power that your
version of BEFDN – '

'BDNFE,' she corrected him.

'Whatever. We have no conscious control over it but you said
that our powerful unconscious desires could affect this version
of reality we're stuck in.'

'Yes. So you're saying your subconscious desire to have your
wife back resulted in her manifestation here?'

'Well,' he said, hesitantly, 'it's not so much that I wanted her
back . . . I think it has more to do with the guilt I feel over her

death. The guilt I've always felt.' He looked at Stephanie. 'I
think my *guilt* recreated her. Do you understand?'

'Yes, I think so.'

'And I believe the same thing applies to Scott.'

She looked puzzled. 'What's your guilt got to do with that
bastard's appearance?'

'Not my guilt. Yours.'

First she looked astonished, then angry. 'You're saying that
my subconscious felt so guilty over my indirect involvement in
his death that I conjured up his dead body in order to have him
beat me up and sexually assault me? That's crazy! I regret
what happened to him because of my dream but I as sure as
hell don't feel *that* guilty about it. Besides, I never liked the
creep.'

'It's not just your guilt about Scott; you feel guilty about
being responsible for' – he made a gesture with his hands – 'all
this. I mean, if you hadn't experimented on Gilmour, none of
this would have happened.'

She glared at him. 'Thanks a lot. Look, I accept some – okay,
a *lot* – of the responsibility for what's going on but no matter
how guilty I feel I did not, and do not, have an unconscious
desire to be stripped, tied up and sexually abused by the Dead
Lager Lout Yuppie from Hell!'

'I'm not saying you did. I'm saying that your guilt created
Scott, but from then on it was a free agent. Your unconscious
mind had nothing to do with its actions. No more than I had
any control over Judith once she'd appeared.'

She pondered on this and then said, 'Yes, I see. You might
have a point.'

'It's the only explanation. If Gilmour had been responsible
the BDNFE, or whatever, would have protected you from Scott.
That's why Gilmour intervened. Scott might have killed you.'

'Yes, he very nearly did,' she admitted as she remembered
how close she had been to choking to death. She then muttered,
'Gilmour certainly left it until the last moment.'

'Yeah, well I'm sure he enjoyed what happened to you but he
didn't want to lose you completely. He wants you for himself.'

Stephanie shivered. 'Yes.' She suddenly looked so anxious
that Hamilton wanted to go over and put his arm around her
but he didn't think she would interpret the gesture in the right
way. Not after what had just happened to her. Instead he got
up and went to the window. It was now nearing 3 p.m. The
sickly, yellow murk had become thicker, making the hour seem
much later. As before, the murk was at its thickest around the
summit of the Hill and it was still completely obscuring the
church spire. He wondered if he had seen the last of Judith.
He hoped so . . .

She had to admit to herself that he was probably right about
all this buried guilt shit. She'd certainly buried the guilt she
felt over her young sister's death. Even the actual memory of
the event. How long had it been since she'd consciously thought
about the fire? Not for years. Incredible, considering how much
it had changed her life. Relations with her parents had certainly never been the same again. They blamed her for Gloria's
death. They tried their best to hide their true feelings but it
was clear to her that they held her responsible. Gloria had
been the favourite. They had drifted apart since she had left
home to go to college. Nowadays the only contact she had with
her parents was a card on her birthday and at Christmas. It
had been, she realised, over four years since she had spoken to
them on the phone.

And she remembered now how much, at first, she had blamed
herself. She had been tortured with guilt, attending Mass every
day to pray for forgiveness, convinced that she would go to Hell
for what she'd done. She also changed in other ways. Prior to
the fire she'd been a kind of wild child. Rebellious and unruly.
And she'd hated school, playing truant on a regular basis. After
the fire she became a model student. She stopped hanging
around with her group of similarly wild friends and became a
solitary child. She spent all her spare time studying. She supposed now that this was another way of dealing with her guilt.
She had been, vainly, trying to make amends to her parents.

When, she wondered, had she begun burying the guilt, along

with the memories? University, perhaps, when her obsession with her work took over her life? And why had it all come flooding back on this particular day? The answer to that was easy. Gilmour. Bloody Gilmour.

As Hamilton stared glumly at the murk-shrouded Hill it occurred to him that the stuff appeared to be emanating from the top of the Hill itself. 'Come here,' he said to Stephanie. Something in his tone made her obey without questioning him. When she had joined him at the window he pointed at the Hill. 'That's where the Institute is. And Gilmour. Up there.'

'What makes you think that?'

'Remember what Gilmour said just before he faded away in that doctor's kitchen? "I'm the King of the Castle, and you're the dirty rascals." Didn't you ever play that game when you were a kid?'

'What game?'

'King of the Castle, of course! The aim was to shove your way to the top of some sandpile or whatever without being shoved off by someone else. When you did manage to get to the top you cried, "I'm the King of the Castle!"'

'I obviously had a deprived childhood. I've never heard of the game.'

'Well, Gilmour has. He's up there, on top of the hill, lording it over his conquered subjects. He's the King of the Castle, and we're up shit creek.'

She gazed at the Hill for a while. 'If the Institute's up there, where is the church now?'

'How the hell should I know? He shifted it somewhere else. Or maybe he simply made it disappear into thin air. But I'll bet my pension that your damned Institute is sitting right up where the church was!'

'Well, it's certainly worth checking out.'

'Right, but before we go charging off half-cocked, let's think about making some preparations for this little expedition.'

'Like what?'

'You wouldn't happen to have something like a crowbar around the place?'

'No. Sainsburys never seem to have them in stock whenever I ask,' she said dryly. 'So what do you need a crowbar for?'

'Somehow I don't think Gilmour will have left the front door of the building open for us. We're going to have to force our way in. How about a hammer and chisel?'

'Yes, those I do have. What else?'

He ran through a short list of things. One of the items was inflammable liquid of any kind. She told him she had a spare can of petrol in the boot of her car. 'Great,' he told her. 'Let's go fetch it!'

They went down to her car together, their new policy being not to go anywhere alone. They returned with the can of petrol and her car tool box. They had seen nobody outside and Hillview House had remained thankfully silent, and inert, though Hamilton had got the strong impression that there were still other people in the building, behind those closed doors.

Stephanie watched as he made six Molotov cocktails, using milk and wine bottles and wicks made of strips from a torn-up sheet. 'We need something to carry all this in,' he said. She went off and came back with an old rucksack. 'I used to belong to a ramblers' association once upon a time, but I got better,' she told him.

After he had packed everything into the rucksack and reloaded his gun, and checked hers, he said, 'Well, time to go pay a call on the King. Ready?'

She gave him a strained smile. 'Sure.'

They went back downstairs. As they entered the car park something landed with a *splat* on the concrete just in front of them. They both stopped and stared at it.

It was a foetus.

It was about four inches long and it was alive. It squirmed and wriggled, waving and kicking its tiny arms and legs. Hamilton assumed it was a human foetus but he wasn't sure.

Then another landed nearby, and another. They squirmed and wriggled too. 'Oh God,' whispered Stephanie.

Suddenly it began to rain foetuses. When the first of them landed on Stephanie she screamed hysterically, swatted madly at herself and then flung herself into Hamilton's arms, her face buried against his chest. The shower turned into a deluge and all he could hear, apart from her muffled screams, were the sickening *splat! splat! splat!* sounds of the foetuses hitting the concrete.

'Come on, this way!' he cried, and, head down, hustled her in the direction of her car. As they ran they couldn't avoid stepping on some of the wriggling, twitching creatures and Hamilton's stomach lurched as he felt the tiny bodies burst under his shoes. Stephanie's screams became even more hysterical.

They reached the car. He tried to pull the door open. It was locked, of course. 'Keys!' he yelled at Stephanie. 'Where are the goddamned car keys?' But she was out of it completely, screaming and sobbing while trying to burrow her head under his coat. He shook her hard. 'The *keys!*' he yelled. 'Where are they?' It was no good so he began digging through the pockets of her jacket. Meanwhile the downpour of foetuses continued unabated. He found the keys, got the door open and shoved Stephanie into the car. He quickly followed her and slammed the door shut. 'Bloody hell!' he cried.

He touched the side of his face. It was sticky with fluid. So was his hair. The foetuses pounded down on the car and the bonnet was covered with the pink, squirming little creatures. His stomach lurched again. Stephanie, hunched forward with her arms wrapped around herself, was still screaming. He dug his elbow sharply into her shoulder. 'Shut up, will you!' She kept on screaming. He was surprised by her reaction. She didn't seem the type to go to pieces completely. He put his arm around her shoulders and hugged her. 'Hey, it's okay, calm down. Everything's going to be okay.' *Hah!* he said to himself. *That old lie.*

The rain of foetuses continued and the little wriggling bodies

began to pile up against the windshield. Then, slowly, the
downpour lessened and finally stopped. Stephanie had stopped
screaming as well, but her body shook with convulsive sobs as
she rocked back and forth. He held her tightly. 'It's stopped,
Stephanie. It's stopped.'

Her sobbing subsided. After a while she raised her head . . .
and when she saw the heap of little, pink, squirming creatures
piled against the windshield she let out a terrible wail and
buried her face in her hands again. 'Get rid of them!' she
screamed. *'Get rid of them!'*

'Okay, okay, I will,' he assured her hurriedly. With extreme
reluctance, he opened the door and got out of the car. He fought
to keep control of the contents of his stomach as he felt and
heard the small bodies crunch beneath his feet. Shutting his
mind to what he was doing, he began brushing the things off
the bonnet with his arm, trying to avoid making any contact
with them with his hand. But direct contact was impossible to
avoid and he shuddered as he touched them and felt the
warmth of their bodies.

Finally he'd completely cleared the bonnet and then turned
his attention to the foetuses lying on the car's roof. He hoped
it was imagination that was providing the thin, high-pitched
cries he thought he could hear as he brushed the things off the
car. He was surprised he hadn't vomited.

With relief, after wiping the soles of his shoes clean on the
bottom of the door frame, he got back into the car. 'All clear,'
he told Stephanie, who was still hiding her face. 'I promise.'

She warily raised her head and looked. 'Thank God. Oh, that
was horrible . . . *horrible.*'

He wished that among the things he had packed into her
rucksack he had included either the whisky or the brandy
bottle. He considered going to fetch them, but the thought of
having to step on any more of those creatures made him
immediately abandon the idea. He looked at Stephanie. Her
former pale complexion had turned into a shade of grey.

'Want to talk about it?'

'About what?' she asked listlessly.

'Well, I'm pretty certain that nasty little shower didn't have its roots in *my* subconscious.'

'No, I suppose not.'

'So you had an abortion at some time?'

'I've had two. One before my marriage, and one during it.'

'They must have hit you hard.'

'No. Not really. I suffered some depression after each one, but nothing serious.'

'But deep down they must have affected you worse than you realised.'

'So it would seem,' she said bitterly. She produced a paper handkerchief, wiped her eyes then blew her nose.

He stared into space for a short time, then said, 'I think I have to modify my theory. I still think Judith came out of my subconscious, or unconscious, and you created the late Douglas Scott and now these things . . . but now I believe that Gilmour is making us do it. He's digging around inside our minds and finding our weak spots. Getting us to hurt ourselves where it really counts. So don't blame yourself for what happened just then. It's Gilmour . . . It's all Gilmour.'

She sniffed, then patted him on the hand.

'Shall we go back to your flat so you can have a rest?' he asked her. 'We could postpone our expedition until later.'

She shook her head. 'No, let's get it over with. Before he springs something even more terrible on us.'

As he was in the driver's seat he decided he might as well drive. She made no objection so he started the engine. He drove out of the car park, trying to ignore the sounds coming from beneath the car as the tyres crushed countless numbers of the . . . things.

He went to the end of Lower Road then drove up the Hill along West Street which led into High Street. Now they were surrounded by various sections and off-shoots of the famous Harrow School. On their right was the Harrow School Book- shop, while on the left they were just passing the Harrow School Outfitters. Ahead, also on the left, was the original Harrow School building, completed, someone had told him once, way back in 1615. Hamilton wondered how many Harrow students and staff had been sucked into Gilmour's sick little universe, and what had happened to them since. There was no one in evidence in the area now. In fact, they had not seen a soul since leaving Hillview House.

His intention had been to turn into the small street called Church Hill which led directly up to where the church had once stood, but he braked the car when he saw that would be impossible. Church Hill was blocked off with a high mound of broken masonry. 'Shit,' said Hamilton and absent-mindedly thumped his bad hand on the steering wheel. '*Shit!*' he cried, wincing from the pain.

'What is all that stuff?' asked Stephanie.

'From the look of it, that's the church. Or it's part of it. Gilmour stomped on it and recycled it as a barrier in the roads around the Institute.'

He drove a short way on and they saw that Grove Hill was also blocked with the aged and shattered masonry from the church. They were obliged to go on down the Hill along Peterborough Road to Tyburn Lane. A short time later they had confirmed that the other two roads that led straight up to the Grove, the name of the woods that had surrounded the church and now undoubtedly surrounded the Institute, were similarly blocked with stone.

'I think the message is clear,' Hamilton said to Stephanie. 'Gilmour wants us to leave the car and make the journey on foot.'

Chapter Fourteen

They were back in her flat. Stephanie had made no objection when Hamilton suggested that they wait until dark before going up the Hill on foot. She knew that it really wouldn't make a scrap of difference – Gilmour could just as easily keep track of them at night as he could during the day – but she was secretly grateful for the excuse to postpone the attempt to reach the Institute. Also she agreed with Hamilton that they both needed some fortification, in the form of food and drink, before setting off. With the exception of those few mouthfuls of that ghastly meal cooked by Hamilton's wife, she hadn't eaten all day. She wasn't hungry but she was feeling weak and she knew she ought to eat something.

When they'd returned to Hillview House she'd been relieved to see there was no trace of any of the foetuses. It was as if they'd never existed. The building remained as eerily quiet as before, but it took some willpower to walk past the door of Douglas Scott's flat, even with Hamilton by her side.

She made them both a grilled cheese sandwich with salad. She'd had to force her food down but noted that Hamilton seemed to have no difficulty. He'd eaten with gusto and was now attacking the whisky bottle with equal enthusiasm as he pored over a map of the central Harrow area which was spread out over the dining table. She hoped he wouldn't drink to the point where he was hopelessly drunk. That was all she needed.

She was sitting on the sofa with Gilmour's file open on her

lap. Even though she had read it several times before she was going through it again in the desperate hope that she might spot something that she'd missed before. Something that they could use against Gilmour when it came to the crunch . . .

Crunch. She didn't like that word.

'What did you people do in that Institute of yours, apart from experiment on dangerous psychopaths?' Hamilton asked her.

She looked up from the file. 'What did we do? We had a whole range of research programmes dealing with various areas of brain function on the biochemical level. A lot of the work concerned research into brain diseases, such as Parkinson's and Alzheimer's diseases. My colleagues in that department were attempting to discover whether there was genetic predisposition to such diseases.'

'But you weren't involved in that?'

'No. My area was in identifying the neurotransmitters in the brain that are connected with the emotional processes. For example, different neurotransmitters control the firing of neurons when you're in a happy state of mind to the ones involved when you're in a state of extreme anger. I was also interested in those that govern mood. I and my staff were trying to find an endogenous tranquilliser in the brain that would be the equivalent to the endogenous opoids, the enkephalins or endorphins, that act on the same receptors in the brain as narcotic drugs such as morphine. This led to the accidental discovery of BDNFE last year and – '

She was interrupted by the ringing of her doorbell.

She and Hamilton looked at each other. The doorbell rang again. Hamilton picked up the .38 that had been sitting on the table near the map. He rose. 'Come on, let's go see who it is.'

She remained sitting. 'It might be Gilmour.'

'Good. If it's him in the flesh it will save us a long walk up the Hill. I can blow his brains out here.'

'Or it could be Scott again.'

'Yeah, well that would present a problem. I've already blown *his* brains out.' He went into the hallway. Reluctantly, she got up and followed him.

He was peering out through the door's spy-hole. 'It's an old lady,' he said. 'Seems harmless enough. Do you know her?' He stepped aside for her and Stephanie peered into the hole. 'Yes, I know her. It's Miss Coope. From the first floor.' Stephanie gave a jump as the bell rang again.

'Do we let her in?' Hamilton asked.

She looked at him. 'I'd rather we didn't,' she said in a flat voice. 'Don't you remember? You told me in my office that Miss Coope had hung herself yesterday morning.'

'Oh shit . . . yeah. Delia Coope.' He shook his head. 'Christ, we've got dead people coming out of the woodwork.'

The bell rang again. 'Let's ignore her,' said Stephanie, and headed back towards the living room. 'Maybe she'll get tired and go off and haunt someone else.'

Stephanie stepped into the living room and froze. Sitting very upright in one of the armchairs was Miss Delia Coope. She fixed a cool, disapproving eye on Stephanie and said, frostily, 'I hope you don't mind, Dr Lyell, but I took the liberty of letting myself in.'

'Bloody hell,' muttered Hamilton as he came in behind Stephanie and saw the old woman sitting there.

'Is that kind of language really necessary?' Miss Coope asked him.

'Uh, sorry.'

'Is there something you want, Miss Coope?' Stephanie asked her, uneasily. She couldn't understand why Miss Coope had been resurrected here. She had had nothing to do with her suicide so there couldn't be any subconscious guilt involved in this particular manifestation.

'Yes. We need to talk. Please sit down, Dr Lyell. And you too, sir.'

Both Stephanie and Hamilton dutifully obeyed her. Stephanie remembered that Miss Coope had been a former headmistress. It showed, even now.

'What do we need to talk about?' Stephanie asked her.

Miss Coope glared at Stephanie and said, 'My death, young lady.'

'You . . . you committed suicide, Miss Coope.'

'I'm well aware of that,' she said crisply. 'It's the reason why that concerns you. Concerns you intimately.'

'No, that's not true. I had nothing to do with your death,' protested Stephanie.

'Oh, I'm afraid you did, Dr Lyell. Most certainly you did.'

'How?'

'For two nights in a row you invaded my mind with your filth. Your filthy, disgusting dream.' Miss Coope's nostrils twitched with distaste.

'I don't understand what you're talking about,' said Stephanie, genuinely mystified.

'I'm talking about your dream where you fornicated with that unpleasant young man with the moustache. "Derek", I believe his name is. Do you remember now?'

Stephanie put her hand to her mouth as she realised what Miss Coope was talking about. Her recurring erotic dream involving the young lab technician, Derek Leycott. 'Oh my God, you mean you . . . you shared *my* dream about Derek?'

'Every foul, disgusting second of it,' Miss Coope told her.

Stephanie felt her cheeks redden. 'I'm sorry. I had no idea . . .'

'What's she talking about?' asked Hamilton. 'And who is Derek?'

'Someone at work,' she told him quickly, then she said to Miss Coope. 'I'm sorry if my dream upset you, Miss Coope.'

'It did more than upset me, Miss Lyell. It drove me to suicide.'

'But why? I mean, you obviously found it distressing, but surely the . . . experience . . . wasn't bad enough to make you want to kill yourself.'

'Dr Lyell, all my life I have had a profound physical and emotional aversion to the thought of having any form of sexual contact with a man. I knew that, in the modern psychological context, this aversion would be regarded as "unnatural" but I was quite content to accept things as they were. I never attempted to delve into the reason for my desire for celibacy. And then your dream happened to me.'

'And?' asked Stephanie anxiously.

'The first occasion was bad enough, but it was the second time that did the crucial damage. It caused me to remember something that I had successfully kept buried for nearly sixty years. And it was more than I could bear.'

'What was?' asked Stephanie, pretty certain that she wasn't going to like the answer.

'The memory of a night when I was nine years old. The night that my father came, drunk, into my bedroom and raped me.'

'Oh,' said Stephanie, in a small voice.

'The memory was too much to take. So I hung myself. You see, Dr Lyell, I loved my father.'

'I . . . I don't know what to say,' Stephanie told her. She felt terrible.

'There's not much you can say now. It's all rather too late, me being dead and everything,' said Miss Coope and smiled at her. It wasn't a nice smile. 'If I'd been thinking more clearly I wouldn't have chosen hanging as the means of my self-destruction. I was under the delusion that it would be quick. That my neck would be instantly broken. But it wasn't quick, Dr Lyell. It wasn't at all. After I'd kicked the chair away from under my feet I spent some considerable time suffocating. It was very, *very* unpleasant, Miss Lyell.'

Stephanie could say nothing.

'By the time I was found yesterday my neck had literally been stretched. Caused by the weight of my body hanging there all those hours. I appeared quite grotesque, which annoyed me because I have always taken a pride in my appearance. To appear undignified, even in death, was greatly upsetting to me. Do you want to see how I looked, Dr Lyell?'

'No,' said Stephanie, truthfully.

But then she saw, to her dismay, that Miss Coope's neck had started to stretch. She could hear the crackle of vertebrae dislocating as Miss Coope's neck continued to stretch and her head rose higher and higher. 'Stop it!' screamed Stephanie. 'Stop it!'

Miss Coope smiled down at her from the top of her now

absurdly elongated neck. 'Not a very nice sight, is it Dr Lyell?'

Stephanie, screaming, leapt up from her chair and ran from the room. She frantically unlocked and opened the front door, then rushed out and down the corridor towards the stairs in the rear of the building. She had no idea where she was going; she only knew that she had to get away from that old, dead, woman.

'Hey, Stephanie! Wait! Don't go off by yourself!' cried Hamilton as Stephanie ran from the room. He'd got to his feet to follow her but suddenly Miss Coope had reached out with an arm that stretched itself like her neck and seized him by the wrist. 'I think she wants to be by herself,' she said.

He shook off her grip. 'You have no power over me!' he yelled at her. 'Piss off!'

As he ran for the hallway he heard her say behind him, disapprovingly, 'That kind of language really is completely uncalled for.'

In the hallway he skidded to a halt. Standing there in the doorway was a man in his mid-twenties. He was dressed like something out of the early or mid-seventies, right down to the flared trousers. And he was holding a revolver . . . which was pointed straight at Hamilton. 'Stop right there, fatso, and raise your hands,' ordered the man.

Hamilton raised his hands. 'Who the fuck are you?' he asked.

'Shut your face and back up into the living room,' said the man coldly. He seemed extremely angry.

Again, Hamilton did as he was told. Glancing round, he saw that Miss Delia Coope was gone. He looked back at the young man with the gun and was struck by the realisation that he seemed oddly familiar. 'Do I know you?' he asked.

'You used to, fatso,' said the man. 'Now get your clothes off.'

Startled, Hamilton said, *'What?'*

'You heard me, fatso,' the man made a gesture with the gun. 'Strip.'

Hamilton began to undress. 'Just what exactly are you? Another one of Gilmour's sick little jokes?'

'Shut up.'

When Hamilton was naked the man said, 'All right, into the bedroom, fatso.'

'The *bedroom*?' said Hamilton, incredulously. 'Hey, just what have you got in mind?'

'I said, get into the bedroom,' said the man and he raised the gun until it was level with Hamilton's face. Hamilton began to back towards Stephanie's bedroom. He was now feeling very worried. Did this reject from the seventies intend *raping* him? He must be crazy . . .

'Look, whatever your name is . . . nothing personal, but if you find me a turn-on then you've got to be pretty damned desperate – '

'Don't make me puke!' said the younger man angrily. Then he quickly stepped forward and rammed the gun barrel into the pit of Hamilton's stomach. Hamilton fell, retching, to his knees as his belly exploded in pain. He hugged his lower stomach as he tried desperately to draw air into his lungs. Then he felt his left arm pulled violently behind his back and then levered upwards. The pain was excruciating and, despite being completely winded, he was forced to his feet. 'Move it, fatman!' snarled a voice in his ear and he was expertly propelled into Stephanie's bedroom. Hamilton was familiar with the grip being used on his arm. Through all his pain he said to himself, *The bastard's a cop.*

The next thing he knew he was on his knees in front of a full-length mirror attached to one of the walls in Stephanie's bedroom. The man stood just behind him, hand gripping him by the back of his neck. The revolver was now tucked into his waistband. He clearly thought he no longer needed it to handle Hamilton. The way Hamilton was feeling he agreed with him.

'Look at yourself!' ordered the man.

Hamilton did, and he also looked at the reflection of the man's face. And in that reflected image he recognised who the man was. 'Christ,' gasped Hamilton, 'You're – '

The man hit him across the face. 'Shut up! I said, look at *yourself!*'

Hamilton stared at his own naked image in the mirror. It wasn't a pretty sight.

'What do you see?'

'I see . . . me.'

He was hit across the face again. Then the man grabbed him by the hair and jerked his head up. 'Describe yourself! What do you *see*?'

His face and scalp stinging, Hamilton said haltingly, 'I . . . see a middle-aged bloke who could do to lose some . . . weight.'

'Is that all you see?' sneered the man. 'Well, I see a run-down, out-of-condition slob with a big, fat gut! You're *pathetic*!' The man pulled painfully on his hair. 'Look at yourself, I said! Bloated flesh the colour of a fish's belly, apart from your bloated face which is so red it looks like its going to explode. You make me sick just to look at you.'

'We all get older,' gasped Hamilton. 'Nothing you can do about that.'

'I'm not talking about old age, fatso, I'm talking about what you let happen to yourself! To *me*!'

The man had confirmed the awful truth. When he had seen the reflection in the mirror he knew why the man's face had seemed so familiar. He had seen it every day nearly twenty years ago. In a bathroom mirror. It was his own face. Or rather the way it had been . . .

'Look at me!' cried his younger, slim and even good-looking self. He patted his flat stomach. 'A thirty-two-inch waist. I weighed one hundred and sixty pounds. I worked out in the gym three times a week. I played rugby every weekend when I wasn't on duty. I watched my diet. And for what? To end up like . . . *you*.' He spat the latter word out.

'Look, Terry . . . Do you mind if I call you Terry?'

'Why not? It's my fucking name.'

'Terry, things change as you get older. Things don't always work out the way you think they're going to do when you're younger – '

His younger self jerked his hair again, making him wince with pain. 'Don't give me that bullshit. I was a Detective Constable at twenty-four. I was *good*. By now I should be a DCI at the very least. And what are you? Nearly twenty years later and you're a lousy Detective Sergeant.'

'Hey, I made it to Detective Superintendent,' said Hamilton, 'but then ... then ...'

'You fucked up.'

'No! *Gilmour* happened.'

'He didn't kill Judith. *You're* the one who shot her.'

'It was an accident!'

'It was a fuck-up. Yours. And then you went to pieces. Boozed yourself down the toilet. You lost everything after that, including your son. Your career isn't going anywhere now, you're just marking time till they give you the gold handcuffs and a pension. My bet is you'll have drunk yourself to death within a year of being retired. Face it, fatso, you have nothing to live for. *Look* at yourself.'

Hamilton stared in the mirror, and saw himself as his younger self perceived him. And suddenly he was filled with profound self-loathing and disgust. Everything his younger self had said was true. He closed his eyes as they filled with tears.

'Why bother going on?' asked his younger self. 'Why not finish it now, before you become an even more pathetic mess?'

Hamilton nodded, feeling himself sinking into a bottomless pit of despair. He heard something heavy land on the floor right in front of him. He opened his eyes and looked. It was the revolver.

'You know what to do,' he heard himself say.

He nodded again and, with a rush of gratitude, picked up the gun. He cocked it and put the barrel in his mouth.

Then he closed his eyes again.

Chapter Fifteen

Stephanie was on the roof of Hillview House. She wasn't sure how she'd got there or how long she'd been on the roof. Standing in front of her was someone she hadn't thought of for a very long time. Sister Romulus. The nun who had terrified her during that year she was obliged to spend at a ghastly convent in Hove. She had been ten at the time. Her parents had sent her there in the hope the experience would turn her into a more obedient and studious child. It hadn't worked, despite her fear of Sister Romulus. She hadn't thought of the nun for years but now all her old feelings about her were flooding back . . .

'I'm very disappointed in you, Stephanie,' Sister Romulus told her in that severe tone Stephanie had known so well all those years ago.

'I'm sorry, Sister Romulus,' she said in a small voice. She could feel herself shedding years at a fast rate, turning into a young, intimidated girl again.

'You have let us down, badly, Stephanie. You turned your back on the Church and have led a very sinful life.'

'No . . . I haven't,' she protested, but weakly. All the terrible fear this woman once induced within her had fully returned. 'I don't believe in any of that any more. I became an agnostic . . . at university.'

'Stephanie, you know you can never leave the Church, no matter what you may think. And you know, in your heart of hearts, that the reason you rejected the Church at university was *sex*. You wanted to have a sex life there but you didn't want to feel guilty about it. So you rationalised away your belief in the Church . . . and God.'

'No,' said Stephanie, feeling dazed. 'It wasn't that way at all. I just didn't *believe* any more . . . I *don't* believe . . .'

'You can't wish God away, Stephanie. Pretending that He doesn't exist doesn't mean you can commit mortal sins and avoid the consequences. You *know* that, Stephanie, in your heart of hearts. Don't you, Stephanie?'

'I . . . I . . .' Suddenly she didn't know what she thought any more. Her adult self was rapidly dwindling away. She was now very scared.

'You have committed many, many sins since leaving the Church, haven't you, Stephanie?' said Sister Romulus.

'. . . Yes, I suppose I have,' Stephanie admitted.

'And the most serious of them all was the murder of your unborn children. Do you admit it?'

'No . . . no . . .' she protested. 'I don't!'

'You're saying you didn't have two abortions?'

'No . . . I did, but . . .'

'Abortion is murder. And you know that. In your heart of hearts. Don't you?'

'No . . .' she cried, but then the last of her adult self collapsed. She trembled with fear before Sister Romulus whose eyes seemed to blaze with white light. 'Yes, Sister Romulus. I do. I . . . beg forgiveness, please. I want absolution.'

'It's too late for that, Stephanie. There are no priests *here*. You must suffer the consequences for your actions. And you know what that means, don't you?'

Terror filled Stephanie. 'Yes,' she whispered. 'Eternal damnation.'

Hamilton pulled the trigger and blew himself to pieces.

Sister Romulus floated upwards some three feet above the roof, then began to float backwards. She drifted right over the edge of the roof then hung there, suspended in space. 'Come forward, girl,' she commanded. Stephanie, shaking with fear, walked to the edge of the roof.

'Look down. What do you see?'

Stephanie looked down over the edge of the roof and gasped. Far, far below her she could see the burning, incandescent depths of Hell. She could feel its heat on her face, smell the sickening smell of sulphur and could hear the heart-rending screams of the Damned. She immediately lost control of her bladder and felt warm urine running down her legs. 'No,' she pleaded. 'No, please, don't . . .'

'I told you, Stephanie, it's too late now. And as I warned you all those years ago, those who commit mortal sins and are not absolved of them must spend eternity within the flames of Hell. You will suffer agonising pain for ever and ever. And why, Stephanie?'

'Because . . . because,' she said as she shook with terror, 'because I *deserve* to, Sister Romulus.'

'Yes, Stephanie. Now kneel and apologise to God, Jesus and the Holy Mother for your sins. When you have done so you will stand and step off the roof to begin your punishment in Hell. Your *eternal* punishment.'

The mirror had exploded into fragments when the bullet struck it. His reflection vanished, and so did the reflection of his younger self. 'Shit,' he'd heard his younger self say. He turned. He was alone in Stephanie's bedroom.

Cursing and weeping, Hamilton staggered back into the living room, found his clothes and hurriedly started to dress. He was hopping back and forth on one foot as he struggled to get his trousers on when he heard a familiar voice say, 'He was right, you know, Terry. As I told you before, you have let yourself go rather badly. Nothing at all like the man I used to be married to.'

He spun round, almost losing his balance. It was Judith. She was back. She was standing in the kitchen doorway, her arms folded, and was regarding him with a look of pity in her eyes. 'Oh no,' he groaned. 'Not you again.'

'You're a sad sight, Terry. You really are.'

He managed to pull his trousers up. Then he grabbed his shirt and jacket. And his gun. 'At least I'm alive,' he called to her as he headed into the hallway. 'Which is more than I can say for you.'

'And whose fault is that?' he heard her say just before he slammed the front door behind him.

Touché, he thought bitterly as he looked up and down the corridor and wondered where the hell Stephanie could have got to. He ran towards the elevator and had just reached it when he heard a 'ping' sound and the elevator doors opened.

'Terry! Am I glad to see you!'

He stared. It was Josie Welch. She was dressed in the same clothes she'd been wearing yesterday afternoon. She ran out of the elevator and hugged him. He felt her warm breath against his cheek. 'I've been so frightened!'

He gently prised her arms from around him and pushed her a step away from him. He scrutinised her face. She did look frightened and her running mascara showed that she'd been crying. She also looked very alive but that was no longer a reliable criteria. 'Josie, what are you doing here?'

'I saw the lights on up here. I was hoping I'd find some ... some *normal* people ... It's been terrible. You just wouldn't believe the day I've had! Terry, just what the fuck is going on?'

He hesitated, then said, 'Josie, don't take this the wrong way but are you by any chance, er, *dead*?'

'Stephanie, you must do as I say. Step forward!'

Tears were streaming down Stephanie's face. 'I can't!' she wailed. 'I don't want to! Please, don't make me!'

'Snivelling won't help you now, Stephanie. You knew what the consequences would be for your sins. You were warned over and over again. By *me*, in Hove. Now step forward!'

Josie had reacted with wide-eyed alarm. 'What do you mean *am I dead*? Have you gone crazy like all the other fucking weirdos running around out there?'

'Look, if you are dead you know what I'm talking about and if you're not dead I apologise. I haven't time to explain right now. I've got to find someone before something awful happens to her. Well, before something even *more* awful than what's happened to her already. You can wait for us in there –' He pointed at the open door of Stephanie's flat. 'My wife will keep you company. She, by the way, *is* dead.'

She grabbed him by the arm. 'You're not leaving me! Now that I've found you I'm not letting you out of my sight!'

'Okay, come with me then. Not that I know where I'm going.' A thought occurred to him. 'You didn't see Stephanie outside, did you? She has dark hair and was wearing jeans and a black leather jacket.'

After a pause Josie nodded vigorously. 'Yeah, I did! She came running out of the front gate as I arrived. She took off down the street. That way.' Josie pointed towards Harrow-on-the-Hill.

'Right. Let's go.' He was about to press the button to open the elevator doors but stopped and turned to her. 'How did you get in here?'

She shrugged. 'Through the front door. It was open. Your friend must have been in too much of a hurry to shut it behind her.'

'No. It shuts automatically. And locks. You'd need a key to open it. So how did you get in?'

'I told you. It was open.'

He backed away from her, having made his decision. 'You almost fooled me, Josie. If you are Josie.'

She looked sad. 'Oh, I *was* Josie . . . but you guessed right. Gilmour got me. And he's going to get you too, Terry. It's inevitable. You can't fight him . . .'

Hamilton turned and began to hurry back down the corridor. An unpleasant, *wet* sound of several things landing on the floor made him pause and look back. Josie's dismembered body lay scattered in front of the elevator. There was blood everywhere. Her decapitated head lay on its side, the eyes open and staring at him. Her lips moved. 'By the way, Terry,' she said, 'yester-

day afternoon was fucking fantastic. Maybe we can do it again
sometime soon.'

'Fine. I'll call you,' he said, and continued along the corridor.

She shut her eyes. The screams from the suffering souls below
grew more shrill and desperate. She couldn't do it. She couldn't
step over the edge and let herself fall into the pit of everlasting
fire. She started to pray. 'Please God, forgive me! Please don't
make me go to Hell! I'll do *anything*!'

'It's too late to pray now,' said Sister Romulus. 'You must
abandon all hope . . . for ever.'

'Help me!' screamed Stephanie. 'Somebody please *help me*!'

'Step forward. You have no choice.'

Stephanie took a step forward, opened her eyes and looked
down. She was teetering on the very edge of the roof. The
eternity of Hell waited below her, its heat growing more
intense. She knew it was nothing to what it would feel like on
her flesh once she was in the Pit. She shut her eyes again.
Tight.

'One more step,' ordered Sister Romulus.

Against her wishes, her right leg began to rise and she
leaned forward . . .

A hand closed on the collar of her leather jacket and she was
jerked backwards.

Then there were arms around her, catching her as she fell.
She was pulled away from the edge of the roof. 'What the fuck
were you trying to do?' growled a voice in her ear. It was
Hamilton.

She opened her eyes. Sister Romulus had gone. So had the
screams and the smell of sulphur. As an indescribable feeling
of relief engulfed her she felt consciousness slip away . . .

When she woke up she was lying on her back on the roof and
Hamilton was bending over, his expression anxious. He was
holding her hand and massaging it. 'Ah, thank God you're
back,' he told her. 'I was getting really worried.'

'How long was I out?' The images of Hell flashed through her mind and she shivered. Could she possibly hope that none of it was real?

'Over ten minutes. What happened? Why were you trying to throw yourself off the roof?'

'I'll . . . I'll tell you later.' She didn't want to talk about it. 'How did you find me?'

'Indirectly, it was thanks to Gilmour. He arranged for an ex-acquaintance of mine to turn up and throw me off the track. When she said she saw you downstairs in the street and I realised she was lying I decided to start looking for you in the opposite direction. I came up the fire stairs to the roof, and was just in time to stop you from breaking your neck.'

'No. You saved me from a lot worse.' She sat up. 'Help me, please.' He pulled her gently to her feet. She was dizzy and had to lean against him.

As he helped her down the stairs she asked, 'Is she still in my flat? Miss Coope?'

'What? Christ, I'd forgotten about her. No, she's gone, but my wife's back.'

'Oh.'

'Yeah, I know exactly what you mean. Also there's a hell of a mess in the hallway.'

But when they went downstairs he saw that Josie's remains had vanished from in front of the elevator. However, when they entered Stephanie's flat Hamilton's wife emerged from the kitchen with a tray containing a tea pot and cups and saucers. 'I'm sure you can both do with a nice cup of tea,' she said as she set the tray down on the dining table. 'I know I could.'

'Give me strength,' muttered Hamilton. He helped Stephanie to the sofa then went to the drinks cabinet and poured a large brandy for her and a large Scotch for himself.

'That's no answer,' said his wife disapprovingly as he gave the glass to Stephanie. 'Alcohol only causes problems, it never solves any.'

'Judith, shut up,' he said. Then he asked Stephanie, 'How are you feeling?' He was shocked by the way she was looking and he wondered if whatever she had just experienced had been even worse than his encounter with his younger self.

She drank half the brandy then lit a cigarette with shaking hands. 'Not too good,' she admitted.

'You want to tell me what happened yet?'

She shook her head. 'No, not yet.' She was staring at something he couldn't see. She clearly didn't want to see what she was seeing but it was as if she was unable to stop herself.

'I had a bad trip too,' he said, hoping to distract her.

'Yes?' she said, without interest.

'Another visitor from my past. *Myself* . . . from nearly twenty years ago. Complete with side-burns, flares and a wide paisley tie. Jesus, I hadn't realised what a little shit I used to be then.' He shook his head in wonder. 'Tried to convince me I was a total loss and that I and the world would be better off if I topped myself. Nearly worked too. I ended up agreeing with him. I was about to put a bullet through my brains when I realised what Gilmour was doing, playing his usual game of working on your deepest feelings of guilt and turning them into a weapon to use against yourself. So I thought, fuck that, if Gilmour wants me dead then that's a bloody good reason to stay alive.'

'But you must admit, Terry,' said his wife, 'that there was a lot of substance in what your younger self told you. It really is disgraceful the way you've let yourself go to pot.'

He turned and glared at her. 'Judith, why don't you go and make yourself another nice cup of tea.'

'You almost killed yourself?' Stephanie asked. He turned back to her. He saw he had her attention now.

'Yeah. I came that close.' He held up his hand, showing her a tiny gap between his thumb and forefinger. 'And I guess, from what I saw on the roof, you were being persuaded to top yourself as well?'

'Yes.' Her eyes clouded. 'Like you said, guilt from the past. Guilt I didn't know I had. Or felt so deeply about. She convinced me I *deserved* what was about to happen to me . . .'

'She?'

'It doesn't matter.' She finished the rest of her brandy. He saw that her hand was still shaking.

'What Gilmour does is *amplify* these guilt feelings,' Hamilton told her. 'Blows them up out of all proportion. We've got to resist any more of his attempts.'

'Easier said than done,' she said, bitterly.

'Look on the bright side, Stephanie . . .'

'*Bright* side?' she asked, and gave a hollow laugh. 'There's no bright side. We're trapped in the private world of a sadistic maniac and we're totally at his mercy. He'll keep at us until he wins. And Terry' – she looked him in the eyes – 'I really can't take much more of this. I feel that my mind is going to snap. I'm going to be as insane as Gilmour.'

'No!' he said firmly. 'You've got to keep fighting! We've still got the advantage of your drug. It gives us some protection against him. And we've got to defeat him before we run out of the stuff!'

'Defeat Gilmour? We haven't a hope in . . .' She didn't finish the sentence.

'Well, Gilmour seems to think we have.'

'What do you mean?' she asked quickly. He saw a flicker of desperate hope appear in her eyes.

'Don't you see? He was trying to kill both of us. Or rather, he was trying to persuade us to kill ourselves. Yet before he said he was saving us for something special. He even had me rescue you from Scott. Why has the situation changed? Why is Gilmour now afraid of us? It's because he now knows we present a threat to him. Something is different. Something has changed!'

'Yes,' she said slowly, 'I see what you mean. But what's changed? What's our new advantage?'

'I'm not sure. Maybe the fact that we know now that he's shifted the Institute to the top of the Hill,' said Hamilton. 'But then, he more or less gave the game away when he sang that he was the "King of the Castle".'

'Perhaps not deliberately,' she said, some vitality returning to her voice. 'He couldn't resist taunting us with the song but that doesn't mean he wanted us to know where he was. And when we prepared to set off up the Hill he did what he did . . . to both of us.'

'You could be right,' said Hamilton, glad that he had managed to lessen her mood of black despair, 'But I can't help wondering if it isn't something else as well. Maybe we've accidentally uncovered his Achilles' heel but we don't know it yet . . .'

'You think so? But what could it be?'

'Well, it's probably something staring us right in the face –'

The television set suddenly came to life. They all turned towards it as the *Neighbours* theme tune filled the room. For a brief moment Hamilton allowed himself the wild hope that the world had returned to normal but he quickly realised that it could never be this easy. And things had to be pretty low if *Neighbours* constituted normality.

'What's this?' asked Judith as the *Neighbours*' credits ran over shots of the cast having a barbecue beside a swimming pool.

'It's an Australian soap opera,' Hamilton told her as it occurred to him that it must be an old episode, as the more recent series had dropped this opening sequence. 'It's pretty awful but it's become very popular since you were . . . last here.'

'You watch soap operas?' Stephanie asked him, sounding surprised.

'Well, yeah,' he said, embarrassed. 'When I'm on night shift I tend to watch a lot of daytime TV crap. It kind of numbs the mind, and it's cheaper than alcohol.'

As the credits continued to roll various members of the cast fell into the pool while the others laughed. The camera panned and there, laughing as well beside the pool, was Gilmour. He was standing between the two attractive young sisters, Chrissie and Caroline, who were supposedly identical twins but who Hamilton never had any trouble telling apart. Gilmour had his arms around their shoulders. The theme music faded away. The camera closed in on Gilmour's face. 'G'day,

sports!' he said cheerfully, in a bad Australian accent. 'How ya
doin'?'

'Oh, it's that *dreadful* man!' cried Hamilton's wife.

'Gilmour, now you're *really* being sick,' muttered Hamilton.
'You can't get much lower than *Neighbours.*'

'You shouldn't knock this show, Terry,' Gilmour told him
from the screen. 'It's my all-time favourite. In fact, it rates as
one of the most popular TV shows among all the residents of
Broadmoor.'

'That figures. So what's on the menu now, Gilmour? A TV
trailer for whatever horror show you've got lined up for us
next?'

Gilmour kissed Chrissie on the cheek. She giggled prettily.
In the background Harold, the short, stocky one, cooked ham-
burgers on the barbecue. 'I just wanted to put you straight,'
said Gilmour from the screen, 'I couldn't help overhearing what
you were saying about me and I'm afraid you're barking up
the wrong tree. Nothing's changed. And there's nothing you
can do that will, in any way, put me at risk. Absolutely
nothing.'

'Then why did you try and make us both commit suicide?'
Stephanie asked him.

'Oh, just for fun. I wouldn't have let either of you actually
die, of course. As I said, I have special plans for you. So as soon
as you can make it up the Hill the sooner we can all get
together. I'll be waiting.'

The camera then pulled back. At the same time Gilmour
removed his arms from the twins' shoulders and stepped behind
them. An axe materialised in his hands. He swung the blade
at the neck of the twin standing on the right of the screen.
Caroline. The more attractive of the two, in Hamilton's
opinion. The axe chopped right through her neck. Her head
went flying through the air and her body toppled forward as
blood jetted from her open neck. The head landed in the swimming pool, causing Chrissie to burst out laughing.

Gilmour waved the bloody axe at the camera. 'G'day, mates!
Be seein' ya!' Then the TV set switched itself off.

After several moments' silence in the room, Hamilton's wife said, 'Well, I can see what you mean about it being an awful programme.'

Hamilton got up and went over to the drinks cabinet for a refill. 'Actually, that episode had much more substance than usual,' he told her.

Chapter Sixteen

'I think he's bluffing.'

'Yeah. Maybe.'

'He's afraid of us, believe me. All that stuff on the TV was an act. He still doesn't want us to pay the Institute a visit.'

'I wish I was as confident as you,' said Stephanie.

'Would anyone like a cup of tea?'

Hamilton ignored his wife's question. He was pacing restlessly up and down the room. Then he paused at the main window. It had got very dark outside . . . at least three hours ahead of schedule for the time of the year. He could barely make out the Hill.

'Oh damn!' cried Stephanie.

He turned quickly, alarmed. 'What's wrong?' he asked anxiously.

'I've run out of cigarettes.'

He relaxed. 'Why don't you try conjuring some out of thin air. If you want them bad enough it should work. It certainly works for Gilmour.'

Stephanie stared at the empty packet in her hand, frowning with concentration. Then she shook her head. 'Nothing.'

'Perhaps you have a strong unconscious desire to give up smoking and it's working against your conscious desire,' he suggested wryly.

She flipped the packet into a wastepaper bin in the corner of the room. 'It's not fair. The synthetic BDNFE provides Gilmour

with practically omnipotent powers and I can't even material-
ise a lousy menthol cigarette.'

'Why is that?' he asked. 'Why has your drug had such an
extraordinary effect on Gilmour and not us? Have you given it
any more thought?'

'Not really. I've had other things on my mind, as you may
have noticed.'

'Well, how about giving it some thought now.'

She sighed. 'I'm not sure what to think any more. Nothing
makes sense. But I guess you were right about Gilmour.'

'I was?' he asked, surprised. 'When? And about what?'

'When we were discussing his nature in my office that day
. . . God, it was only *yesterday*. It seems so long ago. Anyway,
you described Gilmour as being basically evil and now I'm
inclined to agree with you.'

'Yeah? You said I was being unscientific by using that word.'

'I know, but in the light of what's happened my faith in
science has been rather shaken. You also said a man like Gilmour exudes some sort of malign aura, a bad atmosphere. I
pooh-poohed the idea but now I think you're right there as
well. Gilmour was born with some kind of evil dimension to
him. It enabled him to manipulate and negatively influence
other people to some extent, and now I've come along and,
thanks to my stupid experiment, I've somehow increased his
"talent" out of all proportion.'

'Goodness, look at the time,' said Judith. 'I should think
about getting dinner ready.'

Hamilton turned to his late wife. 'I wouldn't bother,' he told
her. 'Stephanie and I are going out.'

'Oh, really? Somewhere nice?' Judith asked brightly, but also
conveying, in her tone of voice, that typical hint of martyrdom
over the fact that she hadn't been invited to join them.

He stared at her, wondering what was going on behind the
familiar façade of her face. Was she conscious at all, or just a
mere puppet being manipulated either by his guilty subconscious or by Gilmour?

He said, 'We're going for a stroll up the Hill where, if we're lucky, we're going to find and then kill Gilmour and bring all this madness to an end. And that includes you.'

His wife said, 'Tsk, tsk,' and shook her head. 'Same old Terry. Drinking whisky always did turn you into such a sorehead.'

'Good grief.' He turned back to Stephanie. 'So now you think Gilmour had supernatural powers all along?'

She nodded. 'And I've increased them.'

'By scientific means? That doesn't make sense, science and the supernatural mixed up.'

'Well, you'd better believe it because it's happened. And Gilmour has this natural . . . *supernatural* . . . advantage over us. The synthetic BDNFE gives us some ability to manipulate reality but only unconsciously.'

'Yet he's afraid of us now, I'd swear it,' said Hamilton.

'But I can't imagine why,' she said wearily. She glanced at her watch. 'And speaking of BDNFE, it's time we topped ourselves up.' She rose and went to her attaché case. While she prepared an injection for him he rolled up his sleeve. His wife watched them, then said blandly, 'I've never liked needles. The only needles I like are knitting needles.' She smiled at her little joke.

He studied her coldly, trying and failing to remember the time when he'd been in love with her. Then he reminded himself again that this wasn't the real Judith, merely a crude facsimile put together from his memories of her. But if this was how he remembered his wife it showed just how much he'd come to dislike her by the time of her . . . death.

He barely felt it when Stephanie gave him the injection. As usual, he didn't feel any different afterwards. The only time there had been any noticeable effect was on the first occasion when he'd regained the missing sections from his memory.

'Are you ready?' he asked Stephanie after she had injected herself.

She nodded. 'Give me five minutes,' she said and disappeared into the bathroom. He took the opportunity to finish the remaining dregs in the whisky bottle, then he checked the contents of Stephanie's rucksack again and made sure the revolvers were fully loaded. He handed one of the guns to Stephanie when she returned from the bathroom. 'Don't forget the safety catch next time,' he said.

She gave a wan smile as she slipped the gun into the pocket of her leather jacket. 'I won't,' she said. She was clearly reluctant to leave the flat and he felt the same way, but they couldn't just sit here until they ran out of BDNFE and became completely at the mercy of Gilmour. They had no choice but to go up the Hill to the Institute, no matter what horrors lay lurking out there in the dark.

And no matter what lay waiting for them within the Institute.

According to the map there was a path leading straight up the Hill that started beside the boundary fence of the cricket field a short distance down the road from Hillview House, just past where Lower Road turned into Bessborough Road. The path appeared to lead straight through the woods right to the church itself. Except now, hopefully, it would lead straight to the Institute.

It was pitch black when they emerged from the building. None of the street lights were working and there was no sign of any stars or the moon. They both carried flashlights and warily swept the beams around. They saw nobody in the immediate vicinity. Nor did they hear anything. The unpleasant-smelling air felt warm and viscous. It seemed to muffle sound, including their footsteps.

'Into the valley of death rode the four hundred . . .' said Stephanie quietly.

'Hey, let's try and keep a positive attitude here, shall we?' he said.

They set off along the footpath. Hamilton was carrying the heavy rucksack. He kept his hand on the butt of the revolver in his jacket pocket. In his other pocket was a wrench. Taped to the calf of his right leg was one of Stephanie's serrated steak knives. He wished he also had a bazooka and flame-thrower, not to mention a tactical nuke.

'No one about, thank goodness,' said Stephanie as she swept her flashlight beam up the side of the block of flats next to Hillview House. All the windows were in darkness.

'Yeah,' said Hamilton. 'By now everyone around here except us must be totally in Gilmour's power.'

'Those who are still alive.'

They walked on. They were now in the section of Lower Road where the cricket fields extended on both sides. Hamilton shone his beam into the dark expanse of the field on their left. He'd thought he'd glimpsed movement out in its centre but the beam only extended about fifty feet before dissipating. Then Stephanie came to a stop. He looked round. She had stuck her flashlight under her arm and was struggling to get something out of one of her jacket pockets. He saw her produce a packet of menthol cigarettes and her lighter. She lit a cigarette and offered the pack to him. 'Want one?' she asked.

He walked back to her and took a cigarette from the pack. 'Found a pack you'd forgotten about, did you?' he said as she lit it for him.

'Another pack?'

'I thought you were all out.'

She frowned. 'Yes, I was . . .' She stared at the pack in her hand. 'I'd forgotten. I just reached for the pack automatically. Do you think . . . ?'

He drew on the cigarette. 'Tastes real. Smells real. If you did produce them out of thin air then it's a good sign. We have *some* power here. Perhaps my deep-rooted desire for a bazooka will bear similar fruit.'

They continued on, reaching the corner of Whitmore Road where the cricket field on their left came to an end. They crossed over. There were houses to the left now. They both shone their flashlights over the fronts of the buildings as they walked. Like the block of flats the houses were in darkness. Some had shattered windows. Discarded childrens' bikes lay in the gardens. All was silent.

'Did you see that?' asked Stephanie, in an alarmed voice.

'What?' he asked, coming to a stop.

'There!' she said, indicating the top floor of a nearby house with her beam. He shone his flashlight on the same place but could see nothing out of the ordinary.

'I thought I saw something up there. Climbing up the side of the house.'

'A man?'

'Not exactly.'

'What's *that* supposed to mean?'

'I only saw it briefly. It seemed sort of shapeless . . . and it wasn't exactly climbing . . . it was sort of *flowing* up the side of the house.'

'Oh, marvellous.' He stared hard at the upper corner of the house and fancied he could see something glistening on the white paintwork. Like the trail a snail or slug would leave behind. A *big* snail or slug. He decided he didn't want to see whatever it was. 'Let's forget it and move on,' he said to Stephanie. But as they walked on he kept nervously playing his beam over the fronts and rooftops of the houses.

'There it is,' Stephanie said, pointing across the road. Between the side of the cricket field and a block of flats there was a narrow gap with a footpath leading into the darkness. It was their way up to the Hill.

They crossed the road, Hamilton out of habit looking in both directions for oncoming traffic. There was, of course, none.

At the start of the footpath they stopped and peered upwards. The Hill was simply a black mass looming ahead of them. They could only dimly make out the wood that surrounded the summit. And drifting down sluggishly through the thick, torpid air came faint cries, whoops and shrieks. It sounded to Hamilton as if a bunch of adolescents were running wild up there in the woods. And it sounded like they were having fun.

The path they were standing on veered to the left. According to the map another path should branch off and go straight up the Hill. Hamilton could see no sign of it. He shone his beam on the signpost that stood next to them. There were two signs. One, pointing to the left, said: 'Public Footpath to Harrow-on-the-Hill', the other, pointing straight up the Hill, said: 'Public

Footpath to the Hill and West Street'. 'So where is it?' he asked in irritation.

'There's a kind of track in the grass running alongside the fence,' said Stephanie, shining her torch down. 'See? Maybe that's it. Maybe it's an historical pathway that no one has ever bothered to cover with a proper surface.'

'Yeah. Or maybe Gilmour has removed it just to make things even more difficult for us.' He angrily stamped out the stub of his cigarette. 'Well, we have no choice but to go this way.' Then he drew his gun and told Stephanie to do likewise. 'Don't take any chances – shoot at anything you see coming in our direction. Just try not to shoot me.'

'I'll do my best,' she said grimly.

They set off along the track, Hamilton in the lead. He kept sweeping his flashlight beam back and forth but saw nothing suspicious in the immediate vicinity. The gradient wasn't very steep but very soon Hamilton was panting from the effort of the climb. His pissy younger self, and his late wife, were both right, he reflected bitterly. He was *definitely* in bad shape.

'Do you think it's wise to keep our flashlights on?' Stephanie asked him. 'Anybody will be able to see us coming.'

'Well, if we switch them off we'll be as good as blind,' he told her over his shoulder, 'and anyway Gilmour must know our exact position at any given time. And if he does you can bet his creatures do as well. So we might as well keep them on.'

Ahead, on their left, loomed a large bush-like tree that resembled a giant blob. As they followed the trail between the tree and the fence running along the side of the cricket field on their right, they heard giggles coming from within the tree's shrubbery. Hamilton and Stephanie both stopped and shone their beams at the giant mound of vegetation but it was impenetrable. Hamilton considered firing a couple of bullets into it but realised he would have to be extremely lucky to hit anybody hiding inside and decided it would be a waste of bullets. 'Let's keep going,' he told Stephanie. He kept his torch beam on the mound of shrubbery as they climbed past it but nothing emerged to pursue them.

As they climbed the gradient grew more steep and Hamilton began making sounds like a steam engine in bad repair. And his heart was pounding alarmingly too. He began to worry that he might be about to suffer a heart attack. Was that what Gilmour had planned for him? He fought back a mounting wave of panic. *Relax*, he told himself, *you're not having a heart attack* . . . and he also tried to convince himself that the pain in his left arm was imaginary.

There came a sudden flapping sound above them and Hamilton felt the air stir. He swung his flashlight upwards and caught briefly in the beam was a huge bat. It gave a piercing shriek and vanished. He heard the beat of its powerful wings as it flew away. 'Did you see its head?' asked Stephanie nervously.

'Yeah.' He didn't elaborate.

When they reached the tall hedgerow that bounded this section of the woods Hamilton, wheezing, called a halt and tried to catch his breath. His heart was still pounding in a worrying manner. 'You all right?' Stephanie asked him.

'No, but I'll live,' he told her, wishing he was sure of that. He shone his beam through the gap in the hedge. It illuminated the tombs and gravestones that lay scattered between the thick trunks of the very old trees – part of the cemetery that had surrounded the church and contained the bodies of old Harrovians. Dead soldiers and other loyal servants of the Empire who had been forged for their tasks by Harrow School. All was now silent. The whoops and yells that they had heard when at the base of the Hill had died away by the time they had reached the halfway point. But Hamilton could sense that the woods contained many presences . . .

When his breathing and heartbeat had both calmed down he motioned to Stephanie that they should go on. They cautiously moved through the gap in the hedge. On their right a row of tombs extended a short distance up the Hill. Hamilton paused to look at the inscription on one of them . . . and got a shock when he saw his own birthdate in the marble. The day and the month, that is; the year on the tomb was 1821, and he wasn't *that* old. The name of the deceased was different too so he presumed it was simply a macabre coincidence rather than one of Gilmour's little jokes.

'What's wrong?' whispered Stephanie.

'Nothing really. For a moment or two I felt someone walking over my grave.'

They continued onwards into the thick wood, winding their way around trees and a haphazard scattering of graves, constantly sweeping their flashlights back and forth.

As they rounded a tree they both saw it at the same time. Stephanie gave a gasp of shock.

A body of a man hung head-down from a lower branch of a nearby tree. His ankles had been tied to the branch and his fingers almost touched the ground. His flesh was red raw and glistening. His upside-down face was like something out of an anatomical text book. Hamilton felt his stomach make a protest at what he was seeing.

The man had been skinned.

And he was still alive.

Chapter Seventeen

Hamilton tried to will the awful truth out of existence but it wouldn't go. The hanging, flayed man stayed terribly alive. Parts of his body kept twitching, his eyes rolled in his lidless sockets and through his clenched teeth came a strange, unnerving hissing sound.

It was Stephanie who acted. She went briskly up to the suspended man, put the gun to the side of his temple and shot him through the head. The sound of the shot, in the muffled air, wasn't very loud. The man's body shuddered and was then still. Stephanie turned away from it, her face expressionless. 'You did the right thing,' Hamilton told her.

'I know.' She dropped the gun into her pocket, stuck her flashlight under her arm again and began to extract her cigarette pack and lighter from her other pocket. Hamilton was about to go over to her when he saw a faceless figure appear from behind a tree some fifteen feet away. The figure was brandishing a spear. 'Look out!' Hamilton yelled to Stephanie as he raised his gun. He fired seconds before the figure threw the spear at Stephanie. The figure fell backwards with a wail. The spear flew too high and passed harmlessly over Stephanie's head as she turned to see what was happening.

Hamilton ran over to the fallen figure and shone his torch down. He saw it was an adolescent boy, naked except for some leaves plastered over his face. His body was smeared all over with blood. It wasn't the boy's own. The bullet hole that

Hamilton had put in the centre of his chest was leaking only a small amount of blood. Stephanie arrived, knelt beside the youth and put her fingers on the side of his throat. She looked up at Hamilton. 'He's dead,' she said accusingly. 'And he's little more than a boy.'

'Yeah, well that "boy" just tried to spear you,' he told her. 'What was I supposed to do before I fired? Ask to see his driving licence?'

There came piercing yells from behind them. Hamilton spun round. His torch beam caught three figures running towards them between the trees. Like the youth he'd shot, they were naked and had their faces covered with leaves. Two of them were carrying spears, the third was holding a large hunting knife. Though they had the advantage of surprise the flashlight clearly dazzled them as they ran. One threw his spear blindly in the general direction of Hamilton and Stephanie and it thudded impotently into the trunk of a tree. Hamilton shot at the other spear carrier, hitting him in the stomach before he could throw it. He went down. The other two, whooping like attacking Red Indians in a bad Western, kept coming. Hamilton fired at the one with the knife, and missed. 'Shoot, damn it!' he yelled to Stephanie, but a brief glance in her direction revealed that she was still trying to get her gun out her pocket.

The two youths were close now. Hamilton fired again, at the nearest one. He fell. Unfortunately, he wasn't the one with the knife. The one who *did* have the knife was now only a couple of yards away. With an ear-splitting shriek, he leapt at Hamilton just as Hamilton swung the gun round towards him. Hamilton fired . . . and the next instant he was falling backwards as the youth collided forcefully with him. He landed with a heavy, bone-shaking thud on his back but immediately began desperately battering at the youth's head with the gun and the flashlight, sure that at any moment he would feel the blade of the hunting knife plunge into him. But the youth just lay limply on top of him. He pushed the body from him and sprang to his feet. The bullet had hit the youth in the face. The leaves were spattered with gore and bone splinters.

Hamilton looked at Stephanie. She appeared stunned but at least she had her gun out now. He just wished she wasn't pointing it at him. Then he heard more whooping calls. They seemed to come from every direction.

'Quickly,' he said, grabbing Stephanie's arm. 'Put your back to the tree.' He pushed her into position and stepped beside her, waving his flashlight quickly back and forth. She started doing the same. Together they were covering a hundred-and-eighty-degree arc. Hamilton glimpsed more naked figures as they ran from tree to tree. Then one of them broke cover and dashed straight towards him, shrieking and yelling like the others. But this one was different. It was a girl.

Hamilton's reluctance to shoot the girl was quickly dispelled by the sight of the blood-stained machete she was waving menacingly above her head. He fired. She staggered from the impact as the bullet struck her shoulder but kept coming. He fired again and the bullet hit her in the throat. She dropped and the machete went spinning through the air to land harmlessly a few yards away.

He heard Stephanie's gun go off. He looked round in time to see a youth, still gripping a make-shift spear, pitch forward on his face. 'Good work,' he told Stephanie.

Three more rushed them. Hamilton shot two of them. Stephanie hit her target on the second attempt. Then there was a respite in the series of attacks and Hamilton asked Stephanie to cover for him while he reloaded, then did the same for her. The attacks resumed.

Fifteen minutes later there were twenty-one dead and dying adolescents scattered around the tree. And both Hamilton and Stephanie were nearly out of ammunition.

They waited apprehensively for further attacks. Apart from the moans of the injured the woods were quiet. More minutes passed and nothing happened. 'I think it's finished,' said Hamilton. 'We must have got them all.'

'I hope so. I can't go on killing like this . . .'

'Well, when we run out of bullets I hope you'll come up with a preferable alternative method. We could sure use it.'

'Bastard.'

'Yeah. How many rounds have you got left?'

She checked. 'Just four.'

'And I've only got two. And we're all out of spare ammo.'

They waited, sweeping the trees with their torch beams.

'You ever been up here before?' he asked her. 'I mean, when it was normal?'

'Only once. When I first moved to Harrow three years ago. I climbed up here with some visiting friends one Sunday afternoon. I remember thinking how marvellous the view was from the top of the Hill. You?'

'Never. Do you remember how far the church was from where we are now?'

'No, not really. But it can't be very far.'

'I hope you're right.'

They waited for another few minutes. Still no sound apart from the moans and groans from those lying on the ground about them. 'Okay, let's go on,' said Hamilton.

They started to thread their way through the scattered bodies. When Stephanie stopped beside a moaning girl, who was lying on her back across a grave, and bent down beside her, Hamilton sighed. The girl had been hit in the stomach and was writhing with pain. 'Stephanie, come on. There's nothing you can do,' he said irritably.

'I just can't leave her like this!' she flashed back. 'I'm a *doctor*, godammit!'

'Well, you shot her, *Doctor*. She's not one of mine.'

'You bastard!' she snarled.

'So you keep telling me. Look, I'm not the one responsible for all this. You know who is. Gilmour turned these kids into a suicide squad against us . . .' He paused as an idea occurred to him. He looked down at the .38 he was holding. 'I think I know why Gilmour did that. He wanted us to use up all our ammunition shooting at them.'

'You think so? Why?'

'Because the guns pose a threat to him. They're something in our control that *he* can't control!'

Stephanie looked from him to the groaning girl. She stroked the girl's forehead for a few moments then slowly rose to her feet. 'If you're right,' she said coldly, 'then we'd better save the remaining bullets for him.'

They continued upward. The yellow mist got thicker and the smell got worse. Stephanie gasped when their torch beams revealed another flayed body of a man hanging upside down from a tree branch. Mercifully, this one was dead. 'Who do you think did this?' she asked. 'And to the other man we found?'

He shrugged. 'Those kids, I guess. That blood they were covered in came from somewhere.'

'But why?'

'You'll have to ask Gilmour about that. But I suspect that this guy and his mate were teachers. And our gang of forest freaks were probably students of theirs.'

'You don't really think so?' she said, sounding shocked. He didn't answer but motioned that they should resume climbing. They then came across a footpath leading upwards to the right. Stephanie said, 'This rings a bell,' and indicated they should follow it. The path led to a look-out point. 'Yes, I remember this from before. This is where I saw the marvellous view.' Hamilton peered over the low wall. All he could see was blackness. Not a sign of a light anywhere. He couldn't even tell where the land ended and the sky began. Some view.

'Yes, I know where we are now. We're almost there. See that?' said Stephanie. Hamilton turned. She was playing her beam over a tomb encased in a protective metal cage. 'There lies Lord Byron himself.'

'Well, I hope he's still in there and not wandering about in these woods.'

She moved the beam to the left. 'And over there is the path that leads straight up to the church. Or it *did*.'

They went up the path, passed through a final line of trees and found themselves facing the Harrow Institute for Neurological Research.

As they shone their flashlights over its front Hamilton saw
that it looked much the same as it had looked on its original
site off Tyburn Lane – albeit with some important differences.
The major, and most striking one, was within the Victorian
archway that framed the main entrance to the Institute. From
top to bottom it was one solid wall of skulls. Hamilton examined them more closely. They were all fresh skulls, not ones
that Gilmour had pilfered from the cemetery as Hamilton had
first assumed. 'I'd say that the Bone Man is definitely at home,'
he said with forced lightness, 'but not receiving visitors.'

'You're being as funny as a tumour,' she told him curtly.

'Sorry,' he said. He ran his beam up the front of the building.
All the windows were dark. 'Speaking of tumours, what do you
make of that?' His torch beam had illuminated one of many
large barnacle-like growths that were attached to the walls of
the Institute. It was nearly three feet in diameter.

'I haven't a clue,' she said, 'but look, it's *moving . . .*'

He saw she was right. The thing was slowly edging its way
out of the light. It made a squelching sound as it moved. Hamilton shivered with disgust. 'If it's like this on the outside I hate
to think what it's like on the inside.'

'Well, at this rate we're never going to find out. We can't get
in through the front door, and the windows are all barred.'

'What about the rear?'

'There's a delivery entrance and two fire exits.'

'Let's take a look.'

They walked cautiously round the side of the building, shining their beams on the darkened, barred windows as they went.
They saw no sign of life within the building, but they did see
more of the barnacle things clinging to the wall. Whether the
things were technically alive or not was open to debate.

They found, as they expected, that doors in the delivery bay
were sealed, as were the fire exit doors, so they explored the
other side of the building. There was no way in there either
and they returned to the front entrance. 'He is definitely not
eager to see us,' said Hamilton. 'If he really had nothing to fear

from us he'd have left the doors wide open and put a giant, illuminated "Welcome" mat on the ground.'

'Maybe, but how are we going to get in?'

'Well, let's try the direct approach. Cover me.' Hamilton pocketed his gun, set the rucksack down, riffled through it and took out Stephanie's tyre iron. 'Keep your light on me,' he instructed her as he pocketed his torch as well. He went up to the wall of skulls that concealed the front doors and tentatively probed between two of the skulls with the end of the tool. Then, using more force, attempted to prise one of them out of the wall. Nothing gave at first and then, without warning, the skull leapt free of the wall with a popping sound. Caught off-balance, Hamilton fell against the wall of skulls . . . and screamed. The jaws of one of the skulls had clamped down hard on his hand, in the exact same place where Policewoman Foster had bitten him earlier that day. He tried to pull his hand free but it was held fast by the skull. He felt his flesh rip as the teeth cut deeper through the bandage into his hand. 'Help me!' he yelled at Stephanie, as he pounded at the skull with the tyre iron, trying to shatter it.

'What can I do?' she cried as she came over.

'*Shoot it! Shoot it!*' The pain was excruciating.

'But we can't afford the bullets! Besides, it's already dead!'

'*You stupid bitch! Shoot it, goddamn you!*' Then, suddenly, the skull came loose from the wall, but remained attached to his hand. He ran around in circles, screaming and frantically trying to shake the thing off. But the skull, with a mocking grin, continued to bite ever deeper into his flesh. Hamilton, through the agony, was filled with overwhelming hatred towards it. '*Damn you to hell!*' he screamed at it with all his heart.

The skull promptly exploded into dust.

For a moment he thought that Stephanie had somehow managed to hit it with a lucky shot but then realised there had been no gunshot. It hadn't been Stephanie.

'What happened?' she asked. 'Why did it do that?'

He took out his torch and shone it on his hand. Blood was

welling out through the bandage and dripping on the ground.
'I think it was me. I think I succeeded in magicking it away.
You want something bad enough, that drug of yours gives it
to you, in spite of us being even closer to Gilmour.'

She came and took a look at his hand then led him over to
the rucksack. She had had the foresight to bring along a first-
aid kit. She cut the bandage from his hand, doused the wounds
with a stinging antiseptic, put a dressing on, and rebandaged
the hand very tightly while he gritted his teeth and swore
under his breath. 'You're going to need more stitches but that
should stop the bleeding for the time being,' she told him.

When she'd finished he went to the rucksack and took out
two of his Molotov cocktails. 'Give me your lighter,' he told her.

'Now what?' she asked as she handed it to him.

'No more Mister Nice Guy,' he said. 'Now stand back.' He lit
the wick of the first petrol bomb and flung the bottle at the
wall of skulls. It shattered and burning petrol exploded across
the skulls with a deep *whooofff* sound. Hamilton lit and threw
the second one, then backed away as the heat from the fire singed
his hair and eyebrows. He watched the inferno with satisfaction.
At last they were hitting back at Gilmour . . .

The skulls blackened and began to fall to the ground. Soon
there was a pile of them at the foot of the doors. Then the
flames began to splutter and Hamilton saw that two streams
of liquid were pouring down from above. He looked up. Two of
the giant barnacle things were directly above the fire. From
their centres protruded two large, penis-like objects that were
hanging down. They were at least eighteen inches long and
three inches wide. The last time Hamilton had seen something
as large it had been hanging from beneath a horse. These were
the source of the liquid.

'Bloody hell!' cried Hamilton as he ran back to the rucksack.
'They're pissing on our fire!' He pulled out another two petrol
bombs. The first he threw at the two things on the wall. They
quivered violently as the fire spread over them and the phal-
luses were quickly withdrawn. Then, with a squeal, one of the
giant barnacles fell from the wall and into the fire below. The

other one soon followed. Hamilton let out a cheer, lit the fourth bomb and flung it at the burning doors.

Ten minutes later the flames died away. The charred doors of the entrance were now devoid of skulls but remained standing. There were just two Molotov cocktails left but Hamilton wanted to test the doors before using them. Kicking the skulls away from the base of the door he then jammed the tyre iron between the doors, just above the large, heavy lock. Smouldering wood fell away. 'I think we're almost there,' he said to Stephanie. He drew his gun, took a few steps backward then launched himself at the doors. His shoulder struck hard, he heard something give way and the doors swung open. Momentum carried him on inside and the next thing he knew, as he fell forwards to the floor, he was surrounded by a blinding white light. Behind him, he heard Stephanie scream.

Chapter Eighteen

'Shit!' cried Hamilton. He had landed hard, banging his knees and an elbow. He blinked furiously, dazzled by the light. Then he saw he was lying on polished white tiles. The walls and ceiling of the entrance hall were also gleaming white. He was sure the hallway hadn't been this way on his previous two visits to the Institute.

'That was quite a nasty fall. I hope you didn't injure yourself.'

Standing at the end of the hallway was an overweight young woman wearing a white lab coat. She was regarding him with concern.

'Pauline!' cried Stephanie as she came in behind him.

The young woman smiled at her. 'Good evening, Dr Lyell. We were hoping you would come. We called your flat but the woman who answered your phone wasn't very helpful.'

'Pauline, what's happened here? Has Gilmour hurt you?' Stephanie asked her anxiously as Hamilton got painfully to his feet.

'I'm fine, and as to the situation here, it is now under control,' said the woman.

'Who the hell is she?' Hamilton asked Stephanie.

'She's Pauline Morrison,' said Stephanie as she stared hard at the woman. 'She's a lab technician. She works for me.'

'She *did* work for you,' said Hamilton grimly as he pointed his gun at her. 'Now she's Gilmour's. Don't let her fool you.'

'I won't.' Then to the woman she said, 'Pauline, what do you mean by the situation now being "under control"?'

'It was all due to Dr Blakeley. He managed to trick Gilmour. He saved us.'

'Jeff tricked Gilmour? How? Where is Gilmour now?' asked Stephanie quickly. Hamilton felt alarmed. Stephanie seemed to be too ready to believe whatever line this woman was spinning. She had to be lying. This was just another one of Gilmour's tricks . . .

'Gilmour is back under our control and we are now trying to repair the damage,' said the young woman to Stephanie. 'But come with me to your lab. Dr Blakeley is there and will explain everything.' She turned and went to the double doors just behind her. She held one open and gestured for Stephanie to go through. Stephanie glanced at Hamilton, her eyebrows raised. Hamilton shook his head. He aimed his gun between the woman's eyes and said, 'Neither of us are going anywhere with you until we get some proof that Gilmour isn't pulling your strings. And unless you convince me pretty damn fast I'm going to shoot you.' Hamilton meant what he said even though he knew that would leave him with only one bullet.

The woman gave him a pained smile. 'It's understandable you're suspicious considering what you've been through, Detective Sergeant, but I assure you the danger is past.'

'How do you know who I am?' he demanded. 'We've never met before.'

'We have direct access to Gilmour's mind now, thanks to Dr Blakeley. We know what he tried to do to you two, and why. He was afraid of you. You represented a real danger to him. He was desperate to destroy you.'

'So we gather. Now just tell us what happened, Pauline,' said Stephanie. 'Tell us how Jeff managed to trick Gilmour. Like Terry says, we need some proof.'

The woman gave a little sigh. 'Really, Dr Blakeley is the one you should talk to about it, but I'll try and explain. You probably know that Gilmour forced us to keep him hooked up on to a continual supply of the synthetic BDNFE in order to keep his brain saturated with the substance. Well, Dr Blakeley managed to inject a neuroleptic drug into the feed line without Gilmour realising it. It tranquillised him and left him in a highly receptive state of mind. Dr Blakeley was then able to put him into a deep hypnotic state and take over control of Gilmour's private world. He is now trying to find the best way to restore things to normality. The redesign of this section of the Institute was a little experiment by Dr Blakeley in controlling Gilmour's power. If you will just come with me you will be able to see all this for yourself, Dr Lyell. So please . . .' She gestured at the door she was holding open. 'Your suspicious policeman friend can remain here for the time being if he wants to.'

Stephanie looked at Hamilton. 'What do you think?'

'What *you* think is the most important thing,' he told her. 'Does it sound plausible?'

'Yes, it *sounds* plausible,' she said hesitantly. 'But . . .'

'But you're not buying it. Neither am I. No one completely under Gilmour's power would be able to take him by surprise. No, I think this is some trick to separate us somehow. Gilmour wants us apart. It'll weaken our power and make us more vulnerable that way.'

Stephanie nodded slowly. 'I'm afraid I agree with you.'

Hamilton gave the young woman a cold smile. 'Good try, but tell Gilmour we're not convinced.'

'Pity,' said the woman and then the lights went out.

Hamilton swore and dropped to the floor, fearing some form of attack in the sudden, pitch-black darkness. 'Terry!' he heard Stephanie cry in alarm. He fumbled in his pocket for his flashlight. He pulled it out and switched it on. Stephanie switched hers on at the same time. They shone their beams at each other. Stephanie was backed up against a wall, her face fearful. 'You okay?' he asked. She nodded. He stood up and swung the beam around the hallway. It had changed.

For the worse. The shiny white floor, walls and ceiling had been replaced by dank stonework. Fungoid growths hung from the stonework and water dripped from the ceiling. The air was foul. 'Well, this is more like it,' he said grimly. 'I thought for a while that Gilmour was losing his touch.'

'What happened to Pauline?' asked Stephanie, pointing her flashlight down the hallway. There was something lying by the double doors. They walked slowly over to it. 'Ugh,' said Stephanie when she got a good look at the transformed Pauline Morrison.

The naked, filth-covered woman lying on the floor had obviously been dead for several hours. And not only that but something had been *nibbling* at her. Her nose was half-eaten away, several of her fingers and toes were missing and there were large bites all over her body.

'Did you used to have rats in this building?' asked Hamilton as he stared down at the gruesome remains of the lab technician.

'A few. We kept getting the exterminators in but they could never get rid of them completely. But then, it was an old building. Not *this* old, of course.'

'Well, looks like you've got a lot of rats around the place now.'

She shuddered. 'I hate rats.'

'Well, I wouldn't have announced that fact to Gilmour then if I were you.'

'I'm sure that Gilmour is already well aware of my phobia. He knows everything else about me.'

'Yeah,' Hamilton agreed. He started back down the hallway, towards the entrance.

'Where are you going?'

'To fetch the rucksack. Better come with me. We were clearly right about Gilmour wanting to separate us.'

They went outside, and immediately saw that something had changed. The mist had vanished and the night sky was now clear. But there were no stars, just an icy blackness. However, there *was* a moon. A vast, bloated yellow moon that seemed close enough to touch. Not that either of them would want to because, etched into its surface, was Gilmour's face. He leered down at them and winked.

'Oh God!' cried Stephanie.

'Gross,' muttered Hamilton and hurriedly picked up the rucksack. It was almost a relief to get back inside the Institute. They went to the end of the entrance hallway. Pauline Morrison's corpse still lay by the doors. Hamilton had half expected to find it gone. He pushed open one of the doors and shone his torch down the corridor beyond it. His beam illuminated more dank stonework. Something went skittering away from the light. He caught a glimpse of something pink with a long tail. 'What was it?' asked Stephanie nervously.

'Don't ask,' he said. The furless rat had been the size of an alley cat. 'Where do we go from here?'

'I don't know. Nothing looks the same any more.'

'Well, we'll just have to wing it. Come on.'

They proceeded slowly along the stone corridor, constantly criss-crossing the floor, walls and ceiling with their flashlight beams. As in the hallway, cold water dripped down on them from the ceiling and ran down the slime-covered walls. There were puddles everywhere and Hamilton's shoes were soon soaked through. Then they came to an intersection. They could keep on going down the corridor or make either a left or right turn. 'Any ideas?' he asked her.

'No. Everything has changed. We might as well go in any direction.'

'Then let's keep going forward.'

As they walked into the intersection there was a loud *cracking* sound overhead and then a deep rumbling. The ceiling was coming down on their heads.

Stephanie felt a violent shove between her shoulder blades and she was sent sprawling along the corridor. Then everything was chaos as the stonework came crashing down with a deafening roar. The floor shook and Stephanie fell forward, dropping the flashlight and hitting her head hard on the floor.

She was stunned but she didn't lose consciousness. She lay there, terrified, as the impossibly loud sound rolled over her, expecting at any moment to be crushed by falling stone. But though she felt small fragments land on her back nothing of a serious size touched her. Then, eventually, the sound, and its rumbling echoes up and down the corridor, died away. She got to her knees and began to crawl towards the flashlight that lay a few yards ahead of her. Its beam had been dimmed by all the dust that the cave-in had produced and she coughed as she crawled. Her relief at still being alive was rapidly being overshadowed by her fear that she had been cut off from Hamilton, or that he had been buried under the stonework. She knew that if she found herself alone in this place she wouldn't be able to cope for very long. She would go mad . . . and then she would be Gilmour's.

She reached the flashlight, snatched it up and shone it behind her. The thick dust obscured everything. She got up and staggered towards the intersection. It was gone, blocked by a solid wall of broken stone. At first she could see no sign of Hamilton, then she spotted him. He was lying face down, and unmoving, near the cave-in. He was covered with fragments of stonework and thick grey dust, the reason she hadn't seen him right away.

'Terry!' she cried as she dropped to her knees beside him. She didn't feel the pain as small fragments of stone bit through her jeans into her knees. She was praying frantically that he wasn't dead. She pulled the rucksack off him, smelling a strong odour of petrol as she did so, then rolled him over on to his back. Underneath the dust she saw blood oozing from a wound on his forehead. She put her fingers to his throat in the same way she had done to the naked youth only a short time before. On that occasion she had felt no pulse but now, to her intense relief, she did. Hamilton was still alive. 'Terry,' she said and slapped him gently on the side of his face. 'Can you hear me? Wake up!'

He groaned and his eyes flickered open. He appeared to have trouble focusing on her. She held up her hand in front of his face, extending only three of her fingers. 'How many fingers am I holding out?'

'Twenty,' he muttered. Then, 'You'll be asking me if I can

remember my name next, you silly cow.' He started to sit up, and groaned again. She helped him. 'Easy. You have a nasty-looking head wound, but I don't think it's serious. I'll clean it up for you but first let's get away from here in case some more of the ceiling comes down.'

'Good idea,' he said. She picked up the rucksack and then helped him to his feet. They moved some hundred feet along the corridor and then came to a halt. She had to sit down again while she got the medical kit out of the rucksack. As she'd expected, one of the remaining Molotov cocktails had broken, saturating everything with petrol but fortunately the medical kit was sealed in a metal box. She cleaned the wound on his forehead, which wasn't deep, put a dressing on it and covered it with a plaster.

'This is getting to be a habit,' he told her, holding up his bandaged hand.

'Yes, like you saving my life. If you hadn't shoved me out of the way back there I'd be closely resembling processed cheese sandwich spread right now.'

'Did I? I can't remember. Everything's kind of hazy. I remember the sound of the ceiling starting to give way and then the next thing I knew you were bending over me and asking me to count fingers.'

'Well, some memory loss is to be expected with a blow to the head.' She put the medical kit back into the rucksack. 'So what now?'

He pointed along the corridor. 'Our options have been severely reduced. We have no choice but to keep going that way.'

'Yes. And I have the strong feeling that's exactly the route Gilmour wants us to take.'

'I'm afraid you could be right.'

Hamilton lay on his stomach holding the flashlight and gun to the back of his head in what was probably a futile gesture of self-protection. Small fragments of rock continued to rain down all around him but the expected crushing impact never came.

Then the noise from the falling stonework faded away. He sat up, choking on the thick dust, and shone his torch behind him. The corridor was completely blocked with broken stone but to his relief he saw Stephanie lying face down only a short distance away. She appeared untouched though covered with dust.

'Stephanie!' he shouted as he got to his feet. 'Stephanie!' He went and knelt beside her. He gently shook her and was relieved to hear her groan. Coughing, she tried to raise herself on her elbows. He took hold of her and lifted her into a sitting position, then shone the torch into her face. She was covered with thick dust but seemed unharmed. 'Am I relieved to see you,' he told her sincerely. 'For a few moments I thought I was trapped in here alone.'

She spat a mixture of dust and saliva on to the floor, coughed again and then looked at him.

'No, Terry, you're not alone,' she said.

Chapter Nineteen

Stephanie, and the person she thought of as Hamilton, trudged along the grim, medieval passageway. She had no idea how far they'd come since leaving the site of the cave-in but she knew they'd walked far beyond the actual length of the Institute building. 'We must be going in circles,' she complained at last. 'The Institute was never *this* big!'

'Gilmour must have made some extensions to the place as well as the, er, modifications.'

'But we walked right round it before we came inside. It wasn't any bigger.'

'Well, no, not from the outside. But the normal laws of physics are no longer working here. Maybe it's like Dr Who's police call box.'

'What?' She had no idea what he was talking about.

'Dr Who's time machine. You know, it was an ordinary call box on the outside but on the inside it was a huge time machine. Didn't you ever watch the show when you were a kid?'

'No. So you're saying this place could be literally endless? As if Gilmour was actually making this up as we go along?'

'Yeah, I suppose so.'

She came to a halt and shone her torch at him. 'Well, this is all rather pointless, isn't it? If we go on we'll just keep walking until we drop from exhaustion.'

'What choice have we got? We can't go back. Besides, we might come across another intersection.'

'Oh sure. Or maybe we'll find an escalator leading to a coffee shop on the mezzanine floor. I could do with a cup of coffee right now. If you're listening, Gilmour, could you take the hint?' She shone her light at the ceiling of the passageway. 'Gilmour, are you listening, you bloody *bastard*!'

'Hey, take it easy, Stephanie. Don't go cracking up on me now.'

She turned on him. 'I think I have a perfect right to have a fit of hysterics considering what I've been through ... and what I'm still *going* through!' she yelled.

He grabbed her arm. 'Shush!'

'Don't shush me, you stupid policeman!' she cried. 'I'll shout as much as – ' She stopped when she saw him suddenly turn and stare up the tunnel. 'What is it?' she asked in a quieter voice.

'Thought I heard something. Might be that rat again.'

'Rat? What rat?'

'Sorry. I shouldn't have mentioned it. But that sound I heard earlier ... it was a rat. I saw it. A big one. Listen.'

She listened. Yes, there was definitely something moving somewhere up the tunnel. She heard splashing sounds as it ran through the puddles. She could picture a huge rat coming in their direction and felt an atavistic horror seize her entire body. She took out the gun and held it ready. She didn't care any more about saving the bullets for Gilmour. The moment she saw the rat she was going to blast it away.

The skittering, splashing sounds grew louder and Stephanie tensed, finger pressing on the trigger. She expected to see the giant rat in her torch beam at any second.

'At last! A doorway!' cried Hamilton. It seemed they had been walking for miles along the passageway since leaving the collapsed intersection. He soon realised that, thanks to Gilmour, the size of the interior of the Institute no longer bore any connection to the size of its exterior. He had been reminded of Dr

Who's deceptive time machine, the Tardis, in the old TV series.

He pulled the heavy wooden door open and shone his torch inside. The beam revealed a series of stone steps leading upwards. He turned to the person he thought to be Stephanie. 'Shall we?' he asked.

She shrugged. 'Why not? At least it looks dry in there. My boots are soaked through.'

He started up the stairs. She followed. As he climbed he shone his torch upwards, hoping to see a landing and another door but all he could see were stairs.

They climbed and they climbed but ahead stretched only more stairs. Finally Hamilton, out of breath and concerned about his pounding heart, called a halt. He leaned, panting, against a greasy wall. 'This is ludicrous,' he gasped. 'These stairs are like the passageway. They just go on and on. We'll never make it to the top because there probably *isn't* one . . .'

'You might be right,' she said. She didn't sound breathless at all.

When his breathing was back to normal and the pounding in his heart had subsided he started back down the stairs. 'Gilmour's got us running around like rats in a maze,' he complained.

'My thoughts exactly,' she replied. And giggled.

The rat didn't appear. And the sounds had stopped. She relaxed a little. 'I can't hear it any more. Can you?'

'No. It must have gone. So let's keep going.'

'All right.' But she was reluctant to continue onwards. She could picture the giant rat waiting silently in the shadows ahead of them . . . waiting to leap at her.

'Come on,' he said, prodding her arm with his flashlight.

'Do you mind going first?' she asked.

He laughed. 'No. Not at all. But if there are rats in front of us there are probably rats behind us as well.'

'Did you *have* to say that!?' she cried as she automatically spun round and shone her light behind her. She saw nothing.

He laughed again. It wasn't a pleasant laugh. She wondered why she hadn't noticed that about Hamilton before.

She nervously followed him along the passageway. She couldn't see any way out of their predicament. How could they possibly locate Gilmour and kill him when he possessed this power to manipulate them so thoroughly? He could keep them running about in this madhouse until they used up all the BDNFE and were then totally at his mercy . . .

'Funny phobia for a medical scientist to have. Being scared of rats.'

'Funny in what way?' she asked him coldly.

'Well, surely you must have a lot of dealings with rats. You know, white rats for experiments and so on.'

'Yes, I do.'

'So how do you cope with handling them?'

'With great difficulty. But these days I try to avoid any direct contact with them. I leave that to my staff. It was much worse when I was a student. After handling a rat I would have to run into the nearest bathroom and throw up.'

'Sounds really bad. Did you always have this phobia or was it set off by something specific?'

'If you mean was I frightened by a rat as a child I have no idea. I can't remember any such experience. Nor could my parents when I asked them. It just seems that I've always felt this way.'

'Ever read *The Rats* by that horror writer, James Herbert? It's about this plague of rats. They eat people in all sorts of really gross ways.' He chuckled unpleasantly. 'You'd love it.'

She stared at his back. What was wrong with him all of a sudden? She'd just told him how much she loathed rats . . .

There was a high-pitched squeal from behind her. She turned and her torch beam illuminated a monstrosity rushing towards her. It was a huge rat, some three feet long from nose to the tip of its tail. But the worst thing about it was that it was completely hairless. Its body gleamed wetly pink in her torch beam . . . like that of a new-born child.

She screamed as it leapt at her. It landed on her right thigh,

clutching her leg tightly with its claws. She felt its sharp teeth
bite into her upper thigh. She began frantically clubbing at its
head with the gun barrel but it remained fastened to her leg.

'Help me! Get it off me!' she screamed to Hamilton. But he
just stood there, watching her with a smile on his face as she
danced about.

'Looks like you've made a friend,' he said, and laughed.

'We should have reached the bottom ages ago,' said Hamilton.

'Yes,' she agreed. 'But it seems it's no longer here.'

'Well, this is bloody marvellous, isn't it!' he said angrily. He
came to a sudden stop, causing her to bump into him. He turned
to her. 'What the hell can we do now? It's pointless going down
and just as pointless going up!'

She smiled at him. 'We could always have a fuck.'

'Pardon?'

'You heard me. It's a waste of time trying to do anything else.
So let's enjoy ourselves while we still can.' She began unfasten-
ing her leather jacket.

He stared at her. 'Are you feeling all right?' He presumed
that she was finally starting to cave in under the pressure. He
wondered what to do. Slap her face? It had worked earlier when
she had done the same to him.

'Don't pretend you haven't thought about fucking me,' she
said as she pulled open her jacket. 'I know you have.'

'Well, yeah, just like I've thought the same about Michelle
Pfeiffer, but in both cases I never thought it would lead anywhere,' he said, and forced a chuckle. He saw she was now
working on the buttons of her shirt. He said quickly, 'Seriously,
Stephanie, right now the thought of having sex with you or
anyone else is the furthest thing from my mind. And I'm kind
of amazed that *you* are thinking about it. I mean, look at our
situation here, Stephanie. We're in deep shit . . .'

She finished unbuttoning her shirt and pulled it open. She
wasn't wearing a bra. And, as breasts went, Hamilton couldn't
help noting for the second time running, that hers were pretty
good.

'All the more reason for us to have a little fun,' she told him as she came closer to him. He backed away until he felt the wall behind him pressing against the rucksack.

'Listen, Stephanie, you're not yourself. And that's perfectly understandable. We're both under quite a . . . well, strain. But when things get back to normal you're going to regret you did this.'

She moved in close, pressing herself against him. 'You really think things are ever going to get back to normal?' Then she kissed him. Her mouth tasted unpleasant but he guessed his did as well.

She drew away from him, switched off her torch and dropped it in her pocket. Then he felt her fingers searching for the zipper on his fly. 'Do you?' she asked.

'I sure *hope* so,' he said, sincerely. His zip was yanked roughly down, then he felt her warm hand slip down inside his underpants. Her fingers encased his penis and scrotum, gently at first, then harder. He gasped. 'Come on, show some enthusiasm,' she told him.

Rather than display any sign of becoming erect, his penis seemed to be shrinking at her touch. 'I don't think there's much chance of anything happening in that department,' he said. 'I haven't had much interest in sex in the years since . . . my wife died.'

She gave his balls a hard squeeze and his eyes filled with tears. 'That's not strictly true, Terry,' she said softly. 'What about yesterday?'

'Yesterday?'

'Yes, yesterday afternoon. When you had your little fling with the Harrow police station groupie. Miss Josie Welch. Don't you remember? You put on an impressive performance for a man who is supposed to be impotent.'

'How in the world did you know about Josie?' he asked, very confused. Then the answer hit him like a brick.

Shit, he thought. *Gilmour*.

*

She had reduced the rat's skull to a bloody pulp with the gun barrel but it continued to hang on to her leg. She stopped pounding on its head and put the gun in her pocket. Then, with extreme distaste, pulled the rat's dead body from her leg. The feel of its pink, slimy, naked flesh made her stomach revolt and as soon as she had succeeded in prying it loose she bent over and vomited on to the floor.

When she was finished she rounded on Hamilton. He was still standing there with an amused grin on his face. 'You bastard! What's the matter with you? Why didn't you help me?'

'I didn't want to spoil the fun, lovely Stephanie.'

Before she could say anything else she heard more sounds from down the passageway. She turned back round. Her beam caught another large, furless rat heading towards her. She fired at it. And was lucky. The bullet took its head off. Then came another one behind it. It made angry squealing sounds as it ran. She fired. And missed. She fired again. She hit it in its back, shattering its spine. It screamed with pain and writhed about for a few moments, then it began to drag itself towards her, using just its forelegs. Its red eyes blazed with hatred. Stephanie waited until it got closer, aimed carefully and blew its head off. She waited. No more sounds. Then she turned to face . . . Hamilton. *Lovely Stephanie*, he had said. She pointed the gun at him and pulled the trigger. There was an empty click. No more bullets.

As he came towards her she realised he was whistling the theme tune from *Neighbours*.

Hamilton's mind, as his mother would have put it, was in a bit of a tizz. Trying to come to terms with the realisation that Stephanie wasn't Stephanie but was actually Gilmour was bad enough; trying to come to terms with the fact that Gilmour literally had him by the balls was even worse.

'Er, look, if we're going to fuck why don't we try and get more comfortable . . . arghhh!'

Stephanie/Gilmour had squeezed him again. Was it his imagination or had the hand holding his balls suddenly become much bigger, not to mention stronger? 'How can we fuck if you can't even get it up?' demanded Gilmour in Stephanie's voice.

'Hey, I'll keep trying . . . I can make it, but it would help if you would let go. You're hurting me . . .' As he spoke he reached into his pocket. He took hold of the gun. Drew it from his pocket. Started to raise it, his finger ready on the trigger . . .

He grunted as his wrist was suddenly seized and jerked to one side. The gun went off. The noise echoed up and down the stone staircase. Stephanie laughed. She started laughing as Stephanie and stopped laughing as Gilmour. Gilmour put his face close to Hamilton's. 'Pull the trigger again,' he commanded.

Hamilton didn't. He knew it was his last bullet. Then he screamed as Gilmour's hand closed even harder around his testicles. He pulled the trigger. The bullet ricocheted harmlessly up the staircase. Gilmour laughed and said, 'Looks like you've shot your wad, Hamilton. A bad case of premature ejaculation. And now here comes a bad case of post-coital depression.' He brutally squeezed Hamilton's testicles and Hamilton threw his head back and screamed.

Chapter Twenty

Stephanie kept pulling the trigger of the empty gun as Hamilton/Gilmour advanced on her. *Click! Click! Click!* Still whistling the theme from *Neighbours*, he reached for the gun, grabbed it by the barrel and wrenched it out of her hand. He threw the useless weapon into the darkness. Then he smiled at her. 'I like you much better without that nasty old gun, lovely Stephanie.'

'Get away from me!' she shouted. 'You can't touch me!'

'I'm not going to touch you, my lovely. But my little friends are ...'

She heard a horrifying sound behind her. The sound of a whole horde of giant rats skittering along the passageway. They squeaked and squealed as they came rushing towards her. There must have been hundreds of them. And she was completely helpless ...

No, she wasn't. She had been carrying the rucksack since she dressed Hamilton's – *Gilmour's* – head. Stepping away from Gilmour, she quickly took it off her back and reached in for the remaining petrol bomb. She was relieved to see it was intact. She got out her lighter, lit the wick then flung the bottle along the passageway. It hit the ground and immediately blazing petrol erupted with a roar. The rats wouldn't get past *that*, she told herself with satisfaction.

Then, suddenly, the flames simply faded away and darkness rushed in to replace them. She heard Gilmour laugh. She turned to him. 'That Molotov cocktail wasn't real,' he told her with amusement. 'Just like this isn't.' He pointed to the dressing on his forehead. It too just faded away. 'Hamilton has the real rucksack and the real Molotov cocktails. The *real* Hamilton, that is.'

She heard the rats come pouring along the passageway towards her.

Hamilton kneed Gilmour as hard as he could in his groin, thankful that Gilmour had changed from Stephanie back to his true form as a man. Gilmour grunted and let go of his wrist. Hamilton clubbed him over the head with the gun, shoved him backwards and then started to run down the stairs. Gilmour's laughter rang out behind him.

He ran and ran, determined to put as much distance as he could between himself and Gilmour. Then he fell. The steps had disappeared and been replaced by a smooth, stony slope. 'Shit!' he cried as he fell on his stomach and began to slide downwards. He was forced to let go of both the flashlight and the gun as he tried desperately to brake himself but couldn't. Instead, he picked up momentum as the downward slope became more acute . . .

He dug his fingernails and the toes of his shoes as hard as he could into the slippery surface. To his relief he felt an almost imperceptible decrease in his rate of descent. Slowly, very slowly, he began to slow. Then his outstretched fingers hit an obstruction – a kind of ridge across the stone ramp – and he was jolted to a complete stop. However, he heard the gun and the flashlight clatter over the ridge . . . and then nothing. He realised he was on the edge of a very long drop.

'Bloody hell,' he muttered to himself in the blackness. He was lying head down at an angle of at least sixty degrees, his arms stretched out in front of him, fingertips pressed against the stone ridge which was only about an inch high. He couldn't move. The incline was too steep for him to push himself back up the slope. Then he heard a distant splash. The gun and flashlight had finally hit bottom. And the bottom was full of water.

A sickening feeling of vertigo seized him.

He considered his options. He saw they were extremely limited. Non-existent, in fact. 'Fuck you, Gilmour!' he snarled.

The incline gradually became even more acute. One more degree . . . two more . . . three more, then the movement stopped. The rucksack, and its contents, bunched up behind his head. The pressure on his fingers and arms intensified. How long before his strength gave out? Christ, the thought of falling into that empty blackness made his heart pound with panic. Then he heard something that made him even more terrified.

A movement in the water far below him. As if something large had surfaced for a few moments and then submerged again.

He knew, he just *knew*, that the Ultimate Horror was down there in that dark water, and waiting. Waiting for him.

The slope moved again, becoming even more acute. Soon it would be almost vertical. 'No, Gilmour, *no! Help me!*'

He heard laughter coming from a long way up the tunnel. Now he was virtually standing on his head. '*NO!*' he screamed.

The inevitable happened. He overbalanced and his body toppled backwards into the void.

He screamed all the way down.

He hit the water and sank deep below the surface. It was cold. It poured into his mouth and nose. He kept trying to scream as he continued to sink, kicking and flaying his arms about, deeper and deeper into the freezing black water. The Thing in the water was coming for him. He could sense it coming closer . . . coming up from below him.

IT was the embodiment of every nightmare that he had ever had. IT was the thing he had always known to be lurking just below the fragile shell of his everyday reality, waiting to reveal ITself to him. The Ultimate Horror. And any second now he would feel ITS touch . . . be engulfed by IT . . .

Something closed around his wrist. In his panic he breathed in water.

'It's me, you twit! Fight it, Terry! Fight it!'

Stephanie's voice, booming inside his head. And it was her hand around his wrist, pulling him upwards.

'Fight it with all your strength! You can do it! You still have the power to resist! You know you can do it!'

But the Thing in the water was very close now . . . it was directly below him . . .

'NO!' he screamed inside his skull.

And the next thing he knew he was lying face down on a hard floor, choking and retching up water.

'Good! We did it!' Stephanie's voice. This time in his ears. Her hand was still around his wrist.

He struggled on to his hands and knees and continued violently to cough up water from his lungs. When he could breathe again he dazedly looked around. Stephanie was sitting beside him, her flashlight resting on her lap. She gave him a reassuring smile. 'Feeling a bit better?'

'Yeah.' They seemed to be in a hospital corridor. 'Where are we? What happened?' He couldn't believe it. He had been absolutely certain that he was doomed – that the Thing in the black water was about to get him.

'Still in the Institute, I'm afraid,' she said as she got up and began pulling the rucksack from his shoulders. 'Take your jacket off and roll up your sleeve.'

As he started to do as she'd instructed it suddenly struck him – this was another trick. 'You're not Stephanie,' he accused her. 'You're still Gilmour!'

'So he did the same thing to you that he did to me? I guessed as much. He must have pulled the switch at the time of the cave-in. We both ended up in different passageways with *doppelgängers* of each other.' She was taking the medical kit out of the rucksack.

'Yeah. And I'm not falling for the same thing two times in a row. You're Gilmour, you fucking bastard!'

'I can understand why you think I am but believe me, I'm not. I'm really Stephanie.' She removed a hypodermic from its sterile packaging.

'Prove it.'

'I'm afraid I'm not equipped to perform a genetic finger-printing test at the moment. You'll just have to take my word for it. Now roll up your sleeve.' She inserted the needle into the top of a small bottle.

'Hah! No way! And what's that stuff?'

She filled the hypodermic and looked him in the eye. 'You know what it is, Terry. The synthetic BDNFE. I'm going to top you up. Then I'm going to top myself up. It's important. It's our only hope. It's what saved you just then.'

'Give it up, Gilmour. It's not going to work this time,' he told her firmly.

She gave an exasperated sigh. Then, after reflecting for a few moments, she said, 'How long was it before you realised, after the cave-in, that you were with Gilmour rather than me?'

'I don't know. Not for quite some time. Not until after you started acting strangely.'

'Strangely? In what way?'

'When you . . .' He hesitated, feeling a little embarrassed. He didn't really believe it, of course, but there was the remote possibility that this *was* Stephanie. 'When you suggested we . . . make love. On the stairway.'

She laughed. 'Well, yes, I can see how that would have been a dead giveaway. So you immediately sussed that I was an impostor?'

'Er, not at first,' he admitted. 'I just thought you were show-ing signs of . . . stress.'

She laughed again. 'I assure you, Terry, that when I finally go over the edge, making sexual propositions to you will *not* be one of the symptoms. But anyway, what happened? You didn't actually screw Gilmour, did you?'

'No, of course not!' he protested. 'He attacked me then. He grabbed my . . . I tried to shoot him and ended up wasting my last two bullets.'

She nodded. 'That's what he did to me too. I don't mean any sexual stuff; he got me to use up all my ammunition. You were right. He was scared of the guns. In our possession they did present a threat to him.'

Hamilton felt himself starting to believe that she was telling the truth. He tried to resist it. *This is Gilmour*, he told himself. *Gilmour!* 'No, no . . . I'm not buying this. If you're Stephanie how did you get me out of that . . . that *place*? Only Gilmour would have the power to do that.'

'Not true. We both have the power as well. Thanks to this.' She held up the hypodermic. 'We don't have the same power as Gilmour but we do have enough to exert an influence in here. More than we did on the outside. Remember my cigarettes? And the way you destroyed that skull? Well, when Gilmour, in your form, tried to freak me out completely with my worst nightmare – a bunch of giant rats – I automatically hit back. The rats vanished, and so did the medieval passageway and the fake you. I found myself here. Then I started looking for you, or rather I started *feeling* around for you, with my senses. And I found you. Just in time. And together we were able to break Gilmour's hold over you and free you from that personal hell he'd designed for you.'

'I wish I could believe you,' he told her.

'Look, Terry, I was in your head back there. You were about to experience the worst thing you could possibly imagine . . . or maybe it was even *beyond* your worst imaginings. Whatever it was it was . . . unspeakable, so do you think Gilmour would have missed the fun by saving you from it?'

He thought about it. 'No,' he said, finally. 'Unless he was saving me for something even worse.'

'Oh, for Christ's sake, roll up your damn sleeve!'

He decided to give her the benefit of the doubt and rolled up his sleeve. I mean, he told himself, why would Gilmour want to do something so mundane as to inject him with poison?

She injected him and then filled another syringe and took off her jacket. As she was rolling up her sleeve Hamilton glanced at the swell of her breasts under her dark shirt and remembered when she had exposed them to him on the stairway.

'Something on your mind?' she asked him. She had caught him looking.

His face reddening, he quickly looked away. 'No . . . nothing.'

'For the last time,' she said as she injected herself, 'I am *not* Gilmour so you can forget it.'

'I don't know what you're talking about,' he muttered. Then, to change the subject, 'Where are we?'

'A corridor on the ground floor of the Institute. My lab is just around the corner. That's where I suspect we'll find Gilmour.'

'But he'll be waiting for us. And we don't have the guns any more.'

'I know.' She put the medical kit back in the rucksack and then pulled out one of the petrol bombs. 'But we still have these.' She pulled the cloth wick out of the bottle and reversed it so that the petrol-soaked section was free. Then she did the same with the other bomb.

'So we just waltz in there and chuck these at him, eh?' he asked her dubiously.

'You have a better plan?'

'You think he's just going to sit there and *let* us barbecue him?'

'Terry, he's at a disadvantage now. We're back together again and we have power. He can't touch us.'

'Well, he's been doing a hell of a job on us up to now for someone who can't touch us.'

'Things have changed. And we have to strike while we have the advantage. So let's go.' She handed him one of the bottles and then rose to her feet. She put on the rucksack. 'Let's pray this will soon be over.'

He got up too. 'Prayers don't seem to rate much in this place. Turn around.' He reached into the rucksack and took out the tyre iron. It felt a more substantial weapon than the milk bottle full of petrol he was holding.

Stephanie led the way down the corridor. When they turned the corner Hamilton couldn't help a small gasp. They were back in medieval territory. Dank stonework, dripping water, mould, slime . . . the works. 'So much for our amazing powers,' he whispered.

'We're close to Gilmour now,' she said. 'Very close.'

There was flickering light up ahead. As they got closer Hamilton saw that the light came from two burning torches set in the wall on each side of a large wooden door. And there was something else too, below the torches . . .

Hamilton hoped he wasn't seeing what he thought he was seeing but, typical of this place, he was. Beneath each torch, impaled on an upward curving spike, was a human male head. And they were both still alive. Their eyes rolled wildly and their mouths opened and closed in silent screams of agony.

'Oh *no* . . .' whispered Stephanie. 'Gary . . . Stewart . . . ?'

'You know them?'

'They're . . . were . . . male nurses. Two of Gilmour's guards at the Institute.'

Gary and Stewart clearly recognised Stephanie. They looked at her imploringly and were desperately trying to speak to her, but lacking lungs couldn't make a single sound. 'I can't do anything to help you now,' she told them. 'But hang on. It won't be for very much longer.'

Hamilton could see that her words, understandably, failed to provide the two severed heads with any consolation, but whatever frantic protests they were making remained unheard.

'Concentrate, Terry,' Stephanie told him. 'We've got to get this door open.' She'd put her flashlight away and was now holding her cigarette lighter near the wick of her Molotov cocktail.

'What do you mean, concentrate?'

'We're going to *will* it open, you moron. Now concentrate, with all your mind! Now!'

He concentrated, and, to his surprise, the door opened. And then another surprise. The door didn't swing slowly open with creaking sound effects but *slid* sideways into the wall. Beyond was a brightly lit room devoid of any furniture. It had a polished wooden floor, grey walls and a white ceiling. Hamilton couldn't see where the light was coming from. There were no obvious sources. In the centre of the room stood a portly middle-aged man with a round, jovial face and very dark eyes. He was wearing a dark grey business suit and red bow-tie. 'Come in, my dears! Come in!' he called to them in a cheerful voice. 'Please.'

Hamilton and Stephanie warily entered the room. The door slid shut behind them.

The man approached them. Hamilton saw then that his eyes had no corneas or pupils. They were both completely black, like twin pits.

'The preliminaries are over, my dears,' he said in his incongruously cheerful voice. 'Now, I'm afraid, your punishment will begin in earnest.' And he gleefully rubbed his hands together.

Chapter Twenty-One

'Oh, come off it, Gilmour!' cried Stephanie in a disgusted tone. 'Don't waste your time with more tricks. It's all over.'

'I assure you, Dr Lyell, that I am not Marc Gilmour,' said the round-faced man with the blank eyes. 'He is not part of this and never has been. You were, of course, encouraged to *think* he was. But where are my manners? Please sit down, my dears.' He waved a perfectly manicured, plump hand. Hamilton glanced over his shoulder and saw two straight-back chairs behind them that hadn't been there just moments ago. He and Stephanie exchanged a worried glance and then, reluctantly, they sat down. The man beamed a smile at them. 'Splendid,' he said.

'All right, we'll humour you for the moment,' Stephanie told him. 'If you aren't Gilmour who are you?'

'Oh, my name is Legion,' he said, and gave them a sly wink. With his dead, matte-black eyes it was an unnerving gesture. 'But you can call me Mister Ende.'

Hamilton said, 'We'll call you whatever you want, Gilmour, but you're still the same crazy fucking maniac.'

The black eyes fixed on his. 'You refuse to understand, don't you, Detective Sergeant? To face up to the truth.'

'What truth?'

'That you are dead. The pair of you.'

'Now you're getting really desperate, Gilmour,' Hamilton told him. 'Sorry, I mean *Mister Ende*.'

The plump man sighed. 'You both died last night. You, Detective Sergeant Terry Hamilton, of vomit inhalation while you lay unconscious, as a result of alcoholic poisoning, in the flat of one Miss Josie Welch.' He turned to Stephanie. 'And you, Dr Stephanie Lyell, died of smoke inhalation, the result of setting fire to your armchair with a dropped cigarette after you had dozed off. Rather appropriate, don't you think, considering your past history with cigarettes and fire?'

'I don't believe it,' said Stephanie firmly.

'Neither do I,' agreed Hamilton. 'If we're both dead, what's this place supposed to be?'

'Can't you guess? You guessed right before, Detective Sergeant, when you recalled a certain novel you had once read . . . *The Third Policeman.* The one where the protagonist discovers he's been in Hell all along.'

'Yeah,' he admitted, feeling uneasy. That had been at the Institute's empty site, when Stephanie had slapped his face. 'But why would I be in Hell? The bloke in the book had murdered someone, but I haven't.'

'I must correct you there,' said the cherubic-faced man with black eyes. 'You have indeed murdered someone. You murdered your wife. Judith.'

'No!' he protested, angrily. 'That was an accident!'

'On the contrary, it wasn't. And in your heart of hearts you know it. Think back to that day. You were aiming the gun at Gilmour, preparing to fire. And then it occurred to you. It was the perfect opportunity to escape from a marriage you could no longer tolerate . . . to be free of a wife you no longer loved . . . a wife who had become even repulsive to you. Admit it.'

Hamilton shook his head. 'No! It was an accident! I was aiming at Gilmour.'

'Look at me,' commanded Mister Ende. And Hamilton looked into those black eyes. 'And remember how it was. Remember what you were feeling at the time.'

Hamilton saw Judith standing there in the kitchen, with Gilmour behind her, holding her. Hamilton had the gun in both hands, aiming it . . . but at who?

Then he saw. He was aiming at Judith's head.

'No!' he cried, despairingly. 'I didn't mean to!'

'You *know* that you did,' said Mister Ende, in a much deeper, more powerful voice. He no longer sounded jovial. And Hamilton saw that he had grown in size. He was at least seven feet tall now and loomed over him, his black eyes glaring down. 'And that's why you are here. For ever. And ever . . .'

'Don't listen to him, Terry,' warned Stephanie. 'Gilmour tried this trick before, on me.'

'But he's right,' moaned Hamilton. 'I did want her dead. And I deliberately shot her.'

'Terry, don't let him get to you.'

Mister Ende turned to her. 'Your previous brush with the Pit was a mere diversion, Miss Lyell. A prelude to the real thing. Which will begin very soon for you.'

'So I'm in Hell because of my two abortions?' she asked, still sounding defiant.

'No. You are here for the murder of your young sister.'

'I didn't murder Gloria!' cried Stephanie. 'It was an accident!'

'Her death was no more an accident than the death of the Detective Sergeant's wife. That is one of the things that links you together. And will continue to link you together throughout your eternal damnation.'

'I did not murder Gloria!' she shouted at the looming figure of Mister Ende.

'How do you know? You can't remember what happened,' he said, tauntingly. 'Let me blow the cobwebs from your mind and refresh your memory. And perhaps this will help . . .'

A young girl suddenly appeared in front of Stephanie. She looked about seven years old, had dark hair and was dressed in blue pyjamas. She was also holding a golliwog. 'Gloria,' whispered Stephanie. The child said nothing but stared at Stephanie with large, accusatory eyes.

'Remember how you felt about her?' Mister Ende asked her, his voice growing louder. 'Remember how jealous you were of her? How envious you were? How you resented her being your parents' favourite? Do you remember how much you *hated* her?'

'No,' protested Stephanie, weakly. She couldn't tear her eyes away from the gaze of her dead sister. 'I didn't . . .'

'You did. Oh yes, you did,' Mister Ende told her. 'You hated her, and you murdered her. You deliberately put your lit cigarette on that pile of newspapers and then you left the room, shutting the door behind you, knowing that Gloria had trouble in working the handle and probably wouldn't be able to get out. And then you waited.'

'No . . . no . . . no . . .' moaned Stephanie. She continued to stare into the eyes of her dead sister.

'You *know* it's the truth,' intoned Mister Ende.

Stephanie suddenly covered her face with her hands and her shoulders shook. 'Yes!' she sobbed. 'Yes, I remember now! I did set that fire . . . I *did* kill her!' She began to cry uncontrollably.

Hamilton was only half aware of what was happening to her; he was too concerned with confronting his own guilt. How had he managed to conceal the dreadful truth from himself for so long? He *had* deliberately fired that first bullet at Judith's head. And killed her. Murdered her.

He looked up at Mister Ende, who was huge now, his head brushing the ceiling. The round face wore a sneer. Red sparks flew in those black eyes. 'Good, my dears. Good. And now it is time to begin your punishment.' Mister Ende took several steps backwards then gestured. A door appeared in the polished wooden floor. Hamilton could see steps leading downwards.

'Descend,' ordered Mister Ende.

Stephanie's dead sister turned and went to the top of the steps. She turned and looked back at her older sister. Stephanie rose slowly and went to her. Hamilton felt himself standing too. He seemed to have no voluntary control over his limbs.

Stephanie was staring anxiously down into the cavity. Mister Ende gave an unpleasant chuckle that reverberated around the room. 'No, Miss Lyell, this is not the Hell of your Catholic upbringing. No flames, no screaming souls, no sulphur and brimstone. The reality is much less theatrical. Hell, as Jean Paul Sartre so accurately noted, is other people. Now go.'

Accompanied by her young sister, Stephanie began to descend the steps. Hamilton followed.

At the base of the steps was another door. It swung open to reveal a very narrow cell. On each side was a wooden bench. Sitting on one of them was, to his profound regret, Judith. She was knitting. As they entered the cell she turned and gave him her pained martyr's smile. 'Hello, Terry. They said you and your friend would turn up sooner or later.'

'Judith . . .' he said, with difficulty. 'I'm so sorry . . . about . . . about . . .'

'Oh, don't give it another thought, Terry. At least we're together now.' She returned her attention to her knitting.

Stephanie had sat down facing her silent sister; Hamilton was obliged to sit facing his wife. The door slammed shut. He turned and saw that there was now no door, only a blank wall identical to the one at the other end of the cell. He took a deep breath. The air in the cell was warm, musty and uncomfortable. And the bench was hard. He glanced at Stephanie. She sat there with slumped shoulders, facing her sister. She appeared transfixed by the steady, accusing gaze of the little girl. The golliwog sitting on the girl's lap also seemed to be staring at Stephanie in an accusatory way. Hamilton guiltily looked again at his wife. She smiled back at him and held up her knitting. 'They said we would be here for some time so I thought I'd better bring something along to occupy my hands.'

There was no answer to that. He smiled weakly at her and wondered what she would do when she'd finished whatever it was that she was knitting. But then he guessed she never actually would finish it. He would be listening to the annoying click-clack of her needles for ever.

He looked at his watch which, as he did so, struck him as a particularly futile thing to do considering the circumstances. It was half past nine in the morning. Not that terms like morning or afternoon would mean anything any more. He saw the seconds tick away and wondered whether his watch would run for ever too.

He looked at Stephanie again. 'Stephanie?' But she wouldn't

202 Harry Adam Knight

answer him. She remained transfixed by her sister's gaze. But the golliwog responded. It turned its head towards Hamilton and gave him a slow wink with one of its large, circular eyes. Hamilton shuddered and quickly looked away. Then he leaned back and rested his head against the hard wall. He closed his eyes.

Click! Clack! Click! Clack!

Time passed. Slowly. He began to feel bored. And hungry. And on top of that he needed to take a leak. That was going to be a problem, considering the lack of toilet facilities in Hell. And if he was dead, why did he still need to have a piss? Maybe he had just had the urge but not the means. He would spend all eternity feeling hungry and with a full bladder. Great, this gets better by the minute . . .

Click! Clack! Click! Clack!

He tried to doze off but couldn't. That was to be expected. In Hell you would be deprived the solace of sleep along with everything else.

More time passed with agonising slowness. He looked at his watch again. Nearly twelve p.m. Two and a half hours in Hell and only an infinite number of other hours to go.

Click! Clack! Click! Clack!

He knew it wasn't his real wife sitting opposite him with those damned knitting needles. Why would she be obliged to suffer eternal punishment for something he had done? No, as before she was merely a facsimile created to intensify his feelings of guilt. And to annoy him.

Click! Clack! Click! Clack!

How long before he grabbed one of those needles and jabbed it through her heart? She would be unkillable, of course. She would merely give him *that* smile, remove the needle and resume her knitting.

More time passed.

And now Hamilton *really* needed to take a leak. The pressure in his bladder was becoming intolerable. Surely he wouldn't have to endure this level of discomfort for eternity? But then, this was Hell after all.

He could stand it no longer. He knew it would probably be a waste of time trying to relieve himself but he had to do it. He stood up. 'Excuse me,' he said to Judith and then turned to where the door had been. He unzipped and took out his penis. *Here goes nothing*, he said to himself.

He expected to be cruelly frustrated but to his delighted surprise a strong jet of urine hit the wall and he felt immediate relief.

'Oh, *really*, Terry,' said his wife in a disgusted tone as he continued to piss against the wall. A large puddle of urine was forming on the floor. She had even stopped knitting. He ignored her.

When he had finished he gave a sigh of satisfaction and zipped himself up again. Then he regarded the puddle of urine on the floor with puzzlement. It didn't seem right. Why should a dead man in Hell be able to urinate?

Not really daring to hope, he thought again about the possibility that this was nothing but another of Gilmour's tricks. *No, no, it couldn't be . . . he* had *remembered deliberately killing Judith and he was being punished for it. For all eternity . . .*

He sat down again and leaned his head against the wall. He closed his eyes. He *did* remember killing Judith, didn't he? Upstairs, he had been certain that he did but now his memory had gone fuzzy again. He reluctantly concentrated, trying to recreate that dreadful afternoon. And then, suddenly, he was no longer in the cell. He was in the back garden of the house they'd owned in Wimbledon. He could feel the sun on the back of his neck, could feel the weight of the revolver in his hand, the sweat from his hand on the butt of the gun.

He was creeping slowly towards the rear of the house, hoping against hope that his fears were wrong. His foot touched something. He looked down. He had almost stepped on the yellow plastic duck that belonged to his daughter. He knew it made a quacking sound if you squeezed it. A close call. He moved on, keeping low. He reached the back of the house. Could he risk a look into the kitchen through the rear window? He hesitated.

He decided against it. The window, by the kitchen sink, was

bare but there were pot plants along the sills of the side windows which would provide him with cover. He crept slowly around to the side of the kitchen then cautiously raised his head . . .

And saw what he dreaded he might see.

He saw Judith and he saw a man. He was holding her by her hair and had a knife at her throat. And then he saw something even worse. Lying on the floor by the kitchen table was his daughter, Kim. She was covered in blood and there was a pool of blood around her. Her throat had been cut.

Hamilton started to retch. He ducked down beneath the window and fought to control himself. He couldn't afford to make a sound. The retching stopped. He wiped his brow then slowly raised his head again. The man – it *had* to be the Bone Man – and his wife were facing the door that led into the hallway that ran through the rest of the house. The Bone Man was expecting him to come in the front way.

What to do? Shoot the bastard, naturally. No crapping about with warnings or any of that stuff. The guy was a complete nutter. If he heard Hamilton shout a warning he'd simply swing Judith round in front of him, and maybe cut her throat into the bargain as well. No, he'd have to take him out with the first shot . . .

But it wasn't going to be easy. Only about nine feet away but he was holding Judith awfully close and Hamilton would be shooting through the window glass. If the glass deflected the bullet he might hit Judith. Better if he broke the glass first but there wouldn't be enough time. The sound of the window breaking would be just like Hamilton yelling a warning.

He had no choice but to fire through the window. It was Judith's only chance of survival.

Hamilton transferred the gun to his left hand and wiped the sweaty palm of his right against his thigh. Then he stood up higher and took careful aim, holding the gun in a two-handed grip. He would have to fire fast before the Bone Man spotted him out of the corner of his eye. He aimed at a point just above the Bone Man's ear. Then he squeezed the trigger . . .

The gun kicked in his hand, a neat hole appeared in the window and an equally neat hole appeared in Judith's right temple. Her head jerked from the impact.

While Hamilton stared in dismay at what he'd done the Bone Man quickly moved. He swung Judith round to face the window. Hamilton could now see blood pouring from the other side of her head. The Bone Man was grinning. Hamilton fired again. Blindly. The bullet hit the Bone Man on the edge of his exposed shoulder, sending him spinning backwards. Judith, no longer being supported, collapsed. The window glass shattered this time, giving Hamilton a clear shot as the Bone Man tried to reach the kitchen door. This bullet caught him in the lower back and he went down . . .

Hamilton opened his eyes. He was back in the cell. In Hell. But he hadn't deliberately shot Judith. He knew that now for certain. It really had been a terrible accident. It was true he had fallen out of love with her by that time but the guilt that had built up within over her death had been based on a groundless fear. He was innocent!

So what was he doing here in Hell?

If it *was* Hell.

What if it *was* another of Gilmour's tricks after all? What if Mister Ende had simply been Gilmour in disguise? But what would be the point of it? Why would Gilmour want them sitting in here? Apart from enjoying their mental torture, that is?

Time. It was wasting time.

And soon they would require another injection of the synthetic BDNFE.

He turned quickly . . . and saw that Stephanie no longer had the rucksack on her back.

Oh shit. He couldn't remember her taking it off but she must have done, upstairs. He'd been too distracted by his own problems to notice. She probably didn't even realise she'd done it herself. Gilmour had manipulated her into doing it.

'Stephanie!' He went over to her, knocking Judith's legs out of the way as he did so. 'Terry!' she cried but he continued to

ignore her. He ignored Stephanie's younger sister too. He
placed himself between them, blocking the girl's gaze, seized
Stephanie roughly by the shoulders and shook her until her
teeth made clicking sounds like his wife's infernal knitting.
'Stephanie! Listen to me! This is another of Gilmour's bloody
games! We are not in Hell!'

He stopped shaking her. Her eyes remained dull and
unfocused. 'Oh, yes we are . . .' she said listlessly. 'And we'll
be here for ever.'

He shook her again. 'Stephanie, Gilmour is trying to dry us
out! He wants the BDNFE out of our systems! We don't have
much time left before we need another injection . . . but Stephanie, *you don't have the rucksack any more!*'

Something stirred in her eyes. 'What?'

'The rucksack,' he said urgently. 'With the medical kit in it.
You were wearing it and now you're not. Gilmour tricked you.
Us. He's got the rucksack. Do you understand me?'

She frowned and felt behind her. 'Yes, it's gone.'

'Gone, right! Now pull yourself together! We've got to get out
of here before it's too late!'

She shook her head. 'No. I killed her. I murdered Gloria.'

'No, you didn't! Gilmour has made you *think* you did! He's
implanted that memory in you just as he implanted a false
memory in me! He's doing what he did to us before . . . amplifying out of all proportion our deep-rooted guilts. *You didn't
deliberately kill your sister! Just as I didn't deliberately kill my
wife!*'

'Yes you did, Terry,' said his wife calmly. 'You know you
did.'

He looked at her. 'PISS OFF!'

Judith vanished. And so did her knitting.

He stepped away from Stephanie and pointed at her mute
sister. 'Go on, tell her to go. You can do it!'

Stephanie stared at the image of her sister. Hesitantly, she
said, 'Gloria, please go away.'

The girl stayed put, her intimidating gaze as intense as
before. The golliwog remained pretty intimidating as well.

'Go on, try again,' he urged Stephanie. 'Put all your will-power into it!'

'Gloria, *please* go away!' cried Stephanie.

The little girl disappeared. So did the damned golliwog.

Stephanie looked at Hamilton. He was overjoyed to see life in her eyes again. He laughed and kissed her briefly on the mouth. Then he asked, 'That guy he quoted, the one who said "Hell is other people"; who was he?'

'A famous French philosopher,' she said. 'And a major prat.'

He grinned. 'Come on, let's go see Gilmour.'

Chapter Twenty-Two

Stephanie watched as Hamilton kicked at the wall where the door had been. The wall crumbled away as his shoe sank into it. He then slammed his shoulder into it and the whole wall just collapsed. Strength, and conviction, was flowing back through her. She saw the stairs beyond. Yellow light shone down.

'See!' he yelled. 'I was right! It's all fake! Come on, let's go and cream that bastard!'

He grabbed Stephanie's hand and they started up the stairs . . .

The cavernous room they emerged into was very different to the one they had left hours before.

Gilmour's banally distinctive decorating style was very much in evidence again. Lots of medieval stonework, mould and fungus. Torches, fastened to the walls, burned with sickly yellow fire. But, incongruously, scattered about on wooden benches were pieces of equipment from Stephanie's laboratory. Also in the room were members of her staff. Stephanie thought she would be immune to any further shocks that might still be in store for her but she gasped when she saw the way they looked . . .

From what she could see of them they were all naked and they appeared to be growing out of the stonework. The nearest to her, Jeff Blakeley, was attached at the waist to the top of a short, stone column next to one of the benches. His face, twisted

with pain, brightened when he saw her. Bernice Blumlein, who
had been completing her Ph.D. in Stephanie's department, was
attached to one of the walls. Her head, one arm, half her torso
and one leg were free but the rest of her body was buried
in the stonework of the wall. Derek Leycott, the young lab
technician whom she'd had those damned dreams about, was
attached to a stone pillar by his . . . well, she supposed it was
his penis. It was a ridiculously long fleshy tube that extended
some fifteen feet. He, like Jeff, had been working at one of the
benches when they'd entered. He too had stopped at the sight
of Stephanie.

'Doc!' he cried. 'Help me!' then gave a shriek when his 'penis'
suddenly jerked him off his feet as it was pulled into the pillar.

'Derek!' she cried as he screamed in agony. Stephanie turned
to Gilmour. 'Stop it, Gilmour. Stop it at once!' she commanded.

Gilmour, dressed in a spotlessly white suit, was on a stone
dais in the centre of the room. He was seated on a throne
constructed from human bones. His hands rested upon two
skulls that made up the ends of the arm-rests. There was a
cluster of screaming skulls on the back of the throne above his
head. Another incongruous touch: beside the throne was a
metal stand with a drip feed bottle attached to it. A tube ran
down into the back of Gilmour's left hand. Stephanie guessed
it was providing a constant supply of her BDNFE.

Derek ceased to be pulled towards the pillar. He lay groaning
on the bare stone floor. Gilmour gave Stephanie a leering
smile. 'Well-hung lad, isn't he? I can see why he got you so
excited, lovely Stephanie.'

'Oh, piss off, you ludicrous prat! Let him go. Let them all go.'

'Heavens, no. I haven't finished with them yet. As for you
two, you disappoint me. I expected your sojourn in Hell to have
lasted a little longer. Eternity isn't what it used to be. Never
mind. A small inconvenience, that's all.'

'Face it, Gilmour!' shouted Hamilton. 'You've run out of
tricks. You can't fool us any more. You're helpless!'

'Helpless? Far from it. There is nothing you can do to harm
me. Admittedly, for the moment, I can't hurt you. But it is

merely a temporary stalemate while I wait for the remainder of the synthetic BDNFE to disappear from your brains. And then you will be the helpless ones . . . and what fun and games we'll have then! They'll make what you have endured so far seem like a trip to Disneyland. In the meantime you might as well make yourselves comfortable. I estimate you have only half an hour to wait.'

Despite his arrogant words Stephanie sensed he was afraid of them. Why? They no longer had the guns. But he'd been afraid of them ever since he'd started trying to manipulate them into committing suicide. It hadn't been just the guns – they'd had them all along. It was something else. What had changed? It had happened back in her flat. Before Miss Coope had appeared. Something had definitely changed then. But what . . . ? She thought hard. She recalled she had been re-reading Gilmour's file . . .

Then she remembered.

And Gilmour knew it. She could see it in his eyes. She smiled at him. 'I know where you live,' she told him. Then she began to concentrate.

'No,' said Gilmour and raised his right hand. He pointed at her. Dust began to fall around her. She looked up. A large chunk of stonework was starting to slide out of the ceiling above. Then it began to fall towards her.

She looked back at Gilmour. She felt no fear. Nor was she surprised when the stonework crashed to the floor some yards from where she was standing, even though it had originally been directly above her. She pointed her own finger at him.

'You can't hurt me, Gilmour.'

Hamilton, looking puzzled, said, 'Stephanie, what . . . ?'

'Hush,' she cautioned him. 'I have to concentrate. Just be ready to act when I give the word.'

A giant hairless rat, some nine feet from head to tail, appeared in front of Gilmour's throne. 'Kill her!' he shrieked at it. The rat charged towards Stephanie, but then the floor suddenly opened up beneath it and it fell, screeching, into the pit below. The floor closed up over it.

'Bitch!'

'What's next, a giant killer foetus? Your imagination is running dry. It's no good, Gilmour. I told you – I know where you live. Now it's your turn . . .'

And then, from the breast pocket of Gilmour's immaculate white jacket, a tarantula emerged. Gilmour stared at it with an expression of horror. 'No!' he cried and frantically knocked it away. But other large black spiders began to appear . . . from the eye sockets, nasal cavities and jaws of the skulls in his throne of bones.

'Still don't like spiders, do you?' Stephanie asked him pleasantly. 'In fact, according to your file, even seeing a photograph of one when you were a child brought on a panic attack. I'm so glad to see you haven't grown out of your phobia.'

'No!' he cried again as the spiders from the cluster of skulls above him began to drop down on his head and shoulders, to pour down into his lap. Gilmour screamed. He stood up, trying to brush the spiders from him. The needle and tube were torn loose from his hand. The stand holding the bottle of BDNFE solution went crashing from the dais.

Stephanie forced him to sit down again. His screams became more and more high-pitched. Hamilton watched in mystification, then he turned to Stephanie and asked, 'Are *you* doing this?'

Stephanie lost her concentration. In that instant the spiders vanished. Gilmour stopped screaming. He looked down at his white suit, then fearfully patted his pockets, obviously terrified that more spiders lurked within them. Then, when finally convinced they were all gone, he looked at Stephanie. 'Seems your batteries have run out, *bitch!*'

He rose to his feet. 'You think you're so clever! Yes? Well, you're going to pay for doing that, bitch. I'm going to cause you such pain you'll curse your mother for not having you aborted. First I'm going to flay every single inch of skin from your body and then, while you scream for mercy . . . then . . . gah!' Gilmour's voice had become muffled. He started to choke and gag. He reeled back and collapsed onto his throne. And then, out of his open mouth, crawled a large tarantula. It scuttled down his neck and disappeared under his collar. Another tarantula emerged from Gilmour's mouth and another . . . These too vanished under his shirt collar. Gilmour began to tear frantically at his clothing. The spiders continued to emerge from his mouth. Very soon he was vomiting up a veritable torrent of tarantulas. They were flowing down his suit. Some disappeared up the cuffs of his jacket. Others formed a hairy, writhing pool in his lap.

Stephanie said, in a calm and distinct voice, 'Kill him, Terry.'

Hamilton looked at her. 'How?'

'I don't care how, just *do* it! Quickly! I can't keep this up for much longer!'

Hamilton got the message. He bent down, pulled up his right trouser leg and tore something from his calf. Then he moved quickly towards Gilmour. She saw he was holding a knife. One of her serrated steak knives . . .

Hamilton had reached the dais. 'Don't worry about the spiders, Terry!' she cried. 'They won't hurt you!'

He nodded. He was up on the dais now, beside the writhing Gilmour on his throne of bones. Gilmour held up an ineffectual arm to ward him off. Hamilton brushed it aside. 'This is for my wife and child, you bastard!' He struck out with the knife, ramming it into Gilmour's throat. Bright arterial blood jetted from the hole in his neck, splashing the white bones of his throne with streaks of scarlet. Hamilton stabbed him in the throat again.

The spiders disappeared.

Gilmour staggered to his feet and leapt down from the dais. He clamped both hands around his throat in a vain attempt to stop the jet of blood from pumping out of his ravaged throat. He tottered towards Stephanie, eyes blazing with a mixture of a terrible rage and a terrible fear. Then he pitched forward onto the floor and blood quickly pooled around him. His body trembled – one leg jerked violently – and then he was still.

And everything abruptly changed.

She was suddenly back in her lab. It was filled with afternoon sunlight. She could hear the sound of heavy traffic from Tyburn Lane. Everything was as she remembered it to be, apart from three of her staff lying naked and groaning on the floor. And Hamilton standing over Gilmour's dead body in the centre of the room. Gilmour, dressed now in only white, blood-spattered t-shirt and slacks, was sprawled on his stomach in a huge pool of blood. Hamilton, looking haggard and stunned, turned to her. 'What . . . ?'

'We did it,' she said simply.

Hamilton looked around the lab then staggered towards her, still clutching her steak knife. Gilmour's blood dripped from it. 'Yeah,' he said hoarsely. 'But *how?*'

She felt unsteady herself. She went to a nearby chair and fell into it. She was trembling. Now she could hear sirens outside. Ambulances? Fire engines? She couldn't tell. 'Like I said, it was in his file. His childhood, pathological fear of spiders.'

Hamilton dropped the knife in a sink. He turned on the tap and began splashing water onto his face. Behind him, Jeff Blakeley was crawling with painful slowness across the floor on his hands and knees, groaning as he went. Derek and Bernice were still lying on their backs. She was finding it hard to think. She desperately wanted to go to sleep. She knew she should be trying to do something for her staff members but she had no idea what she *could* do.

'It was when I was re-reading his file to see if there was anything in it that would help us. And I did spot something, though it didn't fully register at the time. First you distracted me by asking about the work at the Institute, and then poor Miss Coope put in an appearance. But Gilmour knew it had taken root in my mind, and that's when he started steering us into acts of self-destruction . . .

'It was his major weakness – apart from being a crazy mass murderer, that is. He'd been using our phobias against us so it occurred to me that I could do the same thing to him. Distract him to the point where all his defences were down and he was totally vulnerable.'

Hamilton nodded approvingly as he glanced at Gilmour's

dead body. 'So the mind-fucker ended up getting mind-fucked himself. Good for you, Stephanie.'

'Hey, I couldn't have done it without you. If you hadn't acted so quickly with that knife it's possible Gilmour might have regained control.'

'Yeah,' said Hamilton. 'Maybe.'

Jeff Blakeley had reached a wall and come to a stop. He was sobbing. From other parts of the building Stephanie could hear raised, frightened voices. A woman was crying. The number of screaming sirens outside had increased. She wondered what was happening out there in Harrow-on-the-Hill. For over thirty-six hours several hundred people, perhaps even thousands, had gone inexplicably missing from the area. And now they were suddenly back, either as corpses or as seriously damaged individuals. She thought of the twenty-one adolescents that she and Hamilton had shot down up on the Hill. Were any of them still alive? Maybe all the survivors would be hopelessly insane. Looking at her three colleagues didn't provide her with much encouragement.

She wondered what explanations were being devised to explain the bizarre phenomenon. No doubt some government spokesman was already announcing to the media that there would be a full and thorough public enquiry at the earliest opportunity.

Her little experiment was going to have plenty of grim, long-term consequences. She wondered about her own future – her career – but only briefly. She gave a deep sigh and reached into her jacket pocket for the pack of cigarettes and her lighter. The packet was empty. Shit. She dropped it on the floor.

Hamilton walked slowly over to one of the windows. He peered out into the sunshine. 'So we're back in the real world . . .' he said, somewhat disbelievingly.

'Yes,' she answered. She glanced down at the discarded cigarette pack. It had been empty. She was sure of that. It was now full of cigarettes. She picked the pack up, took out a cigarette and lit it. She drew the smoke thankfully into her lungs.

'Whatever *that* is,' she added. Then, 'Why don't you make a wish, Terry?'

He turned and looked at her. 'What?'

'I said, make a wish.'